Art
Love
Forgery

Art
Love
Forgery

a novel

CAROLYN MORGAN

FLANKER PRESS LIMITED
ST. JOHN'S

Library and Archives Canada Cataloguing in Publication

Morgan, Carolyn
  Art Love Forgery

Issued in print and electronic formats.
ISBN 978-1-77117-579-1 (paperback).--ISBN 978-1-77117-580-7 (epub).--ISBN 978-1-77117-581-4 (kindle).--ISBN 978-1-77117-582-1 (pdf)

A CIP catalogue record for this book is available from Library and Archives Canada.

© 2016 by Carolyn Morgan

ALL RIGHTS RESERVED. No part of the work covered by the copyright hereon may be reproduced or used in any form or by any means—graphic, electronic or mechanical—without the written permission of the publisher. Any request for photocopying, recording, taping, or information storage and retrieval systems of any part of this book shall be directed to Access Copyright, The Canadian Copyright Licensing Agency, 1 Yonge Street, Suite 800, Toronto, ON M5E 1E5. This applies to classroom use as well. For an Access Copyright licence, visit www.accesscopyright.ca or call toll-free to 1-800-893-5777.

PRINTED IN CANADA

This paper has been certified to meet the environmental and social standards of the Forest Stewardship Council® (FSC®) and comes from responsibly managed forests, and verified recycled sources.

Edited by Robin McGrath   Cover Design by Graham Blair

FLANKER PRESS LTD.
PO BOX 2522, STATION C
ST. JOHN'S, NL
CANADA

TELEPHONE: (709) 739-4477   FAX: (709) 739-4420   TOLL-FREE: 1-866-739-4420
WWW.FLANKERPRESS.COM

9 8 7 6 5 4 3 2 1

We acknowledge the [financial] support of the Government of Canada. *Nous reconnaissons l'appui [financier] du gouvernement du Canada.* We acknowledge the support of the Canada Council for the Arts, which last year invested $153 million to bring the arts to Canadians throughout the country. *Nous remercions le Conseil des arts du Canada de son soutien. L'an dernier, le Conseil a investi 153 millions de dollars pour mettre de l'art dans la vie des Canadiennes et des Canadiens de tout le pays.* We acknowledge the financial support of the Government of Newfoundland and Labrador, Department of Tourism, Culture and Recreation for our publishing activities.

Dedicated to the memory of my dearest childhood and forever friend, Cheryl (Cheri) Bell Inkpen

prologue

St. John's, October 1882

With a clarity that Ellen hadn't experienced in a very long time, she knew exactly what she had to do. Tucking the blankets around her sleeping daughter, she walked briskly, pushing the baby carriage to the end of Water Street and then up Prescott Street, which was really not a street at all but a long, winding, steep hill. She pushed the pram, gasping for breath as she reached the top. She crossed Queen's Road to Military Road, dodging horses, carts, manure, and mud.

The Presentation Convent was her destination. It stood to the right of the Roman Catholic Cathedral. The two-towered stone building was the boast of all Catholics in the city and it was the defining structure, seen as soon as a ship passed through the Narrows and into St. John's harbour. Ellen's mission was to talk with Sister Mary Angela. She would confess to her what she hadn't been able to confess to anyone up until now. She entered the foyer of the convent, pulling the pram after her.

Sister Mary Teresa was seated at her desk. No one would get past this desk and into the convent without her permission. She was the gatekeeper, and Ellen hoped that she was in a benign mood because she desperately needed her co-operation today.

"Good morning. I need to speak with Sister Mary Angela on an urgent matter. Could you tell her that Mrs. Alexander Pindikowsky is here?" Ellen spoke with confidence, hoping to project what she didn't feel.

"Sister Mary Angela's quite busy, Miss Dormody. I doubt if she can see you today. You could make an appointment for tomorrow."

Ellen could see that Sister Mary Teresa wasn't going to make her visit easy. She was flexing her power and enjoying herself. Addressing her as Miss Dormody was an intended slight and informed Ellen that she recognized her and knew everything about her.

"I'm sure she's busy," Ellen replied, carefully keeping her temper under control, "but the matter I need to discuss with her is urgent, and I would be grateful if you would at least tell Sister Mary Angela that I am here. I don't mind waiting." She prayed that Johanna would keep sleeping. If she started wailing, her chance of a meeting would be lost.

"Very well, wait here and I'll see if she's available," said Sister. She left, closing the door firmly behind her.

When Ellen heard Sister Mary Angela's lilting voice in the corridor, she sighed with relief.

"Ellen, what a wonderful surprise," she said, walking over to the young woman and kissing her on the cheek. She smelled of Mornay, Lily of the Valley, soap. It was the smell Ellen associated with her, and it reassured her. "Come through into my office and we'll have a visit. Sister Mary Teresa will mind little Johanna. You'll bring her to us if she wakes up, won't you, Sister?"

"Of course I will," said Sister Mary Teresa, as pleasant as could be.

As soon as the door closed behind them, Sister Mary Angela looked at Ellen carefully. "You have something big on your mind, I think. Now, out with it. It won't do you any good to keep it bottled up, you know."

Ellen tried to keep her voice from quavering. "I haven't heard from Alexander since he left almost four months ago. No one else knows. I told Mother that I've been receiving letters all along. I've become really good at making up the news from New York. I'm an expert on a place I've never been. I don't understand what's happened. I'm afraid he's sick or hurt. You know when he's creating his frescoes he has to work high up on scaffolding, and I'm afraid he's injured or worse. I can't stand not knowing any more. You have to help me. I love him so much." It all came out in a rush, and now Ellen couldn't keep back her tears. Sister Mary Angela wrapped her arms around her and patted her back, trying to soothe her.

"Enough now, my dear, dry your eyes and blow your nose," she said, handing her a clean cotton handkerchief that she had pulled out of the pocket hidden in her robe. "I'm sure there's a reasonable explanation for why you haven't heard from Alexander."

"Everyone thinks he's deserted me," Ellen wailed. "They think he just married me because he wanted to look respectable after his prison sentence and that he was just biding his time, waiting for a chance to leave me and Johanna." Her tears started flowing again.

"You're wrong, you know, not everyone feels that way. No one who ever saw the two of you together could deny his love for you. And he's besotted over Johanna. There must be some reason why his letters haven't arrived. Maybe they'll all come in a bunch."

"Even if they do, it's not enough. Not anymore. I've been like someone in a trance, looking after the baby and blocking out everything and everyone. Johanna and I must go to him. I have to find him, and that's where I need your help. You have connections through the archdioceses in New York. When Alexander left he said he was going to try for work at the churches and convents. Would you make inquiries for me? If I knew where he last worked, I'm sure I could find him. I have enough money saved for passage to New York. Johanna and I need to be on the next ship going there. We need to be a family again. I will not wait any more."

"I'll start inquiries immediately and I'll send a messenger to you as soon as I find out any news. Don't worry, dear, have faith in God. We will find your Alexander."

Sister Mary Angela walked with Ellen back to the foyer. She peeked into the carriage at little Johanna, who was still sleeping. "She's so beautiful, just like you," she said, smiling at her. "God be with you both, my child."

"And with you," Ellen said, returning her smile. She left the convent, feeling renewed, and walked down the hill to her mother's house on Victoria Street, remembering the events that had led her to Alexander.

one

St. John's, 1880

"Hurry up, you don't want to be late your first day, do you?" Ellen's mother threw the words back to her as she walked up the pathway to the east entrance of Government House.

Ellen stood staring up at the stone facade of the building, her eyes travelling over the large, long French windows, the glass greenhouse, and the trees outlining the expansive gardens surrounding it. It was not a particularly beautiful building, although its size, in comparison to most of the dwellings in St. John's, made it impressive. The Georgian styling was spoiled by the lack of a proper portico. She remembered hearing the story that the building had cost five times the original estimate and the portico had been scratched from the plans for this reason.

Ellen's mother, Louise Dormody, had been working at The House, as it was called by the staff, for four years now, since 1876, and she took the building for granted. She had been the head housekeeper for the last two years, and she was familiar with every room, cupboard, dish, lamp, and piece of furniture. She held a running inventory of the linens in her head at all times and took great pride in being able to keep The House in an orderly fashion, even when there were important visitors from Scotland, England, or Canada staying there and she had been given only a day's notice of their arrival.

"I'm coming, Mother," Ellen replied, hurrying up the path and wiping her boots on the bristle mat before entering the back cloakroom. She knew she would have to work hard and learn quickly or her mother would dismiss her as soon as she would any of the other maids. In fact, she figured she'd have to work even harder than the other maids because her mother wouldn't want to be accused of favouritism to her daughter. The night before, she had given Ellen a condensed course on the rules of behaviour for The House. She had rattled them off and repeated them again at breakfast that morning.

"Don't ask questions that aren't any of your business, like 'What is the name of the wallpaper?' or 'Where did the carpets come from?' Stick to the job you're given and don't daydream. Don't answer back. Most important, always stay out of the way of guests and Governor and Lady Glover. Don't dare speak to them unless they speak to you first, and if they ask you a question give the short answer, not your usual roundabout one. Keep your hair tidy and not wisping around your face. And don't ever call me Mother. I'm Mrs. Dormody when we're at The House."

Ellen and her mother hung their coats in the cloakroom and then walked into the kitchen. Five women and two men stood staring at them.

"Good morning, everyone," Mrs. Dormody said. "This is my daughter, Ellen. She'll be starting work as a chambermaid today. I won't introduce you all now as I know you're busy. Ellen will get to know all your names in due course. I expect her to be treated just like any new girl. Charlotte, you can take Ellen into the laundry and fit her out with a couple of dresses. Make sure the apron straps don't flop down over her shoulders."

A small girl, who looked around Ellen's age, came forward. "Come with me," she said, taking Ellen's arm.

"I'll see you at home tonight, Ellen," said her mother. "Remember what I told you."

"Yes, Mrs. Dormody," Ellen said, trying hard not to giggle. She followed Charlotte through a door at the back of the kitchen. Ellen was at least five inches taller than Charlotte, the top of whose head only reached Ellen's shoulder.

The laundry was large and filled with activity. Women bustled around and steam rose from the huge pots on the stove and the ironing boards. An older woman, around thirty, Ellen guessed, walked by with a tablecloth laid out over her arms. When she passed by, Ellen asked Charlotte, "Will I be wearing a uniform like that? It's ever so smart."

"That's the new uniform that Lady Glover, Governor Glover's wife, just had made up. She designed the style of it herself," said Charlotte proudly. "The blue serge material was sent from England. But that's for the parlour maids. You'll have to get promoted before you'll get a chance to wear that. For chambermaids, we have striped blue cotton dresses. They're very nice, too." Charlotte walked into a small room at the back of the laundry and selected a dress. "Here, try this one on," she said, waving Ellen into the room and closing the door.

The dress was a little too big around the waist and it was too short, but the apron sash would hold the waist in and Ellen would let the hem down that night. She really wanted the new uniform, though, and she was determined to do everything perfectly so she could be promoted in record time. She couldn't believe her mother hadn't mentioned the uniforms, but then she wasn't interested in fashion. Her mother always wore a standard black dress. She did, however, make sure that the material was of good quality and that the fit was perfect.

"What do you think, Charlotte," Ellen asked, turning around to show off the dress. "It's a bit short, but I'll let the hem down all the way tonight."

"I have to cut my dresses off at least a foot," Charlotte said, laughing. "No one in my family is known for their height."

"I can see that, but you're very well proportioned, and that is everything in terms of looking good, Charlotte."

"Thanks, Ellen. I can tell we're going to be friends, so you can call me Cheri. That's what everyone calls me back home. I can take down that hem for you, too, if you'd like. I'm the seamstress here, but I also look after the cleaning of Lady Glover's personal wardrobe and help with just about everything else when we're short-handed like we are today."

"Well, Cheri, will we get to work? I've got my eye on that parlour maid uniform, so I'd best be learning all I can as soon as I can."

"We'll start with the water closets upstairs, then. There are washstands and chamber pots in all the rooms, but when we have visitors and events here, the guests use the water closets. Come on. You'll get used to all the stairs in no time at all, especially with your long legs. It's one of the problems of being short. I have to make two steps for everyone else's one, but I can fit into tight places, like under beds, so I make up for it. Let me tell you, I've heard some great stories underneath beds, too."

"I'll bet you have," Ellen said, raising her eyebrows. They laughed together, and their friendship was sealed.

ELLEN QUICKLY ADJUSTED TO THE DAILY ROUTINE OF DUSTING, polishing, managing the linens, and keeping the bedchambers spotless. Like all the other maids, she had to do the unpopular jobs like emptying the chamber pots and readying the fireplaces with kindling, coal, and wood in just the right order. She worked hard and, because she had inherited her mother's good health, she didn't miss a day.

The activities of The House were subject to the fluctuations of Newfoundland politics. Often there were government officials from Newfoundland and abroad staying at Government House, and when they were in residence, everyone was a bit tense trying to live up to an imagined British standard. From grooms to scullery maids, no one wanted to be thought of as colonial bumpkins lacking in the social graces. Ellen's mother, in particular, made a point of inspecting every nook and cranny of The House at these times. She could be found everywhere, tapping her foot impatiently while a bed was remade or a mirror was polished till it sparkled. Fortunately, Ellen rarely had to redo anything, but that was only because she had been trained by her mother, at home, since she was a toddler.

Most of the female staff hired for The House came only after they had spent a number of years working for the gentry, the relatively rich merchant class of St. John's. Typically a young girl would come to St. John's from an outport community and be placed in the home of a working-class family. In exchange for room and board, she would be expected to work at everything that needed to be done, from babysitting to cleaning chamber pots, washing dishes, cooking, mending, and caring for the elderly.

The women of the households trained the girls to be good domestic servants, and often this was not an easy task. Many of the girls came from families of twelve to twenty children, and they were so poor that malnutrition and bad hygiene were commonplace. Often the girls had to be deloused before they could be permitted to go into the houses and their clothes had to be burned. Apart from domestic work, they were taught how to groom themselves, how to talk slowly enough to be understood, and how to address people properly.

The girls who learned quickly progressed to the better houses, where they would have a room of their own and a small salary. The initial families always complained that just when they had a girl trained so that she wasn't a drain on their energies and could actually be of help, she left and they would have to start the process all over again. The girls who made it into the best houses were the ones that were recruited for Government House. This didn't stop Ellen's mother from insisting that the new girls needed to be trained the proper way, The House way, Louise's way. Her favourite expression was "improvement calls out for more," and often Ellen would hear the maids repeating it in an imitation of her mother's deep voice, followed by giggles.

Ellen's history was quite different from this pattern. Her father, Patrick Dormody, had been the manager of the Colonial Sails Company in Quidi Vidi Village, on the outskirts of St. John's. Her mother, Louise Hann, had fallen in love with Patrick the moment he had walked into the Downtown General Store where she worked as a salesgirl. They married when Louise was just eighteen and Patrick was thirty-five. Since Louise was a Methodist and Patrick a lapsed Roman Catholic, he was willing to marry Louise in her church. Ellen was born one year later. Their marriage was happy but short. They had just bought a house at the foot of Victoria Street when disaster struck. Ellen's father had been supervising the transportation of a shipment of sails going down to the Labrador when a fully-loaded cargo net had fallen on him, crushing his body. He died a day later as a result of his injuries. Ellen's mother, broken-hearted and with a two-year-old to support, was determined to keep her house on Victoria Street. She refused all the ridiculously low offers on her house from men saying how they were helping her out. Louise knew the property would go up in value, as St. John's was rapidly expanding, and the house was to be her insurance against poverty in her old age.

Most women would have tried to find a man to marry and support them, but although Louise had offers, she had refused them all. She still loved Patrick and she wouldn't remarry until she met a man who made her forget him. Instead, Louise took in boarders to help pay the bills for the house. She never had trouble finding boarders, as she kept her house spotlessly clean and was a great cook as well. It was, in fact, one of her boarders, Mr. Kenneth Robinson, who found her the job at Government House. He was a barrister at the time he boarded with Louise but later became a politician, and when his friend, Governor Glover, needed an experienced housekeeper, he recommended Louise for the job. She still kept boarders at the house, as by that time Ellen was twelve years old and able to cook and clean with the help of a maid. Before Louise closed her eyes to sleep each night, she would check on the house and make long lists of instructions to give to Ellen and their maid, Dora. Ellen would get up at five thirty every morning and have much of the work done before she left for school.

Ellen was ambitious, just like her mother. Louise believed in girls getting an education, and she sent Ellen to the Methodist Girls' School. Unlike most of the girls at the school, Ellen loved it there, even though the teachers were strict. Keeping at the top of her class had never been a problem for her, and Louise allowed her to stay at the school for longer than most girls. In fact, she wanted Ellen to continue her schooling and become a teacher. The teachers at the school, all except the art teacher, Miss Seary, thought Ellen had the aptitude for it. Miss Seary recognized Ellen's artistic talent and her need to be creative. She understood that the school rules wouldn't allow Ellen the freedom she craved. Before she left school, Ellen had devised her own plan that would make her independent and use her creativity.

The job at Government House was only temporary, a means to an end. The money Ellen earned working there would pay for her passage to London, England, where she was going to train to be a milliner. Ellen's mother had taught her how to sew, knit, and embroider before she was eight years old. At ten years of age she was designing and making her own hats and embellishing the ones that she bought. Ellen knew that she could probably set up shop without training, but she wanted to do things right. Of course, if she were honest, that wasn't the real reason she wanted to go to London. She yearned for adventure, and she felt London was just the place to have one. Ellen didn't tell her mother that fact, though. Instead, she told her that the only way she could get the proper training was to travel to London where she could study with millinery experts. Her mother had looked at Ellen closely, nodded her head, and said "Hmm." Ellen knew the meaning of that response well—she hadn't believed her argument at all.

Ellen fully intended to return to Newfoundland and set up her own millinery shop after she had had her adventure. She had even gone so far as to pick out a likely location for her shop at the west end of Water Street, far enough away from the smell of fish brought in on the boats, but still close enough to be convenient for commerce.

two

A year had passed at The House, Ellen's savings had grown, and she had been promoted to the position of parlour maid. She was now the proud wearer of the coveted uniform, and she couldn't resist admiring herself in it every time she passed a mirror. She was eighteen now and her figure had lost its girlish look. The fit of the bright navy serge dress complimented Ellen's figure and made her eyes a deeper blue. The cream-coloured collar, cuffs, and apron enhanced her light copper-coloured hair and softened her complexion. She kept her hair in the prescribed coiled bun at the nape of her neck, but always a few strands would escape the pins. Her mother was forever telling her to tuck the ends under her cap.

Ellen had been promoted when two new maids, Moira and Sarah, were hired. They were five years older than Ellen, and they resented the fact that she was senior over them. A few days after she was promoted, she heard Sarah talking about her. "She thinks she's a lady, she does, lording it over us. Everybody knows she wouldn't have been promoted except for her mother being in charge and all. One of these days she'll get what's coming to her, mark my words, Moira, she'll get what's coming to her, for sure." The loud whispered comments floated right off Ellen's shoulders. She knew that this job wasn't her real life. She held her hat shop inside her, like a gift, and the idea of it kept her happy and immune to their taunts.

This morning, Ellen's destination was the dining room. She was going to retrieve the Georgian candlesticks from the mantel for a thorough cleaning and polish. She had noticed that they didn't sparkle as they should have when she had served tea at Lady Glover's "at home" the previous day. Ellen could have sworn that she had sent the candlesticks for cleaning earlier that week, and she wondered if one of the maids, probably Moira or Sarah, was sabotaging her. She wouldn't put it past them, and it wouldn't be the first time they had made her life difficult. Ellen got along well with most of the staff, but she'd given up trying to be friends with Moira and Sarah.

Ellen heard voices as she approached the dining room. Peeking inside the door, she saw Governor Glover and Mr. Kenneth Robinson talking together. They were smoking their pipes and leaning up against the fireplace. She would have to wait for the candlesticks. She recognized Mr. Robinson from when he had been a boarder at her house on Victoria Street. Ellen really liked him because he always talked to her like she was a grown-up. She doubted if he would recognize her now.

Ellen was about to carry on into the laundry when she heard an interesting snippet of their conversation. She wasn't usually an eavesdropper, but the conversation intrigued her, and since no one was around, she busied herself dusting the pictures in the hall while she listened intently.

Governor Glover was staring up at the dining room ceiling. "It needs some embellishment, don't you think? It needs something grand, something that will make this room more important. Governor Cochrane had the right idea when he built this place. He moved the chimney, you know. It was originally placed where the double doors are now leading into the ballroom. It cost a lot of money since the chimney had to come down and be relocated here, but what a difference it made. It gives elegance to the place and makes it feel more spacious. The House is really only a glorified country manor. When Edward, the Prince of Wales, visited here, he must have been a bit shocked by the place, don't you think?"

"I'm sure he enjoyed roughing it a bit, and the food and hospitality probably made up for any lack," said Mr. Robinson. "I do agree with you, though. The ceiling in here and in the ballroom could do with some fresco work, and I have just the person who could do it for you. His name is Alexander Pindikowsky."

Ellen's mouth dropped open. She knew all about Alexander Pindikowsky, and she moved closer to the open doors, as close as she could without being seen.

"Pindikowsky!" Governor Glover shouted. "You mean the forger? He's in jail, isn't he?"

"Yes, he is," said Mr. Robinson. "He's serving a fifteen-month sentence at Her Majesty's Penitentiary. But he's not a dangerous person. I met him last year when I was visiting the Heart's Content cable station. He was brought over from Poland and hired by the Anglo-American Telegraph Company to teach art to employees and their wives. I saw his artwork, and it was fine. His frescoes were as good as any I've seen in England. He made a huge mistake forging Ezra Weedon's cheques. I guess he thought that because he was in St. John's no one would know him. Pindikowsky obviously didn't know that just about everything that goes on in this colony is known because everyone is a friend, cousin, brother, sister, aunt, or uncle to everyone else. Apparently, when he went to cash his cheque at the bank, the teller recognized him. The teller's sister worked for Weedon, and she had told him all about Pindikowsky. The teller knew it was unlikely for Weedon to write a cheque to Pindikowsky. He would have been paid in cash, or a cheque would have been issued with the telegraph company's name.

"Well, that's all water under the bridge now, but you should think about using his talent here. I see this as a great opportunity. You could get the work done free. It could even be part of his prison sentence." Mr. Robinson was getting excited about his subject now. "In lieu of pay, his sentence could be lessened, and you would have that embellishment you want. There wouldn't be any danger of him escaping. An armed guard could be assigned to be with him at all times. I know the police don't usually carry firearms, but for the safety and peace of mind of the staff here at Government House, I'm sure an exception could be made. I could speak with Judge Prowse about it, if you like."

"It certainly is a novel idea. I'm going to give it some thought," said Governor Glover. "Now, I'd better be getting ready for the concert at the Athenaeum tonight. Lady Glover won't let me out of this one.

Elizabeth loves going to the concerts there since the style of the stone architecture reminds her a little of her home in London. The fact that the auditorium can seat a thousand people is quite impressive, and the cupola-shaped ceiling adds distinction and a bit of grandeur. Just what I want for Government House. The Presentation Sisters' Choir is performing tonight. Elizabeth says they rival any of the choirs back home. Are you going, Kenneth?"

"No, I'm spending a quiet night at home. I'm looking forward to it, as a matter of fact."

Ellen ducked out of the way just as they were walking out of the dining room. She was bursting to talk to someone about what she had heard, but then she'd have to confess to listening. She decided to confide in Cheri. They had become good friends since her first day working at The House, and they told each other everything. Ellen knew Cheri wouldn't tell anyone about her eavesdropping. It was a delicious piece of information, really exciting. Like everyone else in St. John's, she had read about Pindikowsky's arrest in the newspaper. She had even caught a glimpse of him when he was brought to the courthouse for sentencing. She remembered how handsome he was, tall, and well built, his dark hair falling over his forehead as he climbed out of the prison wagon. The thought of him working at Government House was a thrilling prospect. She knew Governor Glover well enough to know that when he said he'd give something some thought, it was as good as done.

"What are you smiling about?" asked Moira as she passed by Ellen on her way to the kitchen. "You look like the cat that swallowed the canary."

"Nothing," Ellen said, humming to herself as she took the candlesticks from the mantelpiece.

three

Alexander Pindikowsky paced around his ten-by-seven-foot prison cell at the penitentiary, not allowing himself to stop until he had completed five hundred laps. He then sat on the cold floor and did a series of sit-ups, push-ups, and jumping jacks. He did this three times a day to break up the monotony of his prison sentence and keep himself fit. He had completed two months of his sentence, and in thirteen months' time he would be free and ready to work again. His work required him to climb on ladders and scaffolding, so he needed to be physically fit. His regimen might be all for nothing, though, if no one would hire him. He tried to block this thought from his mind as he paced.

Alexander was generally an optimistic, cheerful sort of person, but he had never been in prison before, and prison was sucking his optimism dry. The only bright spots in his days were mealtimes, when he was brought a tray of food by prison guard Dan Kielly.

Kielly was not the usual burly prison guard. A former policeman, he was of medium height, slightly built, and soft spoken, with a quirky sense of humour. He often stayed and chatted with Alexander while he ate, and they found out that they had a couple of things in common. Kielly was a card player, which was not too surprising, but he also had a lively interest in art. He was quite knowledgeable about the European master painters, and he seemed to respect Alexander's artistic talent.

Alexander remembered the first time Kielly had spoken to him two months ago. He had been scared and miserable, not knowing how he was going to be treated in a prison in the colony of Newfoundland. The loud clunk of the barred iron door that first day in his prison cell had left him feeling extremely vulnerable.

Kielly stood outside Alexander's cell looking in at him, and without preamble he began talking. "I followed your trial, and I don't understand how you could be so stupid. I mean, you're talented, you're relatively young and good-looking, and you had a great job out at the cable station. What were you thinking about? From what I hear, the women were falling all over you and the company was paying you well. I can't understand it. Now, before I ruin my sleep thinking about it, tell me why you thought you could get away with forgery in this town where secrets can't be kept." Kielly looked penetratingly at Alexander and waited for an answer.

At first Alexander wasn't inclined to answer him, but then he thought better of it. He was in a strange town where he had no friends or relatives, and he was in a prison. He didn't want to antagonize Kielly, since he would need him as an ally in the months to come. Alexander spoke English well, but his accent was strong, revealing that English was not his first language.

"Well, I was stupid, as you say, and I'm afraid I'm not good with money. I like to be generous, and when I have money, I spend it. I like to treat the ladies, and I like nice clothes. I also like to gamble a bit, and I guess I thought no one would know me here and I'd get away with it."

"Well, your mistake. Live and learn. I'll get your supper for you now. Don't go anywhere," Kielly laughed as he walked with a swagger down the corridor.

TIME PASSED SLOWLY, AND ALEXANDER WOULD HAVE HAD A HARD time of it but for Kielly, who he now considered his friend. Kielly brought him drawing materials whenever he could, and by now he had enough artwork to paper a room.

About a month into his sentence, Kielly came to see Alexander. He stood outside his cell grinning like a leprechaun with a full pot of gold.

"I bet you're some sick of those four walls in there," he said. "Well, I've got good news for you. I've persuaded the superintendent to allow you to paint a mural out in the reception room. I showed him your drawings, and he was really impressed. You can start today. You'll be under my supervision, so don't even think about escaping."

"Don't worry, I wouldn't try anything so foolish. Where would I go?" Alexander was thrilled with the prospect of having paints, liquid colour, in his hands again. Pencil work was fine, but it was colour that excited him, even more so since the prison cell and surrounding walls were all painted grey.

His first painting was a mural that portrayed the entrance to St. John's harbour, more commonly referred to as the Narrows. It covered almost the entire east wall, about ten feet by eight feet. He chose to paint the Narrows because he loved the way it looked with the steep cliffs rising out of the sea on either side of the harbour entrance. Alexander remembered his first glimpse of St. John's when he made the voyage from England across the Atlantic. The ship made a sudden turn, and it appeared as if the captain of the ship had aimed the vessel straight at a rocky cliff. Then, a magical narrow opening appeared, and the ship glided into St. John's harbour. Alexander understood why the place had been fought over by the French and the English. You couldn't find a better safe harbour, and whoever held the harbour had a distinct advantage over any warship that might try to gain entrance.

The town was built on a hill, and as the ship entered the Narrows, Alexander's eye was drawn magnetically to the most prominent structure, the two-towered Roman Catholic Cathedral. Although he was not a particularly religious man, he felt comforted by the presence of the church as it represented a bit of home for him.

"I don't know how you do it," said Kielly, gazing at the newly painted wall. "It's so real I feel I could just sail right on out through that wall. I'm curious, though. How do you feel when you paint like that?"

"It is hard to explain," said Alexander. "I feel . . ." He paused before continuing. "I feel . . . real. The tightness in my belly disappears, and I feel together, not in pieces."

"I understand. It means you're doing what you should be doing.

I envy you that. I'm a prison guard, but I don't feel real, I don't know what I should be doing with my life. My wife, Martha, says I should be grateful to have such a good job, but I'm not. I want something more. I just don't know what it is."

"My fodder was a portrait artist, a very fine one. But he died when I was just a little boy. I remember mixing paints for him. Maybe that is why I like the smell of paint. It reminds me of him. My modder worked as a cook in one of the great houses back in Poland. She was a bit of an artist, too. She used to make beautiful cakes with a special icing that would harden into beautiful shapes. I loved to watch her spread the icing in swirls over the cake. The plaster I mix for my fresco work is very much the same." Alexander's voice was wistful.

"Superintendent Quinton was in here the other day," said Kielly. "He was full of praise for your painting, and when you've finished it, he wants you to paint a picture of the prison on his office door. Why he would want a picture of the prison when he works here is beyond me, but to each his own. At least you won't have to go back to rotting away in your cell."

"I am grateful for this work," said Alexander. "The days pass so much more fast. I would almost be happy if I was doing plasterwork again, but I know I am very lucky to have anything at all."

ALEXANDER WORKED ON THE PAINTING FOR THE SUPERINTENDENT for the next two weeks, putting in details that didn't exist in the real building just to keep himself out of his cell for a while longer. Finally, he had to admit that it was finished, and he returned to his cell and his exercise regimen. He was sitting there, measuring time, when he heard the loud tap of Kielly's feet walking toward him.

"Have I got news for you," he announced, smiling widely. "Superintendent Quinton has just informed me that Governor Glover wants you to do some fresco work over at Government House. I couldn't believe it at first, but apparently they have it all sorted out with Judge Prowse. You're to start next Monday and work there every day, except Saturday and Sunday, until the work is done. They want the ballroom, the dining room, and the hall done before Christmas. Some dignitaries are coming, and they want the rooms finished before they arrive."

"That is wonderful news! I can't believe it!" Alexander was jumping around his cell. "Will I be paid for my work?"

"You're something, you know," Kielly replied, shaking his head. "Here you are in jail, and you're talking about your payment. You've got nerve, I'll give you that."

"I really have no choice, and I would do the work anyway. It will be good for my reputation to do an important building like Government House."

"Always thinking ahead, aren't you. I admire that. And to answer your question, they're not going to pay you, but there is talk of maybe lessening your sentence, and that would be as good or better than pay, I'm thinking. I don't know how much time they'll take off, but we'll find out soon, I imagine. In the meantime, you're to make up lists for the supplies you're going to need. Make sure it's a detailed list. The supplies will be sent over to Government House, and you can start on Monday."

"Give me some paper and I'll start right away."

Alexander had the list finished in his head by the time Kielly returned with the lined paper and pencil. He asked Kielly how to spell some of the words, and then he handed the list to him and said, "It is important that nothing is substituted. I must have the proper materials or the plaster will not last. I will need a large mortar and pestle, too. I have asked for finely ground pigments, but they are usually not fine enough for me. The colours will last longer if the pigments are very finely ground, and I want my work to last for all time. The ceilings will be my best work yet. I can hardly wait to get started. Kielly, can you get me some large pieces of drawing paper? I want to begin designing the frescoes."

"I'll get right on it," said Kielly. "I'm going to be your guard, so I'm looking forward to this commission, too. Any day spent away from the penitentiary is well spent, I say."

"I have no argument with that," said Alexander, smiling and dancing around his cell.

four

It was the beginning of October, and Cheri and Ellen were in the dining room draping the furniture with blankets and sheets. Pindikowsky was starting work on the frescoes on Monday, and the whole house was buzzing with the idea of it. Some of the staff thought it was a terrible thing to have a criminal in their midst, but most were excited by the prospect of something happening outside the usual routine. Ellen could barely contain herself.

"I can't wait to see him work. Thank God I have an excuse to be going in and out of here," Ellen said to Cheri as she tucked and pinned sheets around each of the Queen Anne–styled chairs.

"You'll have to tell me everything that goes on and leave no details out," said Cheri. "I'll be stuck in the laundry. You don't suppose he'll try to escape, do you?"

"No, I don't. Judge Prowse gave special permission for Pindikowsky's guard to carry a firearm while he's here. Also, they're going to lessen his sentence because he's doing the work. Why would he spoil that chance? And where would he go? As soon as he tried to get off the island, he'd be caught. I heard that out in Heart's Content, the ladies that he taught were really upset when he went to jail. I imagine having him in the community spiced things up a bit. It's dull enough here in the city. I can just imagine how boring life would be in the outports."

"Well, I'm from an outport, and you're right," said Cheri. "Life in Cape Freels is pretty slow compared to here. Mom and Dad moved out to the Cape right after they were married, and I was born there. They often used to talk about life in St. John's, and I guess that's why I wanted to live here. I miss the Cape, though. It's beautiful there, and the sandy beaches are wonderful. The beaches around here are all rocks."

"I've never been to a beach with sand. What's it like?" asked Ellen.

"It's hard to describe, but in July and August I love to walk at the edge of the water and let the sand squish between my toes. Before July, the water's so cold that your feet would be numb in seconds. I pity the poor fishermen whose boats sink. The only good thing is that they die quickly. Most of the fishermen can't swim, and people from away think that's strange, but being able to swim wouldn't matter in the freezing water. It might prolong the agony for a few more minutes, that's all."

"Well, that's a black thought, although it's only too true. My uncle was a fisherman, and he drowned at sea. They found wreckage from his boat, but they never recovered his body. I hope his death was quick." Ellen shivered, thinking about it. "I would like to walk on a sandy beach, though. I hate trying to walk over the rocks on the beaches around here. More than once I've turned my ankle over on them."

"Why don't we take our holidays together, and you can come home with me for a visit? Mom would love to meet you. I've written letters telling her all about you."

"Not everything, I hope."

"You know your secrets are safe with me, El."

"I know. You're the best," Ellen said. "Now grab the end of that blanket and help me cover the sideboard. It has to be well padded in case some of the plaster drops. We can't have the furniture scratched. I thought all of the furnishings would be moved out, but apparently they're just going to shift it around as Pindikowsky works. We'll have to do a good job of protecting every piece of furniture, because I don't want to be blamed for any damage."

WHEN ELLEN'S MOTHER ARRIVED HOME THAT NIGHT SHE WENT DIRECTLY to the kitchen and put the kettle on. Ellen knew they were going to have a chat, and she had a pretty good idea what it would be about.

Louise poured a cup of tea for Ellen and took a sip from her favourite rose-patterned cup before she spoke.

"I hear you've switched your day off with Mabel. When she mentioned it, she told me that you'd cleared the change with me."

Ellen looked across the table at her mother, guilt spreading across her face.

"Don't worry. I told her you had, but I don't like being surprised like that. What were you thinking about? Why didn't you ask me first before you went to Mabel?" Ellen's mother held up her hand. "Never mind, don't bother answering. You thought I'd say no, didn't you? You want to be at The House on Monday when that Pindikowsky fellow starts working, don't you?"

"Yes, and what's wrong with that," Ellen said defensively. "I don't want to miss all the excitement. You know what I'm like."

"Yes, I do. That's the problem. You're too easily excited, and from what I hear this Polish fellow is a charmer, and I don't want you being charmed by him. I don't think it's a very smart idea having him do the work at The House. He is a criminal, after all."

"He's not dangerous, Mother. He forged cheques, that's all. He didn't kill anyone."

"That's all, that's all! Just listen to yourself. You're defending him already." Ellen's mother was shouting and pacing around the kitchen. "Just watch yourself, my lady. Don't talk to him or the guard. You'll be expected to carry in tea and bring in lunch, but other than that I want you to stay out of the way. You can help with the silver polishing. You won't have much to do, anyway. Lady Glover has cancelled her 'at homes' while the work is being done. At least she's sensible enough not to endanger the lives of her friends while a criminal is at The House. I hope Pindikowsky is a fast worker, although he'll probably want to drag it out rather than be in a jail cell. I don't like the feel of this, not at all. Just be careful, mind. I'll be keeping my eye on you."

"Yes, Mother, don't worry. It's not as if he can ask me out or anything, and he will be guarded all the time. Besides, what makes you think I'll like him?" Ellen put her arms around her mother and kissed her cheek.

"Hmm," said Louise.

ON FRIDAY MORNING, THE ART SUPPLIES ARRIVED AT THE HOUSE. George and Stanley, who usually worked at the stables, had been recruited to roll up the carpets in the ballroom and dining room and store them in one of the upstairs rooms. They had then laid down canvas to protect the floors and had set up a large work table, as well as a couple of wooden chairs and a stool that they had carried over from the greenhouse along with ladders and long wooden planks.

Ellen directed the delivery men to place the bags of sand and lime and the other supplies on the floor alongside the planks, and she carefully draped the table with canvas. She could have left all the supplies on the floor, but she was bored without her regular duties to attend to, so she started to arrange the equipment in a way that she thought made sense. She spread out trowels of different sizes, small metal tools, assorted paintbrushes, large and small bowls, glass jars and small bags containing coloured powder. She placed a long-handled tool shaped like a garden hoe and a tool like a gigantic egg beater next to the table. She could pretty much figure out what most of the materials would be used for, but she was mystified by the large mortar and pestle. At first she thought it had been ordered for the kitchen, but she was assured that it was part of the list of supplies that Mr. Pindikowsky had requested. She put it in the middle of the table. Everything was ready for Monday, and Ellen was so excited she knew she wouldn't sleep much the next few nights.

five

Monday morning finally arrived, and Ellen was at work early. Cheri had a view of the east entrance from the window in the laundry, and she'd promised she would come and get Ellen as soon as she saw the police wagon arrive. It was five minutes to six when Ellen heard Cheri's footsteps in the hall.

"They're here," Cheri said in a loud whisper, grabbing Ellen's arm and pulling her toward the back entrance.

"I can't come," Ellen said. "I have to wait here, Mother's orders. You go back inside and see what's happening. I want to hear every detail later."

Cheri rushed off, and Ellen was left waiting and wondering about what was going on. Her mother's specific orders had been to stay at her post, do as she was told, to speak only when spoken to, and under no circumstances stand around chatting. Following her orders was another thing entirely, but Ellen knew her mother would be watching her closely, and she was going to try to behave.

Ellen heard loud footsteps and a dragging sound that she couldn't identify. She looked in the direction of the sound and saw black boots shackled together. She looked up, and her eyes connected with Pindikowsky's. He was better-looking than she remembered from his court appearance. His hair was not long anymore, and because of this

his eyes stood out, revealing their beautiful greenish-grey colour. Ellen quickly looked away, but she could still feel his eyes on her.

Just then, Ellen's mother came down the stairs and into the hall. She was fairly bristling with energy. "What's this, then, Officer? Surely it isn't necessary to have your prisoner shackled once he's in The House, is it? Those chains are going to have the floors ruined. It will be no good to have fancy ceilings but splintered floors."

"Good morning," said the guard, smiling at Ellen's mother. "I'm Officer Kielly. I think you're totally right about the floors. I'll remove the shackles immediately." Kielly removed a key from his jacket and bent to release the chains from Pindikowsky's ankles. "From here on in, the handcuffs will be enough. I have my pistol for protection," he said, patting his holster, "and you and your staff won't have to worry one bit. Prisoner Pindikowsky will be no trouble to you. I can guarantee it."

"I'm counting on it, Officer Kielly. I'll be in the kitchen if I'm needed. In the meantime, Ellen can look after you," said Louise, gesturing to where Ellen stood. Kielly walked toward her and smiled.

"Are the supplies all here, miss?" he asked her.

"Yes, they're all in here," Ellen said, her voice shaking with nervousness. She indicated the door which led into the dining room and stepped back, allowing them to enter. Her heart was pounding, and she wondered if they could hear it.

When Kielly removed his handcuffs, Alexander rubbed his wrists and walked directly over to the table that Ellen had prepared. He carefully inspected the tools and brushes, turning each one over in his hands. He rubbed the trowel handles and ran his fingers along the blades. Then he walked to the north wall of the room, where the bags of sand and lime were piled. He randomly selected five bags, crouched down, and pulled the strings to reveal the contents. He then scooped a handful of sand from the first bag and rubbed it between his fingers, sniffing it before returning it to the bag. He did the same for the first bag of lime. He repeated this ritual for all five bags before retying them.

"Excellent," he said. "Everything is here, and the quality of the materials is good. All I need is a large tub of water and I can start."

Alexander walked over to the table again and began caressing the tools as if they were precious jewels. Ellen guessed that, to him, they were. She realized she had been thinking of him as Alexander ever since their eyes had met. When he spoke, Ellen felt inexplicably drawn to him. His voice was deep and warm, and she loved the sound of his accent. Her mother would not be happy about that, and Ellen reminded herself to refer to him as "the prisoner," or Mr. Pindikowsky, in her mother's presence.

"Please bring us a large tub of water, miss, and if you could get us some tea, too, that would be grand," said Kielly.

Ellen wasn't used to being ordered around by an armed guard, but there was something about Kielly that she liked, so she wasn't going to complain. She did want to establish her position as parlour maid, however. "My name is Miss Ellen Dormody," she said in her most proper voice. "I'll inform the staff of your needs, and I'll be back shortly with your tea." Ellen left the room with her back straight and her head held high. She could feel Alexander's eyes on her, and she felt herself blushing. She took a few deep breaths to gain her composure before she went into the kitchen.

When Ellen returned with the tea, she didn't see Alexander at first. Then she noticed that the large ladder had been moved to the vestibule.

"I think I will be starting here," said Alexander, his voice floating down from the top of the ladder. "My design of the flowers and vines will work well here, I think." Ellen could hear the excitement in his voice.

"Your tea is ready, Officer Kielly," she said. "You should take it now so it doesn't get cold. The shortbread is just out of the oven, too. The water for the plaster will be here directly."

"Come down from there, Pindikowsky. Miss Dormody has brought us a treat. I know you haven't had shortbread like this in a while, if ever," Kielly said, biting into a piece.

Alexander descended the ladder, and Ellen couldn't help but notice his strong calf muscles. "What is shortbread? Is it bread that is not tall?" he said, laughing.

Alexander definitely wasn't what Ellen had expected from a prisoner. He was so relaxed, and somehow he looked like he belonged in the grand room. His accent just added to his charm.

Just then Louise Dormody passed by the doorway, and Ellen quickly left the room, telling them she'd be back for the tray in a few minutes. As it turned out, her mother had different plans.

"Ellen, we need some help with the silver polishing," her mother said. "I've instructed George to bring the tea tray back when he and Stanley bring the water to the dining room, so you'll not be needed in the reception rooms for the next couple of hours. Did I hear that you brought shortbread in with the tea?" she asked as they approached the kitchen. "That was hardly necessary, was it? Prisoner Pindikowsky is not a guest here, you know." Louise was tapping her foot—not a good sign.

"The shortbread was for Officer Kielly," said Ellen. "We should treat him well, shouldn't we? And I couldn't put just one shortbread cookie on the plate, could I?"

"You've an answer for everything, haven't you? Remember, I've got my eye on you."

"Yes, Mrs. Dormody. I'll start polishing the salt cellars, shall I?" Ellen said, in her most pleasant voice.

six

The next day, Ellen barely spent any time in the dining room. Her mother kept her away as much as possible, finding errands for her to do that seemed totally unnecessary. She did serve tea to Kielly and Alexander around nine o'clock, but they hardly noticed her since they were so absorbed in their work.

When she set up the small luncheon table at noon, Kielly had his jacket off, his sleeves rolled up, and he was pouring sand and lime into a large bucket that contained water. He still had his gun strapped into a holster on his left side, but it was getting in his way, and before long he took it off, hanging it over the wooden garden chair that had been brought in for their convenience. The upholstered chairs were too precious to be left in the way of the fresco work and had been shifted into the ballroom.

It was clear, from the ease between them as they worked together, that Kielly and Alexander trusted one another. Kielly fed the sand and lime plaster mixture into a long wooden trough while Alexander mixed it with the long-handled metal hoe. Then he switched to using the metal egg beater tool, vigorously whipping it around and around with his strong, sinewy arms. He didn't seem to notice Ellen's presence at all, so immersed was he in his work, but she watched and listened to everything he did and said. She was so used to his accent now that she hardly noticed it, understanding everything that he said without difficulty.

"I must mix the plaster very smooth, and then it must rest," Alexander said to Kielly. "It will take a couple of days to set right, and then I will begin the real work."

"My back is gone," said Kielly, straightening up and arching upwards with his hands at his waist.

"Your back is gone?" questioned Pindikowsky. "What do you mean your back is gone? How can your back be gone? It is where it always is."

Both Kielly and Ellen started to laugh, and they could hardly stop. Alexander just looked mystified. When they finally got themselves under control, Kielly said, "It's just an expression. It means my back is sore. I'm surprised you haven't heard it before."

"Just when I think I understand English, I hear something like this," said Alexander, shaking his head. "Now I will set up the scaffold." He moved over to the planks and carried them one by one to the back of the room. Ellen heard her mother's footsteps coming out the hall, and she reluctantly left the room.

WEDNESDAY WAS LOUISE DORMODY'S DAY OFF, AND ELLEN WAS determined to spend as much time as she could watching Alexander work. She knew she was attracted to him, but she was also intrigued by the whole fresco project. It was so exciting to have something different going on after all the mundane household tasks that made up her usual workdays. She served tea at nine o'clock, and this time Alexander looked her way and kept gazing at her until she could feel herself blushing.

"Forgive me, Miss Dormody," he said. "I am staring at you. Your hair with the light from the window is like shining copper. I am an artist and cannot help but admire beauty."

Ellen nearly dropped the teapot. "Thank you, Mr. Pindikowsky. Excuse me, I'm needed upstairs," she said, leaving the room quickly. She knew her face was as red as fall apples, and she had to get her emotions under control. She used to laugh at all the other maids blushing and going on about this boy or that boy. But then, make no mistake, Alexander was a man.

"Be careful there, Pindikowsky," Kielly said. "Her mother is the head housekeeper here, you know, and if she thinks there's anything going on, you won't be seeing Miss Dormody again."

"I understand," Pindikowsky said. "But she is very hard to ignore, don't you agree?"

"She is very lovely, different-looking, not the usual sort of pretty. She reminds me of my cousin Judith. She's a law unto herself. And if she's like Judith, that's all the more reason not to trifle with her."

"I will put my mind on my work. I intend for the frescoes I do here to last long after I am dead. It will be my legacy. I want to be remembered as an artist and not a criminal."

"Strangely enough, I'm envying you. No one is going to remember my work as a prison guard."

"Maybe you would like to learn how to do frescoes, Kielly. You may not be able to do the designs at first, but you can learn to work the plaster. I will teach you, if you like. It is how I learned. I apprenticed back in Poland with a well-known fresco artist, Johann Blonsky."

"I'd like that," said Kielly. "I also like the fact that I can learn and be paid at the same time. That's my idea of a bargain. On the records I'm your armed guard, but off the records I'm your apprentice. No funny business, though."

"You know I won't try to escape. This is my chance to redeem myself, and I'm going to do the best work I've ever done."

"That's the spirit. Now, what do we do next?"

WHEN ELLEN CAME BACK INTO THE DINING ROOM TO TAKE THE TEA tray away, Kielly and Alexander were standing over by the table. Alexander was pouring the red powder into the mortar basin. She moved closer, curious. Before she could stop herself, she asked, "What are you going to do with the mortar and pestle? I thought it was for the kitchen when it arrived here."

Alexander turned toward her.

"I will show you, Miss Dormody. I am grinding the pigment to make it finer.

"That is my secret. The finer the pigment powder, the better it will mix with the plaster and the longer the fresco will last. I can trust you with my secret, I hope," he said, smiling at her.

"Of course," Ellen said, returning his gaze. "I'll leave you to your work, then." She backed away from the table and Alexander resumed grinding the powder. Within a moment he was engrossed in his work, and Ellen knew she had disappeared from his mind. It was the first time that she'd had a glimpse into the actual work of being an artist. It was strangely fascinating. As she watched, the rhythmic thump, thump of the pestle echoed her heartbeat. Then another sound entered her consciousness.

"Ellen, you're a million miles away," said Cheri. "I've called out to you twice, but it's like you're in a daze. Come on, it's break time. I've got the kettle boiled and everything."

"I'm coming," Ellen said. She walked down the hall knowing she'd have some explaining to do. Cheri knew her so well that she couldn't hide anything from her. They had taken their breaks together from the first day she worked at The House. She usually couldn't wait for break time, but now she wanted to get back to her post and Alexander.

"Tell me what's going on in there, I'm dying of curiosity," said Cheri as they sat down at the small table over by the window, out of the way of the kitchen traffic. "You're like a cat on a hot stove, El. I can see you can't wait to get back to the dining room. It's written all over you. But you're not leaving until you fill me in on what's going on. Now, start talking."

"Alexander—I mean, Mr. Pindikowsky—is working on the pigments, or 'peegments,' as he says it. That's what he was using the mortar and pestle for, to grind down the colours. Remember, I thought there was a mistake and that Mrs. Parmender had ordered the mortar and pestle for the kitchen?" Ellen was talking fast, trying to cover up calling Pindikowsky by his first name.

"What's that? Did you say something to me?" asked Mrs. Parmender from across the room. She was rolling out pastry.

"Nothing, Mrs. Parmender," Ellen said. She leaned forward and lowered her voice. "He showed me how it was done. He said the grinding was his secret for making the colours and the frescoes last. It's so interesting to watch him."

"You're saying that watching someone grind up powders is interesting? I'd say it's the person doing the grinding that's interesting and not the process. You've seen Mrs. Parmender grind ingredients often enough, and I don't remember you ever being spellbound while watching her."

"What's that you're saying," called out Mrs. Parmender. "I heard my name."

"We were just saying how much we loved your pastry, Mrs. Parmender," said Cheri, winking at Ellen.

"Well, you can have a taste when the tarts come out of the oven," Mrs. Parmender said, smiling.

"Thanks, Mrs. Parmender," they said in unison.

"I think you're smitten with Mr. Pindikowsky, or rather, Alexander," Cheri said, imitating Ellen's voice and fluttering her eyelashes.

"Shhh," Ellen said, looking around her. "I do like him, but no one can know. He's a prisoner, after all."

"He won't be a prisoner this time next year," said Cheri. "You never know what can happen."

"Don't tell anyone how I feel, will you, Cheri? Mother is already watching me like a hawk."

"Well, be careful not to refer to him as Alexander. I'd go with 'the prisoner,' if I were you."

"Don't worry, I'm being careful. Now, I'd better get back to my work."

"Is that what they call gawking at painters all day?" Cheri said, laughing. "Don't forget, we're going shopping on Saturday."

"I'm looking forward to it. See you tomorrow."

"Here, take a pastry," said Mrs. Parmender, walking over to them, holding out a plate.

They both popped a jam-filled pastry into their mouths. "Yum," they said at the same time, laughing as they went back to their work.

THE REST OF THE DAY ELLEN WATCHED AND LISTENED AS ALEXANDER and Kielly mixed plaster and pounded pigments. She was learning about art as they talked.

"What do you think about those artists—the Impressionists, I think they're calling them?" Kielly asked Alexander. "I was reading about them in the paper. They're causing an uproar in Paris. Apparently the Academy won't allow them to exhibit. They're painting all blurry instead of in detail. I saw a coloured picture in the *Art Journal*, over at the library, last week. I can't decide if I like it or not. What do you think of them?"

"I like their work. They are doing something new. I think it is maybe a reaction to photography. If you want an exact picture of something, you can have it photographed now. It doesn't have to be painted. Painters can be free now to paint as they want. The Impressionists are not trying to be exact. They are painting a mood, a moment in time. It will be interesting to see if people will buy their work. They still have to make the money. I am glad that I do frescoes. They will not change, and people will always want decoration in their homes, I think."

"Good point, Pindikowsky, good point," said Kielly.

Ellen made a mental note to find out all about the Impressionists. She didn't want Alexander to think she knew nothing about art.

seven

Saturday morning, Ellen stood outside her door on Victoria Street waiting for Cheri to go shopping with her. Cheri lived over on Prescott Street with her Aunt Betty, not very far away, and Ellen expected her any minute. Ellen's mother's birthday was in a few weeks, and she needed to buy materials to make her a new hat. She always wanted something practical for her birthday. Ellen remembered when she was eleven and had asked her mother what she wanted for her birthday. She had saved up her allowance for weeks, and she wanted to buy her something special. Her mother had insisted that she wanted a new mixing bowl, and Ellen was so disappointed. She wanted to buy her some cologne in a pretty bottle or some bath powder in a beautiful box, but Louise was adamant. She said she didn't need or like cologne, and she really wanted a mixing bowl. Ellen did buy her one, always wanting to please her, but she picked out the brightest-coloured one she could find. It was rimmed in yellow and had red tulips painted on the side. Her mother still used the bowl, and she always told Ellen how much she loved it.

Ellen's theory on gift giving was that the giver should be just as satisfied with the gift as the recipient. Otherwise, it wasn't better to give rather than to receive—it was disappointing. So this year she was going to satisfy her mother's practical streak and her own need for beauty by making her a hat. Everyone needed a hat. The fact that she made it herself would appeal to her mother's sense of thrift. But Ellen was going to buy the most decadent velvet and satin ribbons, feathers and trims, that she could find. It would probably end up costing more money than if she had bought a ready-made hat, but her mother wouldn't have to know that. That was her plan. She could see it finished in her head, and she couldn't wait to get started.

"Sorry I'm late," said Cheri, suddenly appearing at the top of the Victoria Street steps. "Mrs. Brake came out of her house just as I was leaving and I couldn't get her to draw breath between words. I finally had to tell her that I had a doctor's appointment to get rid of her. By now she's probably telling my whole street that I've got some horrible disease and won't last the winter."

"I'm glad my neighbours are a bit standoffish," said Ellen.

"Yes, you're lucky. Now, where are we heading first?"

"I'm making Mother a hat for her birthday, so we have to go to the Royal Emporium. They'll have the best selection of trims. George told me the *Briston* is in from England. It arrived at the dock on Tuesday, so the stores should all have their supplies sorted by now."

"You should make yourself a new hat, too, and make sure your Alexander sees you wearing it."

"He's not my Alexander. He hardly notices me. When he's working, he's so intent I don't think he knows there's a world out there, let alone me. I like that about him, though. It shows that he really is a fine artist, and I respect him for it."

"It seems he can do no wrong in your eyes. Do you know how much time is going to be taken off his sentence for the work he's doing?"

"No, although I heard Officer Kielly telling Alexander that there's already talk of him working on the Colonial Building ceilings when he finishes at The House."

"I guess everyone wants to take advantage of the free workmanship, especially with someone who is so talented. It's not likely that there will ever be another artist-prisoner."

"I wonder why Lady Glover went with the governor on his trip out to Conception Bay? I thought she'd want to be at The House when the fresco work was being done. She is quite good at drawing and watercolours, and I would think she'd want to be able to observe Alexander at work."

"Maybe Governor Glover was a little afraid of her being exposed to a criminal. He wants to take advantage of Alexander's artistry, but he is still a criminal, after all, and his wife is a lady. Did they take the jolly boat on this trip?"

"Yes, I saw them getting it all rigged out. It's apparently very comfortable to ride in, but it's so big that the road engineers are worried about some of the bridges collapsing under the weight. George told me that it takes two of the huge draft horses to pull it."

"I'd sure like to ride in it. Even taking a carriage out to Topsail, to visit my cousin Joan, makes my teeth rattle, with all the bumping around. Thank goodness we'll be taking the coastal boat out to Cape Freels this summer. You haven't forgotten about it, I hope."

"Of course not. I'm really looking forward to it."

"Why do they call the carriage 'the jolly boat,' do you know?"

"George told me that in five minutes they can take the carriage off its base and use it as a punt. I can't believe it, but George said he saw the men do it. It was designed by a boat builder down on the southern shore. An Irishman, I think."

"It's a fascinating time we live in, isn't it? Prisoners painting ceilings, and carriages that are boats. I'm glad to be part of it, aren't you?"

"Yes, I am. And when we get back from Cape Freels, I'll be getting ready to go to England. I need to get started on the next phase of my life. This hat that I'm making for Mother is going to be my own design and my own look. I'm hoping my sketches as well as the finished hat will impress my millinery teachers. Mother has contacted a couple of her relatives in England, and they're going to check on a few millinery establishments for me."

"I wish I was going with you."

"I do, too. I know you have to send most of the money you earn home to help out your family. There are nine of you, aren't there?"

"There'll be ten by this summer." Cheri sighed. "Mother said this baby will be her last, but she said that when Charles was born two years ago."

"Do you want to have lots of children?"

"No. That's why I'm not getting married for a long, long time. Then I'll be too old to have too many. Mother was only our age when she was married."

"I don't know. It would be wonderful to have a child, especially if he looked like your husband." Ellen was picturing a miniature Alexander.

"This child of yours, he wouldn't be named Peter Pindikowsky, would he?" Cheri was laughing.

Ellen looked at her and started laughing, too. "You read me like a book, don't you?"

They had reached their destination. They walked through the doors of the emporium, and it was very crowded inside.

"I guess we weren't the only ones wanting the latest goods from overseas," said Cheri.

eight

On Monday and Tuesday of the second week of the fresco work, Louise kept Ellen away from the reception rooms—and Alexander—as much as possible. It was probably just as well, since he was too busy laying down preliminary coats of plaster to notice her. Tea and lunchtimes were the only times Ellen still went into the dining room. At these times, Alexander was hunched over at the table, drawing designs, making stencils or mixing pigments and putting them in the small jars. So far there had been no actual painting done—it was all preparation—and Ellen was looking forward to when the painting would begin.

When she arrived at her post on Wednesday, Alexander was already on the scaffolding spreading a thin layer of plaster. He held the plasterboard in his left hand, while with his right hand he wielded the trowel, scooping up the plaster and swirling it onto the ceiling. It was like watching a dance. He did only a small section and then came down the ladder.

"That is done. I feel at last I have begun," said Alexander, laying down his plasterboard and rinsing the trowel in the bucket next to the work table. "The plaster has to set up, now, and then I can inscribe my design."

"Here is your tea, Mr. Pindikowsky, Officer Kielly," Ellen said. "Mrs. Parmender has spared you some strawberry jam tarts today. They're really tasty."

"Thank you, Miss Dormody. You are as kind as you are beautiful."

"I agree," said Kielly. "If she weren't kind, she'd be laughing at you right now."

"What do you mean?" asked Alexander.

"You've got almost as much plaster on your forehead and nose as you have on the ceiling. Here, use my handkerchief. It's clean," said Kielly. He held out the handkerchief, and Alexander wiped his face.

"Pardon me, Miss Dormody. Art is messy as well as difficult." He smiled and winked at her. She smiled back at him, and Kielly made a loud coughing sound.

"Your tea is getting cold, Pindikowsky."

"Thank you," said Alexander. He sat on the wooden stool that had been brought over from the greenhouse along with the table. He didn't make eye contact with Ellen again that morning. She took up her position of fly-on-the-wall, watching and listening as Kielly and Alexander talked and worked.

"How come you only covered a small area with the plaster today?" asked Kielly.

"That is the last layer before I start painting. It is called the *intonaco*. I must work the plaster when it is damp. The colours will dry into the plaster and become one with it. That is what makes the frescoes last so long. If I cover too much area, the plaster will dry before I can paint it and the pigment will not bond with it. The area that I have covered is called, in Italian, the *giornata*. It means 'day,' and the area I have prepared is the space that I think I can finish in one day. Because the weather is cold and damp in Newfoundland, I have almost twenty-four hours that I can work with the plaster before it dries. When I worked in Poland in the summer, I would only have maybe eight hours before the plaster would be too dry."

"I'm glad there's some advantage to the damp, dreary weather here," said Kielly. "What can I help you with, now?"

"There is nothing that you can help me with until we mix more plaster tomorrow. For the rest of the day I will be inscribing my design into the plaster. Once I get started and the design is mapped out, I can paint free and the work will go faster."

Alexander tucked his design sheets in his pants and climbed the ladder. Ellen watched his every move. As he inscribed his designs into the plaster, she wondered how he could keep his head tilted back for such a long time. Her neck was aching just looking up at him.

As if reading her mind, Kielly said, "I can see now why you did all those exercises at the jail. You really need to be in fighting form to do this work. I've discovered muscles that I never knew I had just helping you mix the plaster. I feel better, too. I've gotten soft working at the penitentiary, sitting around all day. What do you think, Miss Dormody? Do you think I look fitter than when I came here?"

"I think you do, Officer Kielly. Does your wife think so?" she queried.

"I caught her staring at me the other day. Of course, that could be because I forgot to fix the fence, or chop wood, or pick up the mail, but you never know," Kielly said, chuckling and strutting around like a rooster.

ELLEN BROUGHT IN THE TEA AT FOUR O'CLOCK AND PLACED IT ON the small side table. Alexander was on the scaffolding, and when she looked up, her eyes filled with the beauty of the colours that followed Alexander's brush as he made flowers and vines appear, as if by magic. She was enthralled.

"How beautiful," she said, throwing her voice to Alexander. "I hate to have you stop painting, but your tea will get cold if you don't come down now." He said something that she didn't understand.

"He won't come down now," said Kielly from his chair in the corner of the room. "It's the golden hour."

"The golden hour, what's that?" Ellen asked.

"The plaster is at the perfect state between wet and dry. The plaster will accept the pigments perfectly now, and he won't want to lose that advantage."

Both Kielly and Ellen watched Alexander in silence while time passed without them. Finally, Alexander stopped painting and descended to their level.

"That is it for today for the painting," said Alexander. "I will lay down the *intonaco* for tomorrow before we leave, but I will have my tea now, Miss Dormody, please."

"Let me get more hot water for you," Ellen said. "The tea will be cold by now."

"Please, do not bother," said Alexander, pouring tea into his cup. "It is so hot up there," he said, indicating the ceiling, "that a cool drink is just what I need. The plaster, when it is drying, produces heat. It is a chemical reaction that causes it to happen. Tomorrow, Kielly, you should come up on the scaffold with me. It is important for you to learn all aspects of the process if you want to become a fresco painter."

"I look forward to it," said Kielly, taking another biscuit. "I'll just have another of these to keep my strength up."

"I'll have one, too. Miss Dormody, you are spoiling us," said Alexander, giving her one of his looks that made her knees go weak.

nine

Ellen spent her day off sewing like a slave, because the following day was her mother's birthday and she was determined to finish her hat. She wanted to fashion it in such a way that it could be worn as a bonnet with the green satin ribbons tied under her chin, or as a hat, tilted to the front and over the brow with only a hatpin to hold it in place. The ribbons could easily be folded inside the hat when she didn't want to wear it as a bonnet. Ellen was sure that her mother would like the flexibility of the design. When a northeast gale was blowing, the bonnet style would be perfect, and when the weather was more civil, the hat style would give an entirely different look. Ellen had used green velvet for the main part of the hat, ruching it up over the high crown and smoothing it out over the wide brim. She bent the brim back along the sides of the hat, securing it at the crown and creating a narrow silhouette in the front. She stitched a pale green ostrich feather and jet beads on the right-hand side. Ellen loved the look of it, and it was so flattering. She was going to make another like it for herself and one for Cheri for Christmas. The thought of Christmas reminded her that Alexander would be finished the frescoes by then, and her good mood disappeared. With an effort, she blocked thoughts of Alexander and focused on the evening ahead.

Cheri was coming over for dinner to help celebrate, and she had persuaded Mrs. Parmender to make a special sponge cake with orange zest glaze. The oranges were a treat, courtesy of the trade ship the *Southwind*. It was in port this week from Jamaica, loaded with a cargo of rum, molasses, and a few crates of oranges. The ship was leaving as soon as the weather was favourable. It was at the dock in Baird's Cove, being loaded up with salt fish for the return voyage.

Ellen often wondered what it would be like to live in a place where it was warm all year round. Cheri's cousin, Simon, was a sailor on the ship, and he was the one responsible for getting the oranges. He also gave Cheri a conch shell. Cheri was going to send the shell home to her brother, Paul, so he could make a foghorn out of it by sawing off one end of the shell. The shell horn would be kept in his dory so that if he was lost in the fog, he could blow the horn and be found. More than one Newfoundland fisherman had been saved by a conch shell from the Caribbean.

Ellen loved to think about how Newfoundland's commercial trade connected the cold northern island with the hot island of Jamaica. The pearly pink of the conch shell resting against the cod jiggers in their dories was a romantic reminder of this connection, and it made her feel expansive and part of the outside world. She hoped that some day she would travel there. Until then she had to content herself with reading stories about exotic places or hearing about them when Cheri's cousin had time to visit.

Ellen's thoughts came back home as she heard her mother opening the door, and she quickly tucked the just-finished hat behind a chair.

"It's freezing out there," Louise said, taking off her gloves and rubbing her hands together.

"Why don't you make some tea and I'll join you in a minute," Ellen said.

As soon as Louise walked into the kitchen, Ellen retrieved the hat and went upstairs. "I've got your favourite meat pie in the oven for supper, so you don't have to do a thing, and I've asked Cheri to come for dinner to help us celebrate your birthday," Ellen said, her voice carrying down the stairs.

When she reached her bedroom at the east end of the hall, she took out the new hat box she had purchased and carefully nestled her mother's hat in a fluff of white tissue paper. She couldn't wait for her mother to see it, but she wanted to present it to her after everyone was fed and relaxed. Ellen and her mother had been a little out of sorts with each other since Alexander had started the frescoes. Her mother knew that Ellen was attracted to him, and her protectiveness was irritating. Ellen kept telling her mother that she could look out for herself, but it didn't matter. To be honest, Ellen didn't know if she could protect her heart. Her feelings for Alexander had already gone beyond that.

Tonight she hoped that she and her mother could enjoy each other's company without any strain. She hated there to be distance between them. They had always been close, even though Louise didn't let her get away with anything. Ellen admired her mother, and she wanted to be her friend as well as her daughter.

"Thank you for getting all this ready," said her mother as she walked into the dining room. "The table looks beautiful with the red dogberries as a centrepiece. I never would have thought of using them."

"Nature always provides inspiration for me. Whenever I'm stuck trying to figure out a hat design, I just go for a walk and I always find the answer."

"Well, I don't. I guess you have a different kind of sensitivity than me. Your father was like you, and it's nice to know you inherited that from him. It makes me feel he's still with us." Her mother's voice was wistful.

The doorbell rang and Ellen answered it, ushering Cheri into the house. Her hands were carefully shielding a large box that Ellen assumed contained her mother's cake.

"Steer me to the table," said Cheri, out of breath. "I don't want to drop this now. I walked over from The House with half the dogs in town following me. It's a good thing I found a box large enough for it, or it probably would have blown right out of my hands, with the wind so high."

"Here, give it to me," Ellen said. She put the cake on the sideboard in the dining room. Mrs. Parmender had outdone herself, even decorating the top of the cake with orange blossom flowers made from royal icing.

"Happy birthday, Mrs. Dormody," said Cheri, giving Louise a kiss on the cheek. At work she was very professional with Ellen's mother, but outside of The House they were relaxed with each other, and Louise thought of her as a second daughter.

"Thank you, Cheri. Let's go into the parlour. We'll light the fireplace and get cozy."

Ellen went up to the second floor to tell Har that it was time for dinner. Har's real name was Miss Suzanne Harding, and she had been boarding with them since Ellen was three years old. When Ellen was little she started calling her Har, the closest she could get to saying Miss Harding, and her nickname stuck. She was part of the family now. Har was the one who fostered Ellen's love of reading. She used most of the money she earned as a bookkeeper to buy books. As a child, Ellen thought that Har went to work to look after storybooks—that's what bookkeeping meant to her. Har thought that it was very funny and used to tell the story over and over again. Har's favourite authors were the Brontë sisters, but she read Austin, Richardson, Fielding, Defoe, Swift, Dickens, Shakespeare, and anything else she could get her hands on. It was unusual for a woman of her age—she was in her late forties—to work, but Har was an unusual woman. She had never married, and she was so clever that Wareham and Sons kept her in their employ and would probably be devastated if she retired. Ellen made a mental note to ask Har about the Impressionists that Alexander and Kielly had discussed. She was sure she'd know all about them.

When they'd finished eating, Ellen lit one candle on the cake to represent thirty-seven years, and they all sang "Happy Birthday" to Louise. She blew out the candle and said she had made a wish and hoped with all her heart that it would come true. She looked at Ellen when she said that, and Ellen didn't need to be a mind reader to know that her mother's wish involved a good marriage and children for her.

Har gave Louise tickets to a piano concert at the Athenaeum as well as a leatherbound copy of Dickens's *A Christmas Carol*, and Cheri gave her a white wool scarf with a long fringe that she had knit. Ellen knew that Cheri had put a lot of time into getting the intricate lacy pattern just right, and her mother was touched that Cheri had made it for her.

Now it was Ellen's turn. She went upstairs and brought down the hat box. She was a little nervous giving it to her. She loved the hat so much she just assumed that her mother would, too, but now she was not so sure. Her mother's approval meant everything to her.

Louise opened the box and lifted the hat from the tissue paper. "Ellen," she exclaimed. "It's exquisite! How ever did you afford to buy it? It must have cost you a fortune."

"The hat is my new design, Mother," Ellen said. "I finished making it today."

"You made it? But it looks so perfect and professional," she said, turning the hat over and examining it. "You're a genius. Maybe you'll have to have that hat shop after all."

"Try it on," Ellen said. "Here, let me show you. It can be a bonnet or a hat." Louise put the hat on, and it looked better than Ellen imagined it would. The colour made her green eyes leap from her face. She was still a relatively young woman, and she looked marvellous.

"I know it's not black, but it is dark green, and you have to wear it because it suits you to perfection," Ellen said.

Cheri and Har added their encouragement and praised Ellen for her design. Louise let Cheri try on the hat, and it suited her, too, although it was a little too small. Ellen would have to make Cheri's Christmas hat at least one size larger. She decided that the hat would be a russet colour that would suit Cheri's olive complexion and dark glossy hair. Ellen was thrilled with the success of her creation, and she felt that the rift between her and her mother was mended.

ten

It was the beginning of December and The House was like a ship, seething and groaning, readying for departure. Governor Glover was due back on Wednesday and everything had to be cleaned, polished, cooked, or ironed. Lady Glover wouldn't be returning until the week before Christmas. She was staying with her friend, Lady Shelbourne, in Topsail. Ellen thought Governor Glover was a bit apprehensive about the whole prisoner/fresco experiment and wanted to make sure everything was in the proper order before Lady Glover returned.

Alexander had finished the frescoes in the hall and dining room. The ceilings were perfection, but Alexander had created a total fantasy illusion in the ballroom: vines, winged Cupids, fanciful urns, medallions, intricate ribbon work, all swirled in a soft palette of Titian red, silvered green and golden flowers. Everyone who gazed at the ceiling was entranced. In fact, Louise had to make a new rule for the maids: "No loitering in the reception rooms, no gawking at the ceilings." Ellen was lucky to have an excuse to be in the rooms, and she filled her eyes and her heart with Alexander and his art.

It was Ellen's task to make sure the room was in pre-fresco condition before Governor Glover's arrival. The carpets had been rolled back into the hall and the dining room, the furniture reinstated. Dust from the plaster was everywhere and had settled into every crevice.

The gaslights were coated with it and bits of plaster had spattered the windows, requiring a putty knife to scrape it off. The ballroom had to be left as it was until the fresco was finished, but Ellen did a cursory job of tidying and dusting anyway.

Over the last few weeks, Kielly had been working closely with Alexander, and he had even done a little of the painting under Alexander's close supervision. He was becoming quite good at laying the *intonaco*.

It struck Ellen that The House staff had all gotten used to seeing Kielly with his jacket off, shirt sleeves rolled up, standing on the scaffolding, but she knew that Governor Glover would be shocked by this. They had all forgotten that Kielly was a prison guard for Alexander. In fact, it was hard for any of them at The House to think of Alexander as a prisoner at all. Kielly still had Alexander handcuffed when he arrived at The House every morning, but this was primarily for the eyes of any curious passersby, and the cuffs were quickly removed once he was inside.

The morning Governor Glover was expected, Kielly was on the ladder handing Alexander different pigment pots. As usual, his jacket was flung over the chair along with his gun and holster.

"Excuse me, Officer Kielly," Ellen said. "It may not be my place to say, but Governor Glover will be arriving any minute, and I think he expects you to be in your official role of prison guard."

"Yes, of course," said Kielly.

He continued talking to Alexander while he handed him various brushes. He didn't seem to take her hint, so Ellen pressed on, blushing at her boldness. She cleared her voice loudly. "Your jacket, Officer Kielly," she said, holding it out to him. "And your gun?"

Kielly looked at her sharply, and then with comprehension. "Right, right you are. Good girl. You've a clear head, I can see that," he said, quickly climbing down the ladder. He grabbed his holster from the chair, belted it around his shoulder, and then secured the gun, safely. He had only just rolled down his sleeves and donned his jacket when they heard the governor's carriage pull up to the front door. As Governor Glover walked in, Kielly leaned over and whispered to Ellen, "I owe you a favour. Don't hesitate to ask."

They were standing straight and proper when Governor Glover entered the ballroom. He stopped with one foot in the room and gazed up, his mouth literally falling open.

"Excellent, perfect," he said, regaining his composure. "More than I ever imagined. Capital!"

Kielly was grinning. "Would you like to meet the artist, Your Honour?" he asked, indicating Alexander, who was, miraculously, still painting, oblivious to the mere mortals below him.

"Yes, by all means," replied Governor Glover, staring up at Alexander.

"Mr. Pindikowsky," said Kielly. "Governor Glover would like to meet you."

Alexander, startled, dropped his paintbrush, and it fell like an arrow to the floor. Governor Glover bent and picked it up, smiling as Alexander descended to the bottom of the ladder. He stood at attention, and Ellen could feel his tension from across the room.

"Relax, Mr. Pindikowsky," said Governor Glover. "Your work is magnificent. You are to be congratulated." He held out his hand to Alexander.

Alexander put out his hand and then quickly drew it back when he realized that it was full of paint and plaster drippings. "Pardon me, Your Honour," he said, bowing his head. "My hands are covered in the paint. I wish to thank Your Honour for the opportunity you have given me to work on these frescoes. I thank you for trusting me."

"Your frescoes prove that I did the right thing. Now, tell me about the work and your design inspirations. I am interested in knowing about the whole process. Shall we go into the dining room? I understand that it is completed."

Ellen quickly opened the doors to the dining room and stood back as they walked through. She couldn't help but smile at Alexander as he passed, and he winked at her. She felt a warm, tingling sensation throughout her body, and she was sure that her hair was standing on end.

Kielly passed through the doorway and stood at attention, the perfect guard, while Alexander spoke about his frescoes. At first Alexander's voice sounded stilted, but as he became caught up in his subject, it lost its tension and his enthusiasm poured out.

Ellen noticed that Governor Glover was still holding Alexander's paintbrush in his hand when they returned to the ballroom. "I think this belongs to you," said the governor, handing the brush to Alexander.

"Thank you, Your Honour," said Alexander, taking the brush from his hand.

"When you are finished your work, I would like that brush as a souvenir, Mr. Pindikowsky," said Governor Glover.

"I am honoured," replied Alexander, bowing. "I will paint a miniature fresco on the handle for you."

"That would be delightful," said Governor Glover. "Good work, Officer Kielly," he said. "Carry on." He looked toward Ellen, inclined his head, and said, "Miss Dormody." She curtsied to him as he walked out of the room.

Kielly, Alexander, and Ellen looked at each other and exhaled in unison, their breaths rushing together in complicity.

eleven

Ellen usually looked forward to Christmas, but all it meant this year was that Alexander would be gone. She tried to hold on to each day, but time conspired against her and the fresco neared completion.

Now that Governor Glover was in residence, the casual atmosphere that had prevailed during his absence had disappeared. Kielly was the guard once more and Ellen was the parlour maid, fetching tea as often as six times a day as Governor Glover's curious friends came by to view the ceilings during Pindikowsky's absences. She also became the tour guide when Governor Glover was called away on official business.

Alexander was working feverishly to make his deadline, and Ellen rarely saw him face to face. She was so used to looking up at him on the scaffold that she could swear her neck had grown longer. Kielly, she knew, was bored and itching to work with Alexander again. He spent most of his time pacing the floor or, like her, looking up at Alexander.

The dreaded day came when Alexander descended the ladder for the last time. Governor Glover was out of The House and Ellen realized that he would be disappointed to have missed the last brush stroke. It was still early in the morning, and Ellen knew Alexander would be gone before noon.

"The fresco is complete," Alexander said, looking exhausted but content. "I am pleased with it. It is my best work so far." He walked around the room, gazing up at his ceiling. "What do you think, Kielly?" he asked.

"A masterpiece," said Kielly, clapping Alexander on the back. "Congratulations!"

"That is a compliment coming from a fellow fresco artist," said Alexander, winking at Kielly.

"A future fresco artist, for sure," said Kielly. "You must continue to teach me. I have a lot to learn, but I'm determined not to be a prison guard all my life."

"And I will not always be a prisoner," said Alexander, looking straight at Ellen.

"What do you think, Miss Dormody—*Alen*?" Alexander asked, his eyes looking deep into hers.

It was the first time Alexander had said her given name, his accent turning the *E* into a long *A*, his voice reaching her ears like a caress.

"You have been part of this painting from the very beginning," he said, smiling at her expectantly.

Without thinking, she exclaimed, "I love it, Alexander!" and reached out to touch him. He took her hands in his, and she felt like her whole body was being consumed with fire.

Kielly cleared his throat and they both jumped away from each other, the spell broken. "I think we should have some tea to celebrate, Miss Dormody, and maybe some of those wonderful shortbread cookies."

"Of course," she said. Her heart was beating so fast when she left the room that, for the first time in her life, she thought she might faint.

When Ellen arrived back with the tea, Governor Glover had returned and was talking with Alexander and Kielly. She was desolate that their quiet time together had been disrupted.

"I understand that you are booked to work at the Colonial Building next," said Governor Glover. "The ceilings of the council chamber and the assembly room need your artistry. It will give a sense of grandeur and importance to the building, just as it has done here."

"Thank you for your kind praise, Your Honour," said Alexander. "I would also like to thank your staff here for treating me so well, especially Miss Dormody. You can see she spoils us with tea and treats," he said, indicating the tea tray.

"Yes, thank you, Miss Dormody," said Governor Glover, looking over at Ellen. She curtsied to him and he continued talking. "And thank you, Officer Kielly, for making everything run so smoothly. I will recommend that you continue as guard for the duration of Pindikowsky's sentence, if you wish."

"Thank you, Your Honour," said Kielly. "I would like that very much."

"You will also be interested to know that Mr. Pindikowsky's prison sentence has been commuted by four weeks because of his work here and his anticipated future work. I spoke with Judge Prowse yesterday, and he told me I could convey the news to you, Mr. Pindikowsky. After seeing all the work you have done, I think more time should have been taken from your sentence, but I have no power in that domain. There is one more concession that has been made, however. I understand that the banishment part of your sentence has also been rescinded. When you are released in August, you will not have to leave Newfoundland. I am very pleased about this, and I hope you are, too. We need your skills here."

Alexander smiled broadly, and his face looked years younger. "Thank you, Your Honour. That is wonderful news. I would like to stay here in Newfoundland," he said, glancing over at Ellen.

"I believe they are expecting you to start work at the Colonial Building tomorrow," said Governor Glover. "I have given instructions for all of your equipment to be sent over there, and you can give a list of any supplies that need replenishing later, when you see what's involved in your new project. I will take my leave now. I hope our paths will cross again in the future when you are a free man, Mr. Pindikowsky."

"Thank you, Your Honour," Alexander said. Then he reached over and picked up a paintbrush from the table, handing it to Governor Glover. "Your souvenir, as promised," said Alexander, bowing to the governor.

"This is quite extraordinary, Pindikowsky," said Governor Glover, turning the paintbrush over in his hand."

"I have painted the same designs as in the ceilings, but in miniature. I am happy that you like it," said Alexander, smiling.

"I will treasure it. Thank you. Goodbye and good luck to you." He left the room, and Kielly, Ellen, and Alexander were alone again.

"Please, have your tea now, before you go," Ellen said. She poured for Alexander and Kielly. She could barely keep her hand from trembling as she held out the cup to Alexander and their hands touched.

"Will you share a not-tall cookie with us before we go," Alexander asked, smiling at his joke as he passed the plate. Ellen giggled and took a shortbread cookie from the plate. It was the first meal they had shared. Her heart felt, in that moment, that Alexander loved her as she loved him, but her mind wanted surety. She was trying to get up enough nerve to ask Alexander if she could visit him in prison, when she heard her mother's footsteps in the hall. She jumped away from Alexander, her last bite of shortbread falling to the floor.

Louise Dormody walked purposefully into the ballroom. "Your conveyance is here, Officer Kielly, Mr. Pindikowsky," she said in her most formal voice. "I trust your stay with us has been satisfactory?"

"It has been excellent," said Kielly. "Thank you."

"Yes, thank you very much for everything," said Alexander. "Your daughter has treated us very well, Mrs. Dormody."

"I'm sure she has," replied Ellen's mother, her voice frosting the air. She stood to one side of the door, making it quite clear that it was time for them to leave. Ellen wouldn't trust herself to look at Alexander. She kept her eyes on the floor as Alexander passed by her, and then Kielly was speaking to her.

"Goodbye, Miss Dormody," he said. "Thank you for everything, and I hope to see you again sometime." He glanced over his shoulder, winked at Ellen, and turned away, revealing a piece of paper that he held behind his back. She quickly took it from him and hid it in the folds of her dress before her mother could see it.

After they had walked down the hall, Ellen's mother turned to her and told her to tidy up and put all the equipment in order. George and Stanley would be coming over from the stables to help remove all of

Alexander's things, and Ellen was to make sure that the drop cloths were removed and included with the materials.

"Well, that's over at last," said Ellen's mother. "I hope you haven't entertained any romantic feelings for Pindikowsky, have you, Ellen?" She looked at her closely, and Ellen decided to tell a half-truth.

"He's a very nice man, Mother," she said. "I will miss seeing him work. You must admit that his frescoes are beautiful," she said, switching the focus away from Alexander and onto his art.

"I do admit his work is wonderful. The frescoes make the rooms look so much grander than before," Louise said, staring up at the ceilings. "But don't forget, artist or not, he did break the law."

"He is paying for his crime, Mother, and we are benefiting from his artistry."

"Hmm," said her mother, leaving the room.

AS SOON AS SHE WAS GONE, ELLEN OPENED THE PAPER AND GASPED. Staring up at her was a charcoal drawing of her face, and it was stunning. She knew she wasn't nearly as beautiful as Alexander had portrayed her, and she felt that his drawing was artistic confirmation that he loved her. At the bottom of the paper, in beautifully executed calligraphy, he had written her name and his together. He had spelled her name as he pronounced it, with an *A*—"Alen." Their names shared the large, beautifully scripted "A," and he had entwined ivy and grape leaves around them in the style of the vines on his frescoes. At the very edge of the paper he had drawn a Cupid with his arrow pointing up. Ellen was so excited she could barely keep herself from jumping up and down. But why was Cupid's arrow pointing up instead of toward their names?

Ellen heard a commotion in the hall, and she hid her drawing behind the curtains as George and Stanley came into the room and started removing Alexander's materials.

"Great job," said George, staring up at the ceiling. "Sure fancies the place up, don't it, Stanley?" Stanley nodded. He wasn't one for words.

"What do you think of it, Miss Dormody?" George asked.

"I love it," Ellen said, smiling.

The men made short work of moving out all of Alexander's supplies and equipment. The room felt empty, and Ellen decided to seek out Cheri for some much-needed conversation. She couldn't wait to show her the drawing and talk about her feelings for Alexander. It was near enough to their break time, so there wouldn't be a problem.

They sat in their usual spot at the kitchen window.

"I must say you look better than I would have expected. I thought you'd be upset by Alexander's departure, but you look like you've just won first place in a hat competition. What's going on? Did he say something to you?"

"No. But look at this." Ellen made sure no one was watching and spread her precious paper out on the table.

"Oh, Ellen," said Cheri. "This is so exciting! Alexander really does care for you. He's drawn you like a goddess and temptress all in one. I was afraid that you were imagining his affection for you and you would be hurt, but this proves that he's just as in love with you as you are with him. I don't understand about your names, though. Why is your name spelled with an *A*?"

"That's how he pronounces it—'Alen,'" Ellen said, imitating his accent. "Remember when I told you I thought my name was too plain? Well, I don't think of it as plain anymore, not the way Alexander says it. What do you make of the Cupid? Why do you think his arrow is pointed up and not at our names?"

"Maybe he wants you to look up at the frescoes. Maybe he has left you a message there."

"He wouldn't risk writing anything on the ceilings, and he wouldn't need to. He could just write me a note."

"There must be some reason. Maybe he just wants you to remember him when you look at the ceilings."

"I don't think so," Ellen said.

"I tell you what. Tomorrow, come in to work half an hour early and we'll have a good look at those frescoes. I haven't seen them properly, anyway. Your mother has been doing a fine job of keeping everyone out. You're the luckiest girl in the world, being able to see them painted. And now about Alexander, what are you going to do about your romance?"

"I don't know, Cheri. All I know is that I can't imagine that I won't see him every day. I feel lonely already, and he's only been gone a couple of hours."

"Never mind, one day at a time. Today—the portrait; tomorrow—the frescoes."

"Thanks," Ellen said, smiling. "Until tomorrow."

twelve

"I don't see anything here, other than a beautiful fresco," whispered Cheri.

She and Ellen were in the vestibule at Government House staring up at Alexander's work. Ellen had left home before her mother that morning, her excuse being that she was helping Cheri with a tricky mending job. No one was about yet at The House, so they were the only ones in the reception rooms. Ellen had borrowed her mother's opera glasses so that she could see the details of Alexander's frescoes.

"You check the ballroom and I'll check the dining room," Ellen whispered. "Here, take the glasses, Cheri. My eyesight is better than yours." She started walking around the dining room table, taking in every inch of the fresco.

"Oh my," whispered Cheri from the ballroom. "This is spectacular, magical. I feel like a princess just being in here."

"I know. I feel the same way every time I look at the frescoes. The illusion of space and depth is extraordinary. Alexander is a genius." There was silence as they both admired Alexander's handiwork.

Then Ellen heard a strange sound, like a yelp, coming from Cheri. She turned toward her and saw that Cheri was standing transfixed, her head tilted upwards, staring at the ceiling through the opera glasses. Ellen rushed over to her and looked up, following her gaze.

There, concealed in the fresco, was her face, the same face from Alexander's portrait of her. She couldn't take it in at first.

"I can't believe my eyes," said Cheri, passing Ellen the opera glasses.

Ellen looked again. It was real—Alexander had painted her image into the ceiling. Ivy leaves wrapped around the base of her face, the same ivy leaves that had encircled their names on her charcoal portrait. Ellen's heart was racing and she was overcome with joy. She couldn't believe Alexander had taken such a risk to show his feelings for her.

"Oh, Ellen," said Cheri. "This is fantastic. You'll be famous, like the *Mona Lisa*."

"No. No one can know," she said quickly. "Alexander would get into trouble if it was found out, and it would be removed. This has to be kept secret. He must have done the painting weeks ago, when he was working on this side of the room. It is well camouflaged. I didn't notice it. You can barely see it without the glasses. The only reason that we saw it was because we were looking for something. Promise me that you'll keep the secret."

"Of course I will. But it's too bad we can't talk about it or show anyone. It's the most romantic thing ever!"

"It is, isn't it?" Ellen said, grinning widely. "Alexander is so wonderful! I have to let him know that I saw his painting of me or I'll burst. Will you help me?"

"You know I will. Let me know when you have a plan. This is so exciting! You're so lucky."

Ellen laughed. "Here I am, in love with a criminal, but strangely enough, I do feel lucky."

They heard voices coming from the back entrance, and Cheri hurried off to the laundry, giving Ellen a hug before she left.

Ellen was a jumble of emotions, her heart beating so fast that her breath couldn't keep up with it. She inhaled and exhaled slowly, counting to ten over and over to calm herself. She had to face her mother in a few minutes to discuss the day's schedule and she had to appear normal, as if nothing had happened when, in reality, her whole life had shifted.

IT WAS A LITTLE AFTER TWO O'CLOCK WHEN GOVERNOR GLOVER walked into the vestibule, stamping his feet to knock the snow from his shoes. He was accompanied by Mr. Robinson.

"Have a look up, Kenneth," said Governor Glover, taking off his coat and hat and handing them to Mr. Grieves, the butler. Mr. Robinson looked up at the ceiling in the vestibule.

"This is just a taste of what is to come," said Governor Glover. "Pindikowsky is a genius. The ceilings are spectacular, and I owe the idea of it all to you. I can't thank you enough for suggesting that Pindikowsky do the ceilings as part of his prison sentence. Your idea was inspired. Come through into the dining room. I'm saving the ballroom, his best work, for last."

Ellen opened the door leading into the dining room and bobbed a curtsy as they passed through.

"I knew Pindikowsky wouldn't disappoint you," said Mr. Robinson. "I saw his work before, but this is better than I expected," he said, looking up at the dining room ceiling. "He is very talented. But credit is due to you, too. There aren't many men who would take the risk of having a prisoner in their home. Tell me, have they commuted his sentence?"

"Yes, by four weeks, and he doesn't have to leave Newfoundland on his release."

"He must be pleased about that."

"He was very grateful. In fact, I found his manners to be quite refined. He's certainly not your usual prisoner type. Apart from his recent breach of the law, he seems like a decent person. I have no doubt that he has learned from his mistake and will probably lead an exemplary life from here on. I'm sure this ceiling project has helped him to see that his talent is appreciated, and it has gone far in re-establishing his feeling of worth."

Ellen was delighted to hear Governor Glover speak so favourably about Alexander. If someone with as much influence as he had would vouch for Alexander, his future would be secure.

Mr. Robinson and Governor Glover walked into the ballroom, and Ellen held her breath as they walked to the west end of the room. "The depth of the colours is quite wonderful," said Mr. Robinson.

He didn't comment on the face in the ceiling, even though he had looked directly at it, and Ellen breathed a sigh of relief. Alexander's secret painting was safe.

"You know that he is going to paint the ceilings over at the Colonial Building next," said Governor Glover.

"Yes. Now that you've broken the ice, so to speak, others want to take advantage of Pindikowsky's artistry before his sentence is served. He'll be a busy man. I hope he's being well looked after. I know he is a prisoner, but he is not a slave."

"No worries there. Officer Kielly has been excellent. I even heard rumours that he assisted him on occasion. Over at the jail, Pindikowsky has been given extra food rations and a better mattress. His work is very physically demanding, and we don't want him unable to complete his frescoes because of a back injury or malnourishment. Also, he has been kept well away from the dangerous prisoners."

"That is good news. Once he gets out of prison, though, he might find it hard to find work. I'll see what I can do in that regard. Once people see these frescoes, I'm sure that they'll want them, but they may not be able to pay for the work. And there is the matter of trusting him as well. Time will tell."

Hearing Mr. Robinson talk about Alexander's future was making Ellen feel optimistic and apprehensive at the same time. She wanted to be part of Alexander's future, so everything that concerned him concerned her. She had forgotten that other people would judge Alexander and he might have trouble becoming part of society again. For the first time Ellen understood her mother's concern for her, but it was too late. She loved him, and that was that.

"Speaking of time, you must excuse me, Kenneth. I'm going out to Topsail to pick up Elizabeth. She hasn't seen any of this yet. I know she'll be over the moon about the frescoes. I can't wait to show them off to her. It's been great catching up with you and all the news from England."

"I had a good visit, but I'm glad to be back in Newfoundland. I know I'm in the minority, but I love it here, despite the weather. In fact, the weather in England wasn't an awful lot better than this. It is colder here, but I don't mind that, and I like a bit of snow."

"Well, don't be a stranger," said Governor Glover, walking toward the door. "You don't have to leave yet. Take your time and enjoy the frescoes. Ellen, here, will look after you, won't you, Ellen," he said, leaving the room.

"Of course, Your Honour," she replied, curtsying.

"Have a safe trip, John," said Mr. Robinson. He walked toward Ellen, looking at her closely. "Ellen. Ellen Dormody?" he asked. "Surely it can't be you?"

"Yes, it's me, Mr. Robinson. I didn't think you'd remember me."

"Of course I do," he said, smiling. "It's so good to see you. You've grown into a beautiful woman, just like your mother. She must be so proud of you. And speaking of your mother, I think she's avoiding me. Every time I come here I ask for her, and I'm always informed that she's busy and not available. Maybe you would intercede for me. I hope she's not avoiding me because of my political position. I'm still the man I was when I boarded with you, just more prosperous. I don't think that should be held against me. Most people think of it as an asset. Your mother, though, has always been different. She definitely thinks for herself, but I like that about her. Please find her for me, Ellen. I'm determined to speak with her before I leave."

"I'll be glad to, Mr. Robinson," she said, smiling. "It's lovely to see you. Mother's office is just down the hall here." They stopped outside her mother's office and she knocked on the door.

"Come in," said Louise.

"There's someone who wishes to speak with you, Mrs. Dormody," Ellen said, ushering Mr. Robinson into the room.

Ellen's mother jumped up. "Kenneth," she said. "What a surprise!"

Ellen closed the door quietly behind her, suppressing a giggle. It wasn't often she saw her mother blushing. She was determined to quiz her mother on Mr. Robinson's visit when she came home that night.

Ellen returned to the ballroom and started lighting the lamps. It was only four o'clock, but because of the time of year, it was already dark outside. She noticed that one of Mr. Robinson's gloves was on the floor. She bent to pick it up and saw something underneath the armchair by the window. She moved the chair back a little and uncovered a bag filled with green pigment powder. She picked it up and smiled. She now had an excuse to see Alexander. The bag of pigment would be her entrance ticket to the Colonial Building.

thirteen

That night, Har and Ellen were in the kitchen washing up the dishes. It was just the two of them since Ellen's mother told her she would be working late and wouldn't be home for supper. At the moment, Har was their only boarder, Miss Davis having gone home to Wesleyville for the Christmas holidays. She wouldn't be coming back until after the New Year, and it was relaxing to have just the three of them at home. Ellen took the opportunity to ask Har about Mr. Robinson and her mother. She had a suspicion that he had something to do with her mother's extra work.

"Mr. Kenneth Robinson was at The House this afternoon," Ellen said. "Mother was really surprised to see him. You were living here when he boarded with us years ago. You remember him, don't you?"

"Yes, I do. What a fine man—a real gentleman. And now he's a member of the government, the Liberal MHA for St. John's East. Your mother should never have turned him down. I don't know why she did. She wouldn't talk to me about it."

"What do you mean, turned him down?" Ellen asked.

"He wanted to marry her. I forgot, you were only a child at the time, so you wouldn't have known. Your mother probably doesn't want you to know, even now. Don't let on that I told you, will you?"

"No, I won't. But I think she's with him tonight. Mr. Robinson really wanted to see her today. He told me that he had asked to see her other times when he was at The House, and she had always avoided him. When Mother saw him today, she blushed. That has to mean that she likes him. Mother never blushes."

"Well, that is interesting. It's about time your mother started going out again. Her whole life revolves around you and work, and it's not right. She's still relatively young and pretty, even though all that black she wears makes her look severe."

"She's always watching me like a hawk. I'd be glad if someone else would take the pressure off me for a change."

"You know she wants the best for you, don't you? We both do."

"Yes, but I'll be nineteen next September. I'm grown up. I don't need to be looked after anymore."

"Well, I don't think your mother wants to face that," said Har, drying the last of the plates and reaching over Ellen's head to put them away.

"What about you, Har? Why didn't you get married?"

Har laughed. "Look at me. I'm not exactly a beauty, am I? I never was much in the looks department. If my face were my fortune, I'd be a pauper. Thank the Lord I have a brain. There was Tony, though, when I was just a young girl, younger than you are now. We grew up together in Burin and he wanted to marry me, but he was Catholic and I knew my parents would disown me if I married outside my faith. At least I thought they would. The odd thing is that my sister Nell ended up marrying a Catholic and not a word was said. To be honest, I used the religion card as an excuse. I'm not really the marrying kind. I never wanted to be a wife or a mother, and I'm hopeless at cooking and sewing—you can vouch for that. There's a reason why I always dry the dishes and don't wash them. Your mother says that I never wash the whole dish, just random parts of it." Har laughed and Ellen joined in with her, knowing that everything she said was true. She sat down on her favourite kitchen chair while Ellen wiped off the table and swept the floor.

"What do you know about those artists called the Impressionists?" Ellen asked, her mind drifting from her mother and Mr. Robinson to Alexander.

"Your conversation jumps around, doesn't it? Why are you interested in the Impressionists all of a sudden? It wouldn't have anything to do with Mr. Pindikowsky, would it?"

"I heard Officer Kielly and Ale . . . Mr. Pindikowsky talking about them the other day and I was just curious," she said. "There was something about them in the paper a while ago, and I know you remember everything you read."

"I do remember reading about them. In fact, I think I saved that paper. There's a serial story that I'm reading, *The Wild Marsh* by Daniel Torrington, in Friday's papers, and I'm saving all of them. There are only two more instalments and the story's finished. I promised my sister Nell that I'd paste all the pages together and send them to her. I'll get the paper for you. It'll be better for you to read about the Impressionists than for me to tell you about them."

Har went upstairs to get the paper and Ellen went into the dining room to lay out the fabric for Cheri's hat. She would have to work quickly to get it done in time for Christmas.

She heard her mother's voice from the hallway. "Sunday, six o'clock, see you then."

"See who on Sunday?" Ellen asked, coming into the hall.

"Kenneth," said Louise. "He's coming for supper, this Sunday. He loved my hat, by the way. I told him you made it, and he was very impressed. I hope you don't mind, but I'm going straight to bed. I'm very tired. I'll see you in the morning." She started up the stairs, meeting Har on her way down. "Beautiful evening, isn't it, Har? I hope you had a good supper. I'm off to bed. Good night."

"What's wrong with your mother?" asked Har as she came into the dining room.

"Well, I can guess, but I can scarcely believe it. Mr. Robinson is coming to supper this Sunday," Ellen said.

"Wonders will never cease. You never know what the day will bring."

"No, you don't."

"Here's the paper, and you can keep it. I cut out the story part already."

"Thanks, Har. I'll read it before I go to sleep, unless I'm asleep now. Mother's acting so strangely that I think I just might be dreaming."

"Maybe we're both dreaming, but I hope not," said Har, smiling.

fourteen

Ellen didn't know how she got through the next morning. She didn't sleep at all the night before, her mind jumbled around thoughts of Alexander, her mother, and Mr. Robinson. She woke up late, and so her original plan of going over to the Colonial Building before work had to be scuttled. She decided that she would go over there during her afternoon break. Cheri would cover for her and make up excuses for her whereabouts if anyone asked. Ellen was grateful that her mother was preoccupied with Mr. Robinson. She'd barely noticed her existence that morning.

    Lady Glover had returned, and The House was bustling with her Christmas preparations. She had been so impressed with the frescoes that she'd decided there would be a Christmas Ball to celebrate them. Ellen overheard her saying to Governor Glover, "We have to have this ball, John. If we don't, we're going to be inundated with all the people who want to see the frescoes. Our home already feels like a grand tour destination. If we have the ball, everyone will be willing to wait and see the frescoes then. It makes perfect sense." Governor Glover agreed with her, and Ellen knew that all the staff would have to work really hard to get everything ready in time. Ellen was pleased about it because it would give her something to take her mind off the loneliness she felt with Alexander's departure.

    It was thirty minutes past two when Ellen left The House to walk the short distance to the Colonial Building. The neoclassical style of the building was impressive and the white limestone columns made her feel dwarfed as she climbed the steps to the large, heavily carved doors. She remembered visiting there when she was a young girl, and the building's facade was no less impressive now. At that time there had been a number of geological specimens and artifacts that were being displayed at the Colonial Building before they made their way to the Paris Exhibition. The Beothuk Indian arrows and bone carvings as well as some caribou skin clothing had drawn Ellen's attention. She remembered reaching out to pick up a carving and her mother telling her that she wasn't allowed to touch anything.

Now, she had to consciously remind herself that she was a grown woman on a mission. She took a deep breath and tentatively pulled on the door handle. She was surprised to find that it wasn't bolted. Ellen opened the door just wide enough to gain entrance. It took a few moments for her eyes to adjust to the altered light.

"May I help you, miss?" asked a man dressed in police uniform.

"Yes," she said, trying to sound confident. "I need to speak with Officer Kielly, please." Ellen didn't give her name and she was hoping she wouldn't be asked for it. Thankfully, Kielly came into the hall at that moment.

"Everything's fine, Officer Blake," said Kielly. "I know this woman." He ushered Ellen into the privacy of the assembly room without revealing her identity. As he closed the door behind them, Alexander turned toward Ellen and smiled, lighting her up inside. He walked over and took her hands in his.

"I saw your portrait of me in the ceiling, Alexander, and I just had to see you and let you know how touched I am that you would take such a risk for me. Only Cheri and I know about it. No one else has noticed it. We will keep it a secret, and I will keep your drawing in a safe place, too." Ellen's heart was beating so fast that her words came out in gulps.

"Alen, thank you for coming, but it was a risk, too, for you to come here. You must go now, before Officer Blake comes in and starts asking questions."

For the first time since entering the room, Ellen took it in, gazing up at the criss-crossed wooden scaffolding and the ceiling. "You're a fine one to talk of risk, Alexander. You're up there, at least twenty-five feet off the floor, on that scaffold."

"It is nothing for me. I don't mind heights."

"Promise me that you will wear a rope and tie yourself to the scaffolding when you work. I won't be able to breathe for worrying if you don't. Promise me, Alexander."

He leaned in close to her and whispered, "I want you to know that I love you, Alen. And I will be careful and wear the rope, for you."

His words fell on her heart like a blessing. "I love you, too, Alexander," she whispered back. "You must let me visit you in jail."

Alexander shook his head. "The penitentiary is no place for a young lady like you, Alen. I will be free in seven months, and we will be together then. You will wait for me to be free?" He looked at her and his eyes penetrated her very being.

"Yes, I will," Ellen said, squeezing his hands and returning his gaze.

Kielly's voice broke into their world. "I think you'd better go now, Ellen. I never know when government officials will be passing through, and I don't want there to be any trouble. It is too dangerous for you and for Alexander. Your visits could jeopardize the whole fresco project and cause a scandal."

"Oh, I almost forgot," Ellen said. "I have a legitimate reason for coming." She took the bag of pigment from her purse. "I found this bag of pigment over at The House after you left. If anyone asks, you can honestly say that I was returning government property."

"I must remember never to underestimate you, Miss Dormody," said Kielly, chuckling.

He showed her out and she handed him a note. "I'm redeeming my favour," she said as she left. The scene was almost a reverse duplicate of Alexander's and Kielly's leave-taking yesterday. It seemed impossible that only a day had passed.

Ellen hurried back to The House, feeling weightless. The note she had passed to Kielly was a plea for him to let her know when it would be safe for her to visit Alexander at the prison. She was not going to wait for seven long months to see him again. Life was too short for that.

fifteen

It was December nineteenth and Louise Dormody was standing behind her desk with all of the female staff fanning out around her. She was in her element. "Now then," she said, "the Christmas Ball is to be held on December the twenty-second, so we have only three days to get everything prepared. We're all going to have to look sharp and work hard. We can do it, but it will mean that we'll all have to work overtime. Governor and Lady Glover are depending on us to make this a memorable occasion. It has to be even better than our Victoria Day Ball last May. Remember, improvement calls out for more."

"Yes, Mrs. Dormody," the staff responded.

"There will be no formal dinner served, but we will have plenty of food set up in the dining room. Mrs. Parmender has already started on that, so I have no worries there. Champagne and various wines will be served as well as eggnog. Every one of you will be on duty to help with serving, so don't even dream of taking time off or getting sick. Mr. Grieves is expecting the same dedication from the male staff. We may have to change your duties at a moment's notice, so be prepared for that.

"There will be two house guests, Lord and Lady Shelbourne. I'll need Moira and Sarah to prepare the Royal Suite for them. The Green Room will also have to be prepared in case we have bad weather and we will need to accommodate an out-of-town guest. Jane and Gertrude will be stationed near the water closets and they will attend to the guests' needs there. Charlotte and Susan will be on hand to supply any linens that might be needed. Mabel and Ellen will both be stationed in the ballroom and drawing room to attend to the guests' immediate needs throughout the night. I'll be here, too, of course, in case there are any problems.

"Now, I need you all to listen carefully." Louise looked at everyone present and started to tap her foot. "There will be lots of talk about the frescoes, and I don't want any of you to spread gossip about Mr. Pindikowsky or Officer Kielly. If any of the guests ask personal questions about them, you are not to say anything. Be polite, but say nothing. Is that clear, everyone?" Louise stared at Ellen directly when she said this, and she heard Moira and Sarah giggle over in the corner. Louise glared at them, and the meeting was over.

For the next few days, Ellen was so busy that, for minutes at a time, she didn't think about Alexander. She had not heard a word from Kielly, but she trusted him to get in touch with her as soon as he could. Since Alexander had declared his love for her, she was more determined than ever to visit him, even though she was intimidated by the thought of going to the penitentiary. Before Ellen had met Alexander, she didn't even like walking past the building. She was always afraid one of the prisoners would escape and attack her. Now, her need to see Alexander was all she cared about. She realized, however, that she'd have to be very cautious and plan out every detail of her visits so that her mother wouldn't find out.

In the meantime, Ellen contented herself with decorating the reception rooms for the ball. Holly, boxwood, cedar, ivy, and pine had been gathered from the gardens surrounding Government House, and pots containing amaryllis flowers and paper whites had been sent from the greenhouse. Ellen volunteered to help fashion garlands for the fireplace mantels. She formed the swags by wiring the evergreen branches together, intertwining them with long ropes of ivy and Titian red velvet ribbons. The ribbon colour and the ivy motif subtly linked Alexander's frescoes with the room's mantel decoration. Lady Glover was most impressed, recognizing the effect Ellen was trying to achieve, and she complimented her on her work.

The night of the Christmas Ball was cold, but there was a full moon and not a cloud in the sky. There had been little snow for the last couple of weeks, so road conditions were perfect for the carriages. As expected, very few people had declined the invitation to the ball, and it was rumoured that even the prime minister, Sir William Whiteway, would be coming. Everyone was bursting with excitement.

Ellen's only fear for the evening was that someone might notice her portrait in the ceiling. Because she knew it was there, she saw it every time she looked at the ceiling, but so far no one else had noticed it, and for this she was grateful.

Once the guests started to arrive, Ellen had no time for worrying. Everyone who entered the ballroom stopped and looked up. She had to usher people away from the doorway to avoid collisions.

When Prime Minister Whiteway arrived, he was announced by Mr. Grieves and everyone stopped talking and turned to him. He stood ramrod straight and his thick white beard gave him a very distinguished look. There was an awkward hush until Governor Glover came to Sir William's rescue by launching into a speech about the possibility of a railroad across the interior of the island. This was a pet project of the prime minister, and he was quickly engaged in conversation with Governor Glover, freeing the other guests to return to their own conversations and relax. Sir William did not stay very long. He made an obligatory round of the rooms, stopping to talk with a few of the guests, and then Ellen saw him gazing at the ceilings as Governor Glover gave him the grand tour. She heard him say, "Splendid! Capital!" as he surveyed the ballroom. He gave only a cursory look in the direction of her portrait, so it was safe from detection. It would please Alexander to know that his frescoes were admired by the great man, and Ellen couldn't wait to tell him.

Ellen was thrilled to be seeing all the latest fashions in ball gowns. Of course, some of the older ladies wore gowns from an earlier era, but that was to be expected. Lady Glover looked wonderful in an evening dress of the latest fashion. The underskirt was of pale blue satin, kilted in front and trimmed with Mechlin lace and a garland of cream-coloured silk roses. The overdress of deep blue silk was made like a polonaise with a low neck and short sleeves. Her hair was dressed with a corsage of cream-coloured roses like those on her gown.

The orchestra began playing Strauss's new waltz, *The Blue Danube*. The couples filled the room, the ladies swirling in a mass of bright colours punctuated with the black and white evening dress of the men. Ellen pictured Alexander and herself gliding over the polished floors with the beautiful canopy of his frescoes above them. Snippets of conversation floated around her.

"The frescoes are magnificent. Did you say Pindikowsky was a criminal?"

"I read in the *Royal Gazette* that he's already started painting the ceilings at the Colonial Building."

"I heard that Lady Glover's dress was sent from Paris."

"Are you going to your sister's for Christmas dinner?"

"He's going to be a free man in August next year."

"I heard that Pindikowsky was seen holding hands with one of the maids here at Government House. Surely that can't be true."

That last comment jolted Ellen. Her heart skipped a beat and she felt her face turning red. She wanted to follow the woman in green who had made the comment, but she didn't want to call attention to herself. Who started the rumour? The only people who knew about Alexander and her were Kielly and Cheri, and they wouldn't have been indiscreet. She wondered if anyone at The House had been spying on them. Moira and Sarah came to mind, but Ellen couldn't confront them without giving herself away, so she realized that there was nothing she could do. She just had to hope that the rumour died a quick death. People would speculate about Alexander and her once he was out of prison, but she didn't want their relationship known while he was still incarcerated. Ellen didn't want anything to jeopardize his position. She made a sad decision to forgo visiting him for at least a couple of weeks. By that time the frescoes at Government House would be old news.

sixteen

Christmas Day came soon enough, and Ellen tried to find enjoyment in the usual festivities, but her heart wasn't in it. It resided across town at Her Majesty's Penitentiary with Alexander.

Her family's usual Christmas dinner, a goose and a chicken with dressing, riced potatoes, salt meat, carrots, peas, and turnip, was served at one o'clock. Louise made her wonderful gravy, which was enhanced with wine left over from the mulled wine that they drank before dinner. They had only one guest, Mr. Robinson, so there were four of them.

Louise surprised everyone by wearing a new gown of apricot satin. It even had a slightly lowered bodice. Kenneth Robinson grinned broadly and applauded when she entered the room, and Har and Ellen joined him. Louise laughed and blushed while Har and Ellen looked at each other in amazement.

"Thank you all," Louise said. "I've decided that I need some colour. From now on I'll be wearing black only at work."

"You look splendid, Louise," said Kenneth. "That colour suits you as much as the green of your hat. By the way, Ellen, your mother told me you made that hat. You definitely have talent, and she said that you're thinking of opening a millinery business. I could help you out there. I could invest in your enterprise."

"Thank you, Mr. Robinson," Ellen said, "but I was intending to go to England and apprentice with a milliner there. Mother thinks I could start a business now, without any further training, but I'd be more confident if I had some formal training behind me."

"Well, I applaud you. Education is never wasted, it's easy to carry, and it can't be taken from you. When you feel you're ready to start your business, you must promise to let me invest."

"I will, Mr. Robinson. Your offer is very generous." It was only now that Ellen realized she wouldn't be going to England, not unless Alexander was going with her. Louise rang the little brass dinner bell, and Dora started serving their dinner. Dora was going to spend the evening and the next few days with her cousin, and Louise had given her permission to leave as soon as dinner was finished. Ellen was looking forward to having the kitchen to herself and trying out some new recipes.

Kenneth kept the conversation going, talking about England and the new Gilbert and Sullivan opera, *The Pirates of Penzance*. He had seen it in London the previous summer.

"Didn't the opera make its debut in New York?" asked Har.

"Yes, it did, on December thirty-first, almost a year ago. The London debut was in April of this year at the Opera Comique. It's still playing there to record audiences. It's quite funny and the music is wonderful. George Grossmith played the part of the Major General, and he was marvellous."

"I read about it in the *Ladies' Journal*," said Har. "I guess we'll have to wait a few years before it's performed here. We have the musical expertise in St. John's, so that won't be a problem. The performance of *H.M.S. Pinafore* last year at the Athenaeum was wonderful, wasn't it, Louise?"

"It was a great performance," said Louise. "I love the theatre. It really cheers up a dreary day. We're lucky we have so many talented people living here, even though we are such a small colony."

"To the theatre," said Kenneth, raising his glass of wine, "and to colourful dresses." He winked at Louise.

"Hear, hear," Ellen and Har said in unison. It was a lovely moment for Ellen, seeing her mother so happy.

When they had finished their plum pudding with hard sauce,

they all trooped into the parlour to relax. They had opened their gifts earlier. Louise had given Ellen a pair of black kid gloves and a nightgown, and she had given her mother a green printed silk scarf to match her hat. Har had given Louise Tolstoy's new novel, *Anna Karenina*, and Ellen, Jules Verne's novel *Around the World in Eighty Days*. Ellen couldn't wait to read both of them. She had given Har a new carpet bag. The one Har had been using was disgraceful, and Ellen knew she wouldn't even think about replacing it until it fell apart. Mr. Robinson gave them all a huge five-pound box of chocolates. The box itself was a glorious shade of blue trimmed with gold-coloured edging and tied with a pink satin bow. Ellen already had her eye on the bow for a new summer hat she was planning in her head. She wondered if Mr. Robinson had given her mother a more personal gift in private.

There was a knock on the door and Cheri came in, the cold air following her into the hall. She was wearing the hat Ellen had given her for Christmas, and it suited her to perfection.

"Merry Christmas, everyone," Cheri said, poking her head into the parlour.

"Merry Christmas, Cheri. You remember Mr. Robinson," Louise said, indicating her guest.

"Yes, of course. Merry Christmas, Mr. Robinson," said Cheri.

"Merry Christmas, Miss Bell," he replied.

"Will you have a cup of tea, Cheri?"

"No, thank you. I just need to talk with Ellen for a few minutes, and then I must be going again." She cocked her head in the direction of the stairs, and Ellen knew she wanted to go up to her room. "For your eyes only," she whispered.

Ellen was intrigued. "We're just going up to my room for a minute," she said. "We'll be down in a blink." They ran upstairs and Ellen closed her bedroom door behind them.

"Why all the secrecy?" she asked.

"You'll see," Cheri said, handing Ellen a rectangular-shaped gift wrapped in green paper. Ellen tore off the wrapping revealing a beautiful hinged wooden box inlaid with iridescent shells. It had a keyhole of brass. "It's beautiful," she said. "What a thoughtful gift. Where did you buy it? I've never seen anything like it."

"Simon made it. He gets bored when he's at sea, and he makes them and sells them to earn extra money. This is his best one so far. But that's not the surprise. Open it." She handed Ellen a small brass key.

Ellen unlocked the box and lifted the cover. Inside was a letter addressed to Cheri. She lifted it out. "It's addressed to you," she said, still mystified. "It was hand delivered to my door this morning. Open it."

Ellen lifted the flap revealing another envelope inside. She eased it out and saw her name on the sealed envelope . . . Alen, Alexander's spelling of it! Fancy scrollwork circled her name. She could hardly breathe as she opened the envelope and pulled out a piece of paper identical in size to her portrait picture. On it was a drawing of Alexander's handsome face, his eyes seeming to gaze straight at her. At the bottom of the page he had written: "Our portraits can be together even if we are apart. Merry Christmas, Alen. Love, Alexander." Ellen was overcome with emotion and started to cry.

"Oh no, I thought it would be good news. What's wrong, Ellen?" Cheri sat on the bed and put her arms around her.

"It is good news, the best," Ellen said, tears of happiness rolling down her face as she showed Cheri the picture.

seventeen

Alexander lay on his mattress staring up at the ceiling of his cell. It was Boxing Day and Kielly would be visiting with his wife's sister today, so Alexander would not see him. Yesterday, Kielly had brought him Christmas dinner from his own kitchen. The prison Christmas dinner was little better than the usual fare—just an extra potato, and a small bit of fruitcake. Kielly's dinner was a feast, and Alexander enjoyed every mouthful as well as the company.

It had been two days without painting and, while Alexander's body luxuriated in the imposed rest, his mind balked at being cooped up in his cell with nothing and no one to distract him. He wondered how he would have coped with his imprisonment if he hadn't been indentured into painting the frescoes. Worse, he would never have met Ellen, and now he couldn't imagine his life without her in it.

He hoped that she had received his gift. It was Kielly who suggested using Ellen's friend, Cheri, as a go-between. He yearned to see her. Remembering her as she was when she came to the Colonial Building—standing before him, looking up at him with her glorious Prussian blue eyes—was no substitute for seeing her in the flesh. And what beautiful flesh it was. He imagined painting her, naked, lying on a chaise longue, her arms supporting her head, her copper hair falling over her breasts while she held his gaze, her lips slightly parted with the hint of a smile. He fantasized about making love to her over and over again until they wore grooves into each other's flesh.

He almost regretted telling her that he didn't want her to visit him in jail. While he worked on the frescoes at Government House, he could fool himself into believing that he was a free man, hired to do a job. He was proud of his painting skills, and Ellen had seen him only in the role of a talented fresco painter. She knew he was a convicted criminal, but because she had only seen him as an artist, Alexander felt that she didn't really accept the reality of his situation. He was afraid that if she saw him in his prison cell, she would no longer respect him and he would lose her love. He could not risk that. It seemed unbelievable that it had been only eight days since he had last seen her. How would he be able to wait seven months? He sighed deeply, closed his eyes, and allowed his mind and body to rest. He slept until the familiar sound of Kielly, whistling and jingling his keys, woke him.

"Get up, me son," said Kielly. "It's time we were at those frescoes again. I've had enough idleness for a long while. I've already gained a few pounds eating, drinking, and lounging about. I'll help you mix the plaster today, since it's unlikely that we'll get any visitors. People will still be celebrating or recovering from celebrating."

"I'm more than ready to leave this place," said Alexander. "Yesterday was the longest day of my life."

"I can imagine it was," said Kielly, unlocking the cell door.

"Do you know if Alen received my letter?" asked Alexander, automatically putting his hands behind his back for the handcuffs and spreading his feet to receive the shackles.

"I know it was delivered to Cheri's house, so I'm pretty sure she did. Cheri would want her friend to have a letter from you. She knows that Ellen's gone on you. You're amazing, you know that, don't you? Here you are in jail and you've managed to find yourself a girlfriend, and a beautiful, clever one at that. You're amazing, just amazing."

It was still dark out, but the sky was brightening. Alexander breathed in the cold air and commented, "You can almost eat the air, it is so fresh. I am so happy to be outside again." He hoisted himself into the prison wagon, assisted by Kielly, and they were transported to the Colonial Building in a matter of minutes. Alexander couldn't wait to start work again.

eighteen

St. John's, January 1881 to July 1882

Ellen was grieving for Alexander—there was no other word for her behaviour. Her mother kept asking what was wrong with her, and she told her she had a bad case of the winter blues. It was usually a bit dull after the Christmas celebrations, so everyone was feeling a little low, but Ellen was finding it hard to get up in the morning and she was going to bed as soon as she could. A day without seeing Alexander didn't hold much joy for her.

It was January the fifteenth and Ellen had not heard from Kielly or Alexander. When she saw Cheri she looked at her hopefully, but so far she hadn't received any more letters. Each night Ellen stared at Alexander's portrait, memorizing his face before going to sleep. Then she would lock the picture in her shell box and lay the box on the bureau on the other side of her room. Her only incentive for getting up in the morning was to cross the room to look at his picture once again.

Finally, a few days later, the letter came. Cheri brought it straight to Ellen, making the excuse of bringing her a tea cloth she had just mended. She made sure no one was looking while Ellen read Kielly's note. He had arranged for her to come to the penitentiary at six o'clock on Saturday morning. The superintendent wasn't there on Saturdays, and if she went to the side entrance she wouldn't be seen from the road. He wrote that, because Alexander was adamant that Ellen not have to enter a prison cell, he had lobbied to get permission for Alexander to paint a mural near the side entrance and they could meet there. Kielly would watch out for Ellen and open the door since there was no handle on the door and it was padlocked from the inside. The entrance was only used for deliveries, and none were scheduled for Saturday. Kielly wrote that Ellen would only be able to stay for a brief time, and obviously her visit would be kept secret. At the bottom of the note he instructed her to burn the letter so there would be absolutely no record of their correspondence. Ellen realized that Kielly was taking a big risk, and she was grateful to him. She would be very careful and follow his instructions exactly.

By Friday, Ellen was so excited and fearful that she could barely eat anything. She sipped tea most of the day and was so jittery that she paced back and forth the hallway at The House and made up reasons to climb the stairs. When Ellen finished work she went home and had a bath, washing her hair and rinsing it with vinegar to improve its shine. She ironed her favourite blue dress until there was not a wrinkle showing anywhere. Her new hat was the same shade of blue as her dress, and she hoped that Alexander would notice it. She knew she wouldn't be able to sleep, so she didn't even try. She lit the oil lamp, sat up in bed with the blankets pulled up to her chin, and read until morning.

As soon as her mother left for work at five o'clock, Ellen was out of bed. She was grateful that she wouldn't have to explain why she was leaving the house at six o'clock on her day off. She dressed with care and spent time arranging her hair around her hat so that the wind would not disturb it.

It was still dark outside when she left the house, and she hoped she wouldn't be seen by anyone she knew. Unfortunately, she had to wear her old leather boots, because of the snow, but she hoped her new coat and hat would make up for their lack of style. Ellen smiled at herself, acknowledging the fact that she had spent as much time getting dressed to visit a jail as she had ever spent getting ready for a party. She walked quickly up Victoria Street to Military Road, cutting through the Botanical Gardens and Bannerman's Field to Forest Road and Her Majesty's Penitentiary.

As soon as she arrived at the side entrance, the door opened and Kielly pulled her into the building. Alexander stepped forward and hugged her, kissing her cheek.

"Alen, you came," he said, smiling. "It is so wonderful to see you again. You look so beautiful!"

Alexander had a blob of blue paint on the side of his cheek and Ellen reached over to wipe it off. "I see we are well matched, me in blue and you in blue paint," she said, and they laughed together. Ellen had been fearful that their meeting would be awkward, but now that she was with him, she just felt happy and relaxed.

"I love your hat," he said. "It must be a new style. I have never seen one like it before."

"I designed and made it myself," Ellen said with pride.

"Then you are an artist, too. It is no wonder that I love you."

His words warmed her and she felt special. Alexander talked about the frescoes he was doing at the Colonial Building, and Ellen told him about the Christmas Ball at Government House and the complimentary comments about his frescoes, especially Prime Minister Whiteway's. She didn't tell him about the hand-holding comment, because she was afraid that if he knew about it he wouldn't let her risk coming to see him again.

"I am painting Bannerman's Park in this mural—your mural," Alexander said, pointing to the initial drawings on the wall. "I know it is not officially a park yet, but Sir Bannerman has given this land to the city and the park will become a reality. When I am out of here we will go walking in that park. Until then, I will pretend we are there now."

Kielly cleared his throat. "Just a few more minutes, you two. You can come next Saturday at the same time, Ellen. If there is any problem, I will get a note to you through Cheri."

"I have a small painting for you, Alen," said Alexander. He handed her a watercolour of a bouquet of red roses. "When I am free I will buy you real roses."

"These are much better, Alexander. They will be beautiful forever."

"Like you." He cupped her face in his warm hands and kissed her lips, catching them on fire.

Ellen never knew a kiss could be so transforming. She left the prison with the fire still burning on her lips, and she was amazed that everyone at The House looked at her as though she were just the same. All her mother said to her was that she was glad that her winter blues had left her.

It was odd that both Ellen and her mother were in love at the same time. Louise and Kenneth Robinson were seeing each other on a regular basis now, and Har and Ellen expected every day that she would announce her engagement. Ellen didn't know what they were waiting for. Neither one of them was getting any younger.

Har told Ellen that after her mother had turned down his first proposal, Mr. Robinson had returned to England for a few years and he had married a woman there. Apparently she had died of eclampsia after giving birth to his son. It was a double tragedy, since the child had died a few hours after his mother. Ellen understood Mr. Robinson's caution after that, and she knew her mother was still young enough to have a baby, but it was highly unlikely. If her mother had wanted to have more children, she would have remarried years ago. Ellen thought that the real reason that there was no engagement was that her mother liked her independence and, if she married Kenneth, her whole life would be changed, especially because he was a member of the government. She'd be a part of the very society she had served. Still, Ellen saw how happy she was when she was with Kenneth, and she had a feeling that this time he wouldn't give up on her.

nineteen

Alexander was elated when he found out that his new design for the assembly room at the Colonial Building had been approved. The design incorporated the use of twenty-two-karat gold leaf, and he estimated that he would need about 200 books of the gold leaf to complete the work. It would be expensive, but the twenty-eight-foot ceilings and iconic columns demanded the grandeur of the gilt.

Prime Minister Whiteway had visited the Colonial Building just after the New Year. He was very complimentary about the ceiling frescoes at Government House, but for the Colonial Building he wanted a decorative style that reflected its neoclassical structure. Alexander knew that the use of gold leaf would transform the space into a sophisticated venue worthy of the seat of government for Newfoundland. When the books of gold leaf were delivered to the Colonial Building, the irony of the whole situation was not lost on Kielly or Pindikowsky.

"Well, Pindikowsky," said Kielly, "you pulled it off. Here you are, a convicted forger, working in a room above the Newfoundland Savings Bank, being trusted to spread gold on the ceilings of the government's House of Assembly, while serving a prison sentence. It defies all logic. As I said before, you're amazing." Kielly clapped Alexander on the back and they both laughed heartily. "This will go down in the record books, for sure."

"To be serious, Kielly, I want those books of gold accounted for every day and locked up every night. I will not be accused of theft ever again. When I finish serving my time, I want to marry Alen and start a new life. I will let nothing interfere with that, as long as she will have me."

"When do you intend to ask her to marry you? Will you wait until you're released?"

"I don't know. What is the right thing to do? I love her and I want her to know that I do not play with her affection. But how can I propose to her in prison? And if she accepts me I would want her to have a ring."

"I'm confident that you'll work it all out between you. She's not your usual sort of woman. She's very strong and independent. I'm sure she can handle just about anything. Now, we'd better get back to fresco work, and you can teach me how to gild as well. I've decided that I'm giving up prison work after you're released. Maybe we can go into business together. I think we make a good team."

"I would be honoured to form a business with you. But will anyone hire us? Maybe the fact that you will be a former policeman and prison guard and I will be an ex-convict will cancel each other out. It is worth a try, Kielly, for sure." He went back to preparing the plaster to receive the gold leaf. As he rolled a piece of plaster putty in his hand, he thought of a way he could make a ring for Ellen.

twenty

Ellen lived for Saturdays. The other days went by in a thick cloud of waiting. Thursday was the only tolerable day of the week because, apart from Lady Glover's "at homes" where she entertained ordinary visitors, she hosted a drawing club every Thursday afternoon. Her group consisted of about twelve women ranging in age from twenty-five to sixty. There was a mother-and-daughter pair among them, and Ellen liked the way they helped one another without being competitive. One of the older ladies, Miss Hamilton, painted in a strange manner when she represented colours. They bore little resemblance to the still life subject; a green-leafed plant would be red and purple, and a red scarf would be blue with green shadows. Then Ellen overheard one of the other women say that Miss Hamilton was colour-blind. She saw things in a totally different way than anyone else, but it didn't seem to mar her enjoyment of painting. Her charcoal drawings were completely accurate and quite good.

Lady Glover often called upon Ellen to help her arrange objects to paint in a pleasing composition. She would start setting up possible objects to paint before her group arrived, and then she would ask if Ellen thought it could be improved. She never minded if Ellen spoke her mind, so she often made a suggestion of including a card, a glove, a hat, a scarf, or a bowl to add interest. Sometimes she would just turn a vase a little or move the still life closer to the light to enhance the fall of shadows on the objects. Lady Glover always listened to what Ellen had to say, and most times she carried out her suggestions.

Every couple of weeks, Lady Glover would have an art teacher come to The House and give a lesson to her group. Ellen loved these sessions as she was able to learn artistic terms and impress Alexander with her newly acquired knowledge. She was kept busy, serving tea, trays of sandwiches, cakes, and cookies to the painters. She was also called upon to change the water for the paints and to bring clean cloths when necessary.

The first meeting of the group after Christmas was distressing for Ellen, since the conversation and focus of the session was the frescoes. The ladies who came to the Christmas Ball were familiar with them, but this was the first time any of the artists had seen them in daylight. To make matters worse, it was a rare sunny day and the ladies had the trained eyes of artists. They walked around and around, staring up at the ceilings. Every time they approached her portrait, Ellen would try to distract them, offering sandwiches or cakes or another cup of tea. Her heart stopped cold when Miss Hamilton said, "Is it blue or red flowers that Pindikowsky has painted around the little face?" Ellen didn't know what else to do, so she dropped a cup, and luckily it broke as it hit the floor, causing enough of a distraction to shelve Miss Hamilton's question. The conversation was rerouted to the Paris Exhibition, and she was saved.

Lady Glover and her art group decided to have their own exhibition in April, just after Easter. There was to be musical entertainment as well, featuring the music of Gilbert and Sullivan. Mrs. John Dalton, one of the art ladies, was also an accomplished pianist, and she often played for the ladies at the end of the afternoon painting sessions. One day she played a song called "Poor Wandering One" that was from the opera *The Pirates of Penzance*. The melody was lovely. Ellen couldn't wait to tell Mr. Robinson that some of the music from the opera that he had seen in London would be played at the art show. Mr. Robinson was now a regular for Sunday dinner, and he said Ellen should call him Kenneth. She was still working on that.

twenty-one

Alexander's mural at Her Majesty's, as Ellen preferred to call the prison, was beautiful, but it was progressing faster than she liked. When Alexander finished it, Kielly would have to work out another way for them to meet.

Alexander and Ellen had been courting in the very old-fashioned sense of the word. Kielly was their chaperone and, although he was a very permissive one, they still couldn't stay in each other's arms, lips locked together as they would have liked. So they talked and learned about each other.

Alexander spoke about his childhood growing up in Poland, a country that was occupied by both Germany and Russia. He had to learn to speak German in school, and many of his cultural traditions were suppressed. Alexander's father had been a very talented portrait painter, and because of this he was given employment painting many of the Russian leaders and nobles. This unique position made him a valuable asset to the Polish liberation movement, and he became a leader in the Greater Poland Uprising in 1848. He died in that rebellion when Alexander was just nine years old.

Ellen found it hard to imagine such a life. Her own life growing up in Newfoundland was so idyllic and peaceful in comparison. What they did have in common was that they were only children and had both lost their fathers at a young age. However, Alexander was old enough, when his father was killed, to have a few memories of him. He told Ellen how he used to watch his father work in his studio. The smell of oil paint always made him remember his father, and he thought it was one of the reasons he became an artist. His mother and his mother's sister, Paulina, raised him and gave him the best childhood they could under the circumstances. He told Ellen of his mother's cake decorating and how the decorative icing she used reminded him of the plaster work he did. Then when he was just twenty, his mother had died of tuberculosis. His aunt Paulina helped him through this difficult time and encouraged him in his art career. She paid for his art apprenticeship with Johann Blonsky, who recognized Alexander's talent and kept him working with him long after his apprenticeship. Because of his father's connection to the 1848 uprising, Alexander was unable to get much work in Warsaw as an individual artist, and if it weren't for Johann he probably wouldn't have been employed at all.

It was his Aunt Paulina who saw the Anglo-American Telegraph Company's advertisement for an art teacher in Newfoundland, and she encouraged Alexander to apply for it. Her husband was involved in the underground Polish Nationalist Movement, and she was always fearful that his involvement would be discovered and would further jeopardize Alexander's chances for success. She felt that the New World offered unlimited opportunities for him and freedom from Russian oppression. When he talked about her, Alexander's voice filled with sorrow.

"I had a letter from her last February. She wrote to tell me that my uncle, her husband, was arrested for his involvement in the Polish National Movement. She asked me for money to try to get him out of prison. I had to try and help her. I owe her so much. That is why I forged the cheques. Then I was caught by the police. Just before I was imprisoned, she wrote to tell me that her husband was executed. She told me that it wouldn't have mattered how much money I had sent her: the Russian authorities wanted to make an example of him. I know she is probably right, but I still feel responsible. I have never told anyone but you why I forged those cheques. I don't want to bring my Polish problems here. You won't tell anyone, will you, Alen?"

"Of course not, Alexander, if that is what you wish."

"Thank you, my *kochanie*, my darling. And enough of this gloomy talk. I will talk about the future now."

He told her about his plans to open a decorative painting business with Kielly when he was free. Alexander felt that it would be unlikely for him to get employment teaching art lessons again, now that he had a prison record, but he hoped Kielly's reputation would give him the credibility to work on public buildings and, later, private residences. There were a number of imposing houses being built along Rennie's Mill Road and King's Bridge Road that might want murals.

Ellen told him of her very uneventful life growing up in St. John's, and she shared with him her dreams for opening up a millinery shop. Alexander said, "I will help you with that, Alen. I could sketch and paint your hat designs for you. In fact, I have already finished your first illustration."

He handed Ellen a small, five-by-seven-inch painting. The week before, Alexander had asked her to pose in front of his mural while he sketched, and this was the finished painting. In the painting, she was standing in the rose garden and Alexander was next to her, his arm around her waist. Ellen was wearing her blue dress and her blue bonnet-hat. He had painted her hat with every little detail showing to perfection.

"Every woman will want that hat when they see this picture," Alexander said.

Ellen thought to herself, *Every woman will want this man when they see this picture.*

By the following Saturday, Alexander had added a bandstand to his mural, and the pathway leading to the Rennie's Mill Road entry to the park was lined with large trees.

"I see you've taken liberties with the size of the chestnut and maple trees," Ellen said. "They are only half that size, and the bandstand is only in the planning stages."

"They will grow. I am trying to think in the future when you and I will be strolling there in our old age."

Ellen loved to hear him talk about their future like that. He still hadn't proposed to her, and she figured that he didn't want to while he was in prison. She would have to drop a few hints that she wouldn't mind at all. Ellen stood on tiptoe to kiss Alexander, and she noticed gold flecks all over his face. "Aren't you taking *the golden hour* a little too seriously," she joked, lifting some of the gold with her fingertip.

Alexander laughed. "It is the gold leaf that I am using at the Colonial Building. It is all over me when I leave the building. People must wonder at a thief who is sprinkled with gold," he joked. "Here, see if you can kiss it off my lips." Ellen didn't need a second invitation to do that. Her lips jumped to his like they were magnetized.

It was harder and harder for Ellen to leave Alexander. Every time she saw him she yearned for his sentence to be over so they could be together properly, or rather improperly, as she often imagined them, once they were alone.

twenty-two

It was a Sunday afternoon, the second of April, when Louise Dormody announced her engagement to Kenneth Robinson. They had just returned from a visit to his summer residence near Rennie's River. Supposedly, the purpose of the visit was to make sure there was no damage to the house after the winter weather of ice, snow, and high winds.

"Anyone home?" Louise called out, coming in the door with Mr. Robinson.

"In the kitchen," Ellen and Har answered in unison.

Louise walked in holding Kenneth's hand. "We're getting married, May the fifth," Louise said, smiling like her face would split in two.

"Yes, finally," said Kenneth. "I think I've waited long enough. I was going to ask Louise to marry me yesterday, but since it was April Fool's Day, I thought it would be prudent to wait a day. I'm the happiest man alive. Now the two of you will have to get used to calling me Kenneth, since I'm going to be part of this family."

They hugged one another, and Kenneth went out to the porch and brought in a bottle of champagne. They took out Louise's best Waterford crystal glasses and drank a toast to their future together. Louise's ring was a beautiful solitaire diamond sparkling in the light, and Ellen wondered at its cost.

On Monday, The House was full of talk about the engagement.

Governor and Lady Glover congratulated Louise, pointing out that Kenneth was a lucky man and had made a wise choice. Their comments went a long way to make Louise feel less awkward about the disparity in their social positions. She was clear about keeping on as housekeeper until they could find a replacement. Mabel was the logical choice, and Ellen hoped that she would want to apply for the job.

LADY GLOVER'S ART EXHIBITION WAS SCHEDULED FOR THE FOLLOWING Saturday. It was to be held in the reception room at the Athenaeum, and Ellen was really looking forward to it. On Friday, she was going with Lady Glover and some of the ladies in the art group to hang the show. Lady Glover asked Ellen if she would switch her day off and be available to help serve refreshments at the show from noon, when the show opened, until eight when it would be over. Ellen didn't know what she would have said to her if she had wanted her at The House at six in the morning, but she knew she wouldn't miss seeing Alexander. That was not negotiable.

On Saturday, Ellen dressed with particular care. The snow was all gone and it was unseasonably warm for April. Ellen knew that winter was not finished yet and would make at least one more appearance before anyone could be sure of spring, but she was going to take advantage of the day and wear her pale green dress with the muslin over drape. She knew it looked good on her and showed off her figure. Most of the time when she was with Alexander she had to keep her coat on because it was so cold, but today she was going to go *in her figure*, as Har would say. Ellen needed only her wool shawl to keep her warm, and she walked quickly to Her Majesty's. It was now daylight by six o'clock, and she was always afraid of being seen as she walked to the side entrance and waited for Kielly to open the door.

When she entered the hallway of the prison, Alexander gasped. "You look like the goddess of spring," he said, scooping her into his arms. "You are more beautiful every day."

"And you are still my golden man," she said, smiling and brushing the flecks of gold gilt from his face. Kielly, she noticed, had walked to the end of the hall to give them a little privacy.

"The mural is almost finished, Alen. What do you think of it?"

"It is beautiful! I feel like I'm actually in the park."

"That is what I hoped to achieve. Now, Alen, please stand there next to the chestnut tree and pretend that we are in the park together. I have something to ask you."

Her heart was already beating like hummingbird wings when Alexander went down on one knee.

"Alen, I love you. Will you marry me when I am free? I want to spend all of my *giornatas* with you." His eyes on her were so intense that she felt like she was caught in a beam of light.

"Yes, Alexander, I will marry you. And if you hadn't asked me soon, I was going to ask you myself," she said, her laughter bubbling up, her joy seeking release.

"Oh, Alen, you are one in a thousand million. I am the luckiest man in the world." He picked her up in his arms and spun her around. "I almost forgot," he said, reaching into his pocket. "Here is your ring. It was the best I could make for you in here, but when I am free I will have a real gold ring with a diamond made just like it for you. That is, if you like it. It is very fragile, so you can only wear it for a short time."

He placed the ring on Ellen's finger, and it was almost a perfect fit. The ring was made from plaster that he had carved into the shape of a small square cut diamond surrounded with an intricate etched design of hearts and flowers, winding around a vine. The entire ring was gilded with tiny bits of gold leaf that had been burnished onto it. It was exquisite, but the many hours Ellen knew Alexander must have spent working on it made it a thousand times more valuable. She knew that nothing else she ever owned would mean as much to her as that ring.

"Congratulations, you two," said Kielly, holding his hand out to Alexander and giving Ellen a kiss on the cheek. "I know you will be happy. You are perfect for each other."

"Thank you, Kielly," Ellen said. "I know we have you to thank for helping us be together."

"Yes, well, please don't spread that information around. I still need this job for a little while. A masterpiece, isn't it?" Kielly said, changing the subject and pointing at the ring. "No one else could do that. I am in awe of this man's talent. Now, I hate to bring it up at this time, but the mural will be finished tomorrow and the delivery schedule is changing over to the spring/summer one next week. That means deliveries will be made early every morning, including Saturday. I can't risk anyone seeing you here, Ellen. But don't worry, I'll work something out so you and Alexander can see each other. It might take a few weeks, though."

"I understand," Ellen said. "I don't like it, but I understand. It doesn't matter anyway, because now that Alexander and I are engaged, I'm going to tell Mother about us. No more secrecy. Then I can come to the prison during regular visiting hours and see you, Alexander."

"No, Alen. Please, I do not want that. I do not want people to see us together until I am free. I don't want to shame you. These secret visits have been risky enough. Please, Alen. We will work something out, Kielly and I. We are engaged, we are pledged to one another. We can wait to see each other knowing we will be together for the rest of our lives. Now, give me your best kiss before you go. It must last me for a while, so we will make it sweet." He took Ellen in his arms and Kielly, tactfully, walked away.

Ellen left Her Majesty's and walked home to Victoria Street. At least she must have done, because she arrived there, even though she had no real recollection of her feet touching the ground. She ran to her room and raided her sewing scraps to make a tiny silk pouch to hold her ring. She threaded her gold locket chain through the loop she had made on the back of the pouch and clasped the chain around her neck. It rested above her heart, and only she would know it was there under her House uniform.

Ellen fulfilled her duties for the art exhibition and she heard afterwards that it was a huge success, although she was hardly aware of what she was doing or saying. Her ring pressed against her skin and reminded her of the glorious morning she had spent with Alexander. The setting of her engagement could have been better, but the romance couldn't be improved upon.

twenty-three

As soon as the art exhibition was over, Ellen went to Cheri's house to tell her about her engagement. They went upstairs to Cheri's room where they could have some privacy.

"The exhibition must have gone well. You're positively beaming. I didn't know serving a bunch of people sandwiches could be so exciting," Cheri said.

"That's not what I'm excited about. This morning, Alexander proposed!"

Ellen took the ring from the silk pouch and showed it to Cheri.

"I would love to wear it on my finger, but it's too fragile for that. He made it out of plaster."

Cheri took the ring from Ellen and held it underneath the lamp on her dresser. "I can't believe it! It's amazing! I'm so happy for you!" She gave Ellen a bear hug. "You're going to be Mrs. Alexander Pindikowsky—Ellen Pindikowsky!"

Ellen took the ring and placed it safely back in its pouch. "I can't tell anyone until Alexander is out of Her Majesty's. No one is supposed to know about us or my visiting him."

"What about your mother?"

"I want to tell her, but she's so taken up with her own wedding now that I don't want to spoil her happiness. I don't imagine she's going to be pleased with my engagement to an artist, a criminal, a foreigner, and a Catholic, all rolled into one."

"You're right there. She's definitely going to have to be persuaded, and it'll be a shock to her. I know she was worried about you falling for him when he was at The House, but I think that once he left, she forgot all about him. Of course, she's been a bit preoccupied with her own romance lately."

"Also, if I tell her, I'll have to admit that I've been seeing him behind her back at the prison, no less. No, I can't risk it. I'm going to have to wait until he's free. Then, she'll just have to accept the fact that I'm in love with Alexander. I'm certainly not going to give him up."

"It's so romantic! Now tell me all the details about the proposal, and don't leave anything out." They sat talking the night away. Just being able to tell Cheri about her unusual proposal made it real, gave it substance.

IT WAS SIX WEEKS BEFORE ELLEN SAW ALEXANDER AGAIN; DURING this time he sent her two watercolour paintings, via Cheri, and that helped ease her misery. The first one was a painting of Alexander and her in Bannerman's Park; he was down on one knee and the chestnut tree canopied over the two of them. He had titled it *Our Engagement*. In the years to come, Ellen thought, their children would see this painting and think how idyllic their romance was. Would they tell them the truth? The second painting was a beautiful Georgian-styled house with a lovely garden surrounding it. Below it Alexander had written *Our Future House*. At the bottom of each painting he signed, "I love you, Alen, Alexander." He'd entwined the *A*'s in their names together as in her portrait drawing. He didn't write Ellen a conversational letter, and she realized that his spoken English was far more advanced than his written. Of course, she didn't know a word of Polish, written or spoken, so he was still well ahead of her. Ellen wrote back to him, recounting her days as if she were speaking to him, and when she signed her name, she laboured to duplicate his calligraphic drawing of their linked names, knowing that this would mean more to him than words. She used Kielly's two-envelope method of posting, putting Kielly's name and address on the outside envelope and leaving off the return address.

LOUISE AND KENNETH'S WEDDING WAS TO BE HELD AT GEORGE STREET Methodist Church. Even though Ellen and her mother didn't attend church every Sunday, they still considered themselves part of the George Street congregation. Ellen loved the Gothic-styled architecture of the church; the exposed wooden beams and the stained glass lancet windows lent a warm feeling of peace.

The wedding was to be a small private affair, followed by a luncheon at Kenneth's summer house, Riverside. He and Louise were going to make the house their permanent residence, and Kenneth was going to sell his house on Queen's Road. The storm windows and extra fireplaces that Kenneth had installed would make it comfortable during the winter. Since the fire of 1846, a number of St. John's merchants had moved away from the town core and had built on the land surrounding Rennie's River. With more houses being built there every year, they wouldn't be isolated.

Louise had chosen an ashes-of-roses-hued, peau de soie fabric for her wedding dress. Ellen made her hat, trimming it with soft tulle netting, dyed the same colour as her dress. The style was similar in shape to the green velvet she had made for her, but the netting would soften the lines. The same tulle was ruffled and made to encircle the neckline of her dress and the sleeve cuffs. For contrast, Ellen sewed black soutache braid around the edge of the dress, train, and bustle, looping it in a rosette shape around the front of the dress and at the sleeve cuff, along the ruffle of tulle. She used a small amount of the soutache braid on her hat to tie the ensemble together.

Ellen was her mother's only attendant, and her dress was a deep rose colour trimmed with bias binding that she made from the wedding dress fabric. Her hat was similar in style to her mother's but trimmed in the peau de soie instead of the tulle.

The day of the wedding was cool but sunny. The service was at eleven o'clock and their small party arrived in carriages almost at the same time. Apart from Kenneth and Louise, there was Ellen, Har, Cheri, and Governor and Lady Glover. Mr. Robert Baird, Kenneth's cousin and best man for the ceremony, was already inside the church waiting with Reverend Barbour. Since only Louise and Kenneth knew him, Robert was introduced to everyone and the ceremony began.

Louise and Kenneth held hands as they repeated their vows, and their obvious commitment and love for each other made Ellen cry. She realized that her tears were really about losing her mother. She had had her to herself for all of her life, never even having to share her love with a sibling, and now all of that would change.

Once the ceremony was over, they bundled into the waiting carriages. Cheri reached over and gave Ellen's hand a squeeze, reassuring her. "It'll be you and Alexander next," she whispered. "Just three months to go." Ellen wished she could imagine three months as a short time.

When they arrived at Riverside, Dora and Mrs. Parmender were on the veranda waiting to greet them. Mrs. Parmender had offered to cook the wedding luncheon and make the wedding cake, and Dora offered to help serve. They were both happy that Louise was getting married, and this luncheon was their wedding gift to her. It was the first time Ellen had been to Riverside, and she loved the house with its mansard roof and dormer windows. Best of all was the large veranda, at the back of the house, which overlooked Rennie's River. The house was situated at the top of a rise which prevented the house from being flooded by the river when it rose over its banks. The swiftly flowing water was a deep blue that sparkled when the sun caught the water spraying over the rocks. The river's destination was the Atlantic Ocean, but first it would travel through Quidi Vidi Lake and then Quidi Vidi Gut to the sea.

The luncheon was a great success with plenty of champagne, which Governor Glover had graciously supplied. It was a little strange to be seated next to Governor and Lady Glover instead of serving them, but any awkwardness was soon drowned in drink and goodwill. Cheri sat next to Robert Baird, and every time Ellen tried to catch her attention, she was deep in conversation with him. Even though Robert was Kenneth's cousin, he was at least fifteen years younger than Kenneth. As Ellen's mother would say, *Hmm*.

When Mrs. Parmender and Dora brought in the wedding cake, they were persuaded to join them for more champagne and more toasting to Louise and Kenneth. It was a day to remember, and because of Kenneth's foresight it would be forever commemorated in a photograph. He had hired a young photographer, James Vey, to come to Riverside at three o'clock when he knew everyone would be finished their luncheon, and it was a wonderful surprise. Several pictures were taken, including a picture of Mrs. Parmender next to the wedding cake. Later, Louise had the picture framed and gave it to her as a thank you for the wedding luncheon and for her friendship at Government House. It was displayed proudly in the kitchen of The House for all the years Mrs. Parmender worked there.

Ellen's favourite photograph was taken on the back veranda. Kenneth and her mother were in the centre of the picture, and Kenneth was kissing her mother's hand while she smiled up at him and everyone was looking very happy and relaxed. Ellen always referred to it as the Champagne Photograph.

twenty-four

Work at The House continued as usual. Mabel had taken over the position of housekeeper, and while things did not run quite as smoothly as when Louise was in charge, there were no heavy complaints. They were getting ready for the Victoria Day Ball, which was to be the last big social event before the summer. After that, Governor and Lady Glover would be away for quite a while, visiting around the island.

Since marrying Kenneth, Ellen's mother had decided that she would no longer take on any boarders at their house on Victoria Street, except for Har, who would always have a place with their family. Ellen was happy about that, since she hoped that Alexander and she could live together at the house once they were married. Then, they could save enough money to build their own house or buy the Victoria Street property. Ellen had it all planned out in her mind. All she had to do was convince her mother to accept Alexander. It wasn't going to be easy.

There was no truer adage in life than "Humans make plans and God laughs."

It was Har that shook things up this time. Her employer, Mr. Wareham, had to go to New York City on extended business, and he said he definitely could not cope there unless Miss Harding agreed to go with him to manage his office. Ellen asked her if she was afraid of being a woman alone in such a large city, and in typical Har fashion, she said, "Any man should be so ill-advised as to accost me. I can certainly look after myself." Ellen and her mother laughed at the indignant expression on her face.

In reality, Har was more excited about going away than Ellen thought possible. "I'll have a little adventure," she said. "I've always wanted to see New York." Mr. Wareham had arranged a boarding house for her in New York City and had purchased tickets on the *Belgrave*. They were sailing on July twelfth, and Ellen was happy for her. That is, until she lost her illusion of freedom. Ellen had foolishly thought that her mother would allow her stay at Victoria Street without Har.

"Well, Ellen, you certainly won't be staying at Victoria Street by yourself," Louise said. "You'll come and live at Riverside until Har returns, and I'll close the house up." That meant that Ellen would be under her mother's watchful eye once more. She'd have to invent excuses for the times she was going to see Alexander. One thing Ellen was sure of was that she would see him, come hell or high water.

The letter came from Kielly the day after Har's trip announcement. In the letter, Kielly said that work at the Colonial Building was taking longer than they thought it would. The height of the ceilings combined with the gilt work was very detailed, and in fact the government had hired a couple of men to assist Alexander so that he would complete the work before his prison sentence was over. That was the problem where their visits were concerned. Alexander would not risk the chance of the hired workmen seeing her. Kielly said that the only possible time that they could see each other would be on Mondays, when Alexander was there alone sorting out the work schedule for the week. Ellen was to be at the entrance at the back of the building at five thirty Monday morning. Kielly would watch for her and let her in. She would be allowed only ten minutes with Alexander. If Ellen saw anyone as she approached the building, she was to abort the visit and try again the following week. Ellen reread the letter and destroyed it.

Mondays never came soon enough. Every time Ellen saw Alexander, she felt infused with life. The days in between their visits felt like she was being deprived of oxygen, her energy leaking from her so that by Sunday she felt physically ill. She had lost weight and her mother had commented on it. Ellen told her that she was working hard making hats and, thankfully, that wasn't a lie. Two of the women in Lady Glover's art group had seen her wearing her bonnet-hat when she was leaving the Athenaeum after the art exhibition. They asked her where she had bought it, and when she told them that it was her own design and she had made it herself, they both commissioned her to make similar hats for them. Ellen was thrilled! Then her mother's wedding plans got in the way, and now she was scrambling to get them finished. It would be the first time that she would receive payment for something that she had created, and it felt good. Ellen truly understood the pride Alexander took in his artwork.

Once Har had gone away, Ellen moved in with her mother and Kenneth and needed to be more inventive to get away early on Mondays. There were four bedrooms in the Riverside house, and Louise and Kenneth occupied the largest one upstairs facing north. One bedroom was on the main level at the back of the house facing south, and Ellen told her mother she would prefer that one since she would not have to disturb them when she went to work. She was sure her mother and Kenneth wanted their privacy as well.

Even though Riverside was farther from the town centre, it was a shorter distance to Government House and the Colonial Building than from Victoria Street. On Mondays, Ellen could leave Riverside at five twenty and still arrive at the Colonial Building on time. She told her mother that she was helping train in a new parlour maid and had to go to work a little earlier than usual. That explained one Monday. Then she used Cheri as an excuse, saying that she needed her to help with some special mending for another Monday.

Kenneth suggested Ellen should give up working. He pointed out that she didn't need to wait for September, when she had originally decided that she could afford to go to London, to study millinery. He said he would pay for her expenses and that would be part of his investment in her business. Ellen thanked him and explained that she would have enough money saved herself by the end of August and she would continue to work at The House until then. Ellen thought her mother was secretly pleased at her show of independence. She would tell her mother about her real plan, her marriage plan, in due time. Ellen planned to make and sell hats from her home after she was married, and she believed she could continue until babies came along, and maybe even afterwards. She wasn't living in the dark ages. It was 1881.

twenty-five

Release, Ellen's and Alexander's, came at six o'clock on the morning of August tenth. The day was foggy, but it could have been a raging storm and Ellen wouldn't have cared. She had dressed in Alexander's favourite blue dress and bonnet and was waiting outside Her Majesty's door at a quarter to six. She hadn't slept a wink and would probably have waited outside the prison all night if her good sense hadn't prevailed. If anyone was observing her that early on a Monday morning, she probably looked like a ghostly apparition, the fog was so thick. She was grateful that nature had facilitated her tryst with Alexander, because she would not suffer a chaperone today. Alexander and Ellen had never been alone together, and she was determined that they would be now, if only for a brief time.

Just when Ellen had lost patience and was thinking of barging inside the prison, the door squeaked opened and Kielly appeared, grinning from ear to ear. "Here he is, my darling girl," he said, standing aside for Alexander. "He was afraid you wouldn't be here, silly man. I'll see you both later. Don't do anything I wouldn't do." He laughed and re-entered the prison.

Ellen hardly heard what Kielly was saying. She was totally dazzled by Alexander, dressed in a navy blue suit of impeccable tailoring. He grabbed Ellen's hand and started running, pulling her with him, down Forest Road and up over the barrens behind Government House. Ellen was gasping when they stopped behind a clump of alder bushes.

"Oh, Alen, I am free, finally free," Alexander said, crushing her to his chest and kissing her. Ellen thought she was going to faint from running and from excitement. She was not as fit as Alexander and had the added curse of a tight corset.

"Alexander, wait. I can't breathe." She was laughing and choking and gasping all at the same time.

"Alen, forgive me." He looked at her, his brow wrinkling in concern. "I just had to get away from that prison as fast as I could. I will be happy never to see it again."

"I understand, Alexander. Let's just rest here a moment." Alexander circled her in his arms and her breathing calmed as her heartbeat quickened. Then his lips found hers, igniting a fuse that travelled through her body core starting a liquid fire. Ellen was suffused with desire. She pulled him as close as she could toward her, and it was not enough. Her breasts pushed against the armature of her clothing and she shamelessly rubbed her body against Alexander's. She felt his arousal through the folds of her dress. She was a virgin, but she had read enough books to know exactly what was going on between them. If it hadn't been for the shrieking wheels of a vegetable cart on the road below them, they would have stripped each other's clothing off right then and there. The harsh sound brought them both back to their surroundings, and they reluctantly pulled apart.

Their hands linked them together as they continued to walk in a state of bliss. They didn't speak, but luxuriated in the bliss of being together, with no persons or prison to keep them apart. They reached Bannerman's Park and strolled through it, making Alexander's painting of them come alive with every step. They reached the chestnut tree which barely touched Alexander's shoulder. He took out a small pocket knife and carved their special double-*A* monogram into it.

"One day this tree will be as big as the one I painted, and our initials will be part of it."

"I love our special monogram," Ellen said, tracing the carving with her finger. "I think I will even start spelling my name with an *A*."

"What do you mean, Alen?"

"My name is spelled E-l-l-e-n. But I love the way you spell it." Alexander was frowning, and she reached up, kissing the line between his eyes.

"How stupid of me. I do not know your language very well when I write it."

"Don't you dare spell it any other way, Alexander. It is like our secret code, and the two *A*'s link us together. You are so clever, Alexander. I wish I knew your language. You will have to teach it to me."

"I would be honoured. Speaking of honour, when will I be meeting with your mother? I know that she does not approve of me, and I should have asked her for your hand in marriage. But I could not risk waiting until I was released from prison and losing you."

"Alexander, you will never lose me, I'll love you forever." They kissed again, and Ellen was grateful for the fog that kept people from the park and gave them their privacy.

"When did you know you loved me?" Alexander asked.

"I was attracted to you from the moment I first saw you, but I think I fell in love with you when you made a joke about the shortbread. I loved the fact that you had a sense of humour even though you were in a dire situation. When did you know you loved me?"

"I noticed your beauty straight away, of course, but I think it was when you asked me about the mortar and pestle. You were so earnest and your intelligence shone from you just like the copper in your hair." He took a strand of her hair and curled it around his finger. "You are a very special person, Alen. Kielly told me how lucky I am at least once a day, and he is right."

"You asked when you would be meeting with my mother, and the answer is not yet. I want to wait until after we have a wedding date in place so that I can feel more confident."

"I have a surprise, too, that might help your modder accept me."

"What surprise? Tell me."

"I have a job, a real paying job. I will be starting this Thursday painting the ceilings at the Presentation Convent. Sister Mary Angela has arranged it. Remember I told you she visited me at the penitentiary as part of her mercy mission? She has been kind to me, and she has become a good friend."

"I can't wait to meet her, and I'm so excited about your job. I know that will impress Mother. She's so practical."

"We will go to the convent on Friday and talk with Sister Mary

Angela. I told her about you because I knew I could trust her not to tell anyone. She will be able to help us arrange our marriage."

"Then I will tell Mother about us on Friday night, and she will probably see you on Saturday or Sunday."

"That is good. The sooner the better. I am nervous, but I am hoping that Mr. Robinson will help me win her over. He has already helped me so much. I owe him many favours. I understand why your modder is concerned about our marriage. She wants the best for you. I want the best for you, too. And I need to convince her of that. I am glad I will be able to tell her that I have a job. That is one stroke against me gone. I will have to earn her trust over time, but I know we will be friends eventually. I will look after you so well that she will have to accept me. And speaking of looking after you, I must soon leave you. You must not be seen with me without a chaperone."

"I hate this waiting. If it wasn't for Mother and the church laws, I would marry you today."

"I love you even more for saying that." He smiled at Ellen and kissed her, lighting up her whole being. "I have become used to waiting over the last months, but that doesn't mean that I don't long for us to be truly together, alone." His eyes looked into hers, and her body responded to his message of desire.

"I have another surprise to tell you about before you go. This morning, Kielly told me that the people that I taught art lessons to, at the cable station in Heart's Content, took up a collection of money for me, and Governor Glover added to it. Kielly said that many people felt guilty about me working for nothing as part of my sentence. I couldn't believe it. Such kindness! With Kielly's savings and this money, we now have enough to start our business together. Kielly is quitting his job at the penitentiary this week. I will be living with him until after we are married, and we will be planning our business then."

"That is wonderful, Alexander! This news will go a long way in gaining Mother's blessing." Ellen was jumping up and down in sheer glee.

"Now, Alen, you must go to work and I will go to Kielly's. He lives just over from Mallard Cottage in Quidi Vidi Village. I am going to walk the long way around the lake, since I do not want to walk by the prison ever again. Just being in the fresh air and being free is wonderful."

"Alexander, I have to see you again, tonight. Mother and Kenneth will be sound asleep by eleven o'clock, and I can meet you at the back of the house by the river. Kenneth's house is the only one on the north side of the river, so you can't miss it."

"I know I shouldn't agree to this, that I should wait until I speak with your modder, but I need to be with you so much. I will be at Riverside at eleven, and I will miss you until I see you then." He kissed her and she clung to him, not wanting him to leave. She watched him as he walked away and felt bereft.

Light couldn't leave the sky fast enough. Ellen spent the rest of the day in a haze of anticipation. She hardly ate anything for supper and wasn't listening to the conversation until Kenneth made a comment that jolted her.

"Isn't this the day Pindikowsky is released?"

"I believe so," said Louise.

Ellen started coughing and her mother looked at her sharply. "Are you all right, Ellen?"

"Fine," she said. "I swallowed the wrong way."

"He no longer has to leave the island," said Kenneth. "I wonder will he settle down here in St. John's?"

"Settle is the operative word, isn't it," said Louise. "He had a reputation for being quite the ladies' man. I hope he will get married and be respectable, if he does decide to stay here in the city. He won't be going back to his old job, not with Weedon still superintendent at the cable office."

Ellen hoped her face didn't betray the tumult going on in her mind and body.

"You're very quiet tonight, Ellen," said Kenneth.

"I'm just a bit tired." she said. "I'm going to do a little sewing and then I'm going to bed."

"Good idea. Kenneth and I are going to have an early night tonight, too." Louise smiled at him and he took her hand. Finally, at half past nine, they went to bed.

twenty-six

Ellen dressed simply in her green cotton dress. She had lost so much weight that she could easily fasten the buttons of the dress without wearing her corset. Nothing was going to keep her from being with Alexander tonight—completely. She draped a shawl around her shoulders, but it was an unusually warm night and she didn't really need it. She was pleased that Kenneth hated squeaky doors and had oiled them well. She left the house, hardly making a sound, and ran to the edge of the river.

    Alexander was waiting for her. Ellen rushed into his arms and was enfolded in his warmth. He smelled of soap, mint, and a wonderful scent that was uniquely his own. He must have shaved with a very sharp blade because his face felt as smooth and warm as freshly ironed sheets. They walked hand in hand by the river until they reached a place just below the falls. It was a hollowed-out area, covered in high grass and surrounded by alder bushes. A mature dogberry tree arced over the spot, sheltering it from view. They both gravitated toward the space, ducking under the branches of the dogberry. Alexander laid his jacket on the ground, Ellen laid her shawl beside it, and they were in each other's arms. Swiftly, their bodies responded to their caresses and they were frantic, their hands scrambling like spiders to remove clothing, freeing their skin to revel in each other's touch. Alexander entered her, and for a brief second Ellen felt a sting like lemon juice on a fresh cut. Then she felt Alexander shudder as their bodies rushed together, blending their passion.

Alexander covered their bodies using the skirt of Ellen's dress as a bedsheet. "Oh, Alen, forgive me for being so quick. I should have taken my time. You are so beautiful. I have been dreaming of being with you for so long. But that is no excuse. I should have waited until we were married. I know it was your first time. I never wanted to hurt you." He was kissing her face and neck as he spoke.

"Alexander, there is nothing to forgive. I was definitely ready, as I'm sure you know. I felt only a tiny sting, and having you inside me, part of me, was everything I wanted. You are mine now, we are married in the true sense, and I am content. Our public marriage will just be for everyone else." Ellen lay back, resting her head on Alexander's shoulder. Through the leaf canopy, they could see the stars. "What a beautiful, perfect night."

"Not half as beautiful as you," Alexander whispered.

They gazed at each other as he stroked Ellen's breasts, causing them to swell and her nipples to become erect. Alexander lowered his lips to them, and the stars blurred as Ellen's eyes leaked tears of happiness. His lips roamed her body until she was quivering with desire. Only then did he enter her again, and this time she was transported to a level of being alive that she hadn't known existed. She gripped his tight buttocks and cried out his name. They were liquid, like the river, and the noise of the falls conspired with them to muffle their cries of ecstasy.

twenty-seven

The world looked and felt different to Ellen after that night. She was a different person. A woman. Even her mother remarked on her transformation, although if she had guessed what had brought it about, she would have been appalled.

"Ellen," she said at breakfast. "You're looking much better. That extra bit of sleep must have done you good."

Her mother kissed her cheek and Ellen felt guilty, but not guilty enough to stay away from Alexander and their place by the falls. After last night, she was so sure of Alexander's love that she felt invincible. They met for the next three nights in their special place by the falls and each night their love and passion grew.

On Friday after work, Ellen met Alexander at the Presentation Convent and they went to see Sister Mary Angela. Ellen liked her right away and felt they would be friends. When Alexander asked how soon they could be married, she told them that the banns would have to be announced in church for three consecutive Sundays, and they would have to speak with Father Brennan and tell him about their intention. Since Ellen was not a Catholic, a schedule of instruction would have to be organized for her. It worked in her favour that her father had been baptized a Catholic. Sister Mary Angela estimated that the earliest possible time they could marry would be September thirtieth. Ellen asked her if she could be the one to instruct her in the Catholic faith. She said she would have to get approval from Father Brennan, but she didn't foresee a problem.

When Ellen left Alexander at the church, she told him that they would not be able to meet by the falls again until after she told her mother about them. She was determined to do so that very night.

The script she had prepared went out of her mind when she finally confronted her mother. Kenneth was at a meeting, so she and Ellen were alone. After supper, Ellen took out her shell box, removed Alexander's paintings, and laid them out on the dining room table: her portrait, Alexander's portrait, the roses, the park, the engagement. As her mother stared at the art, Ellen removed her ring from its pouch, laid it next to the last painting, and held her breath. It was a long time before her mother spoke.

"What does this mean? Who is Alen?"

"I am Alen. It is how Alexander says my name. He writes it the way he says it."

"I see . . . I was afraid of this. I think I knew about your feelings for Pindikowsky, but I didn't want to believe it. I certainly had no idea it had gone this far. How was all this possible?" She indicated the pictures and the ring. "He only worked at The House for a few months, and I made sure you kept away from him as much as possible. "You didn't go down to the penitentiary to see him, I hope and pray?"

"No one knows except Cheri," Ellen said, trying to placate her. "Kielly, Officer Kielly, let me in at the side entrance at Her Majesty's, and I saw Alexander there on Saturdays at six o'clock in the morning, my day off. No one saw me. I didn't go to his cell or to the visiting room. He didn't want to shame me by having me go there. He was painting a mural in the hallway of the west entrance, and I saw him there. Just for a few minutes. I only went there four times, and a couple of times at the Colonial Building. We were careful. No one saw us," she said, her voice cracking as her throat constricted. The look on her mother's face was one of shock and betrayal. Ellen felt awful and wanted to deny it all, but she couldn't. She loved Alexander and was committed to him.

"You were careful? He didn't want to shame you?" Louise shouted. "Well, he has." She picked up the ring and turned it around in her hand. "He made this, I suppose," she said, her voice icy. "I'll say one thing for him: he is talented. I suppose he intends to marry you."

Ellen couldn't get her voice to be more than a whisper. "We want to get married as soon as possible, after you give us your permission."

"My permission!" she shouted. "I assume he's Catholic and you would be married in the Catholic Church?"

Ellen nodded. "I don't mind that, Mother. After all, Father was a Catholic, wasn't he? And you always say that religion doesn't matter, that it's how people treat one another that matters."

"Yes, and look how you've treated me—lying to me, sneaking behind my back. I don't recognize who you've become."

"I'm sorry, Mother. I didn't know what else to do. I knew you wouldn't want me to see him."

"You're right about that. What do you really know about this man? All anyone knows for sure is that he's from Poland, that he's an artist, that he's a Catholic. Oh, and let's not forget, a convicted felon."

"You don't know him, Mother. He's kind and funny and just wonderful."

"Not to mention charming and good-looking. I was afraid you'd fall for that. You're a clever girl, Ellen, but you're also very naive. Don't you see? You're his ticket to respectability. He knows that by marrying you he will be able to whitewash his reputation. To think it was Kenneth who gave Governor Glover the idea to have Pindikowsky do the frescoes at Government House! And look what has happened. Maybe Kenneth can talk some sense into you."

"No, Mother. It doesn't matter what anyone says. I love Alexander and I'm going to marry him. But I want your blessing. Once you know Alexander, you will love him, too. I'm sure you will." Ellen reached out to her, wanting to be folded into her mother's arms, but her mother turned away from her.

"Well, I'm not sure of anything right now, Ellen. I'm in shock. I think you'd better go to your room. I need time to think, and Kenneth will be back at any moment. I will discuss this whole situation with him."

Ellen went to her room and collapsed on the bed feeling like a slowly deflating balloon. She always knew it was going to be hard to tell her mother about Alexander, but she wasn't prepared for the pain that she felt over her withdrawal of love and support. In the morning, her pillow was stiff with tears.

twenty-eight

The next day was Saturday, her day off, and Ellen intended to stay in her room until after her mother and Kenneth finished their breakfast. That way she could avoid the inevitable confrontation for as long as possible. Her mother's voice quickly destroyed that dream. "Ellen," she said, knocking on her door. "I know you're awake. Get dressed and come to breakfast. We have some talking to do."

Ellen washed her face and dressed hastily. Her eyes were very swollen, and she hoped that she could gain some sympathy from her appearance. She walked into the parlour and sat down at the round table that had been set up there in order to capture the morning sunlight. Kenneth held out a chair for her and she sat down at his right. Her mother was seated opposite her. The newspaper was folded over a couple of times and rested by Kenneth's cup.

"It says here in the paper that Mr. Pindikowsky has started working on the ceilings at the Presentation Convent since his release." Kenneth tapped the paper with his finger.

Ellen realized that there would be no pleasantries and that they were going to get right to the issue at hand. "Yes," she said. "He started working there on Thursday. He will be paid well." She looked over at her mother, making sure that she had registered that fact. "Also, Alexander and Dan Kielly are going to set up a business together. Officer

Kielly learned a lot about fresco painting when he was guarding Alexander, and he has quit his job at Her Majesty's and will be assisting Alexander at the convent."

"That is all very well, Ellen. It is wonderful that Mr. Pindikowsky has found employment so quickly, but your mother and I are concerned about you and your relationship with him. You are very young and impressionable, Ellen, and we feel that Mr. Pindikowsky has taken advantage of that fact. He is quite a bit older than you, and to court you while he was in prison was unconscionable. It proves that he is not a gentleman and has not had your best interests at heart."

"It wasn't like that. He was always a gentleman with me. It was I who insisted that I see him. I told Mother all about it." Ellen took a deep breath to stop her tears from starting again. She had to remain strong.

"Yes, you did," said Louise. "And I'm ashamed of your behaviour. I don't know how you could have been so bold. You've always been impulsive, but I really thought you had better sense."

"I love him and I know he loves me. If you can't accept him, then I'll just have to move out." Ellen regretted saying the words as soon as they were out of her mouth. She held her breath, hoping that she wouldn't have to make good on her threat.

"Now, there's no need for that," said Kenneth, looking over at her mother and communicating some unspoken message. "I'm sure we can work something out. After all, there's no rush. There is plenty of time for Mr. Pindikowsky to prove himself. If he loves you sincerely, as you claim, then he will wait for you. He can court you properly and establish his business and if, in a year, you still want to marry, you can."

"A year!" Ellen shouted. "We want to be married right away. Why should we wait?"

"Because," said her mother, "I have to be sure that he is marrying you for all the right reasons and not so that he can further his ambitions. I'm sorry, Ellen, but I can't take a chance on your future happiness."

"But Alexander is my happiness."

"Well, let him prove it to us, starting tomorrow. He can join us for dinner tomorrow night and we can get to know him. You can start courting in the proper manner. After all, Kenneth is a member of the

House of Assembly. We have to think of his reputation. You are his stepdaughter, and it would reflect badly on him if you go about alone with a man, especially a man whom everyone recognizes. We are not saying that you can never marry Mr. Pindikowsky, but you must wait until he has established himself both socially and financially. Now, I'll write an invitation to Mr. Pindikowsky and Kenneth will drop it off at his residence. Do you have his address, Ellen?"

"Yes," Ellen said quietly. "Thank you, Mother. Thank you, Kenneth." She gave them Alexander's address and went back to her room, closing the door. She decided that it was best to bide her time. She was fond of Kenneth and respected him, so she would be dutiful and follow the rules for now. She was confident that Alexander would charm them and win them over. Mother and Kenneth would see how much they loved one another and would give their permission for her to marry him long before a year was out. September thirtieth was the date that was imprinted on her heart.

ALEXANDER ARRIVED AT FIVE O'CLOCK SUNDAY EVENING. WHEN ELLEN heard the knock on the door, she jumped up from the couch where she'd been sitting in tense anticipation. Her mother made her sit down again, saying that Jeanette would answer the door.

Jeanette was the maid Louise had recently hired to replace Dora, who had been their maid for many years. Dora had had to return to her hometown of Trepassey to tend to her father, who was very ill. Jeanette was from Brigus and was about ten years Ellen's senior. She was a good-looking woman, with an excellent figure, and Ellen wondered why she wasn't married. She was sure a story lurked there.

She heard Alexander's voice, followed by Jeannette's. She announced him and he stepped past her into the parlour. The sight of him made Ellen's blood surge with desire. His hands were full of roses.

"Mr. Pindikowsky, it's a pleasure to see you again," said Kenneth, getting up from his chair by the window and holding out his hand.

"The pleasure is mine. Thank you for inviting me to your home," said Alexander, shifting the roses to his left hand and shaking Kenneth's right hand. He stood stiffly, his face very serious, making him appear older. Ellen wished he would smile.

Alexander walked over to Ellen's mother and gave her six pink roses. "Mrs. Robinson, thank you for receiving me," he said. Louise nodded and accepted the roses. Then he handed Ellen a single long-stemmed red rose and gazed at her in such a way that her body overheated and she turned a red that matched the rose. "For you, Alen," Alexander said. For a moment they forgot that her mother and Kenneth were in the room. Then Ellen heard her mother's voice.

"Thank you, Mr. Pindikowsky. I'll just give these flowers to Jeanette to put in water." She took the rose from Ellen's hand and walked briskly from the room.

"Please, sit down, Mr. Pindikowsky," said Kenneth, indicating the chair opposite his. "I hear you're working on the ceilings over at the Presentation Convent. You did a marvellous job at Government House. I was very impressed."

Alexander sat down on the edge of the chair. "Thank you, sir. I understand it was you, Mr. Robinson, who suggested to Governor Glover that I do the ceilings at Government House, and I want to thank you very much. I owe you a debt of gratitude."

Ellen's mother walked into the room and the temperature cooled. "I understand that Government House is where you and Ellen developed a fondness for one another. And she tells me that you want to be married."

"That is true, Mrs. Robinson. I love your daughter and I want you to know that I will look after her."

"Mr. Robinson and I do not doubt that you love Ellen. She is a beautiful, talented, and intelligent young woman. Any man would be fortunate to marry her. But your relationship so far has been quite unethical, and Mr. Robinson and I are worried about Ellen's welfare."

"Alexander has a good job and he . . ." Ellen started to say. Her mother held up her hand to silence her.

"I appreciate that you are working now, Mr. Pindikowsky, but what will you do once that job is over? You do have a criminal record, and that will limit the number of places where you will find employment."

"I understand your concern, Mrs. Robinson. I am planning to start a business with Dan Kielly. He is respected as a former police officer and prison guard, and I feel that our partnership will ease the minds of prospective employers. We have already started to work on our business plan."

"That is very commendable, Mr. Pindikowsky, but your confidence is just that, confidence. Mr. Robinson and I want solid proof that you can support Ellen. That is why we want you and Ellen to wait one year to be married. In the meantime, you may see Ellen, but only if you are chaperoned."

"But, Mother," Ellen blurted, "we love . . ."

"That's enough, Ellen," she said. "If at the end of one year you have proven your business to be successful and you still wish to marry Ellen, we won't stand in your way."

"Thank you, Mrs. Robinson, Mr. Robinson. I will always wish to marry Alen, now or next year or eighty years from now." Alexander looked at Ellen with such love in his eyes that she could hardly breathe. They smiled at each other and were again transported to their own world.

Kenneth interrupted their trance. "Well, I think we've cleared the air here. Now, I believe our supper is ready." He stood up and took Louise's arm.

When they were out of the room, Alexander and Ellen stole a quick kiss—too quick. Supper was politely formal.

twenty-nine

Ellen's hat business was growing without her having to do anything. Miss LeDrew and Mrs. Redmond from Lady Glover's art group had both been pleased with their hats and had referred her to their friends. The result was that she had orders for two more hats that needed to be completed by September fifteenth. Ellen was longing to make a new design, but both women wanted the bonnet-hat, so she was happy enough to oblige. Once she and Alexander were married, she would no longer be working at Government House and she could devote all her time to her business. She would have plenty of time to design new styles then.

Louise and Kenneth seemed happy that Ellen wasn't giving them any more trouble about marrying Alexander. He came to the house almost every day after work for a short time, and he was invited to stay for dinner twice. He and Ellen were always chaperoned. If they went for a walk, they were accompanied by Kenneth. In fact, Kenneth enjoyed talking with Alexander and had started calling him by his given name. Ellen's mother still called him Mr. Pindikowsky.

Alexander and Ellen were allowed to sit together alone on the back veranda and talk. They knew they could be overheard, so their conversation was censored and revolved around Alexander's progress at the Presentation Convent and the business that Kielly and Alexander were starting. Alexander calculated that his work at the convent would be completed by the middle of October and he and Kielly were going to start advertising for new work in the paper within the next couple of weeks. Since fresco painting was an expensive process, they were also going to advertise to do murals and wall stencilling as well. Alexander really would have liked to do all fresco work, but he knew that that would be too limiting for the small client base of St. John's. It was Kenneth who suggested that he try for work at the Athenaeum.

"Alexander," he said, walking out onto the veranda two weeks after the initial dinner confrontation, "have you considered looking for work at the Athenaeum? I don't know if you've been at the new theatre, but it really is in dire need of decoration. I know the owner, Mr. Fairmont, and I could give you a reference if you think it would help."

"That is very generous of you, Mr. Robinson. I think that is a wonderful idea. I will go there as soon as I can."

"You can call me Kenneth, Alexander. You're making me feel like an old man, calling me Mr. Robinson."

"Thank you very much, but I think I should still call you Mr. Robinson until Mrs. Robinson calls me Alexander."

"You're probably right there," said Kenneth, winking at Ellen. "Don't stay out much longer, it's getting cold," he said, going back inside.

"Alen," whispered Alexander, "do you think we can meet tonight?"

"I wish we could," she whispered back, "but Mother is watching me too closely. In another week or two she'll stop being so vigilant, and then we can be together."

Alexander passed her an envelope. "Don't open it now. Open it when you are alone. It will tell you how I feel."

They went inside and Alexander said good night to Ellen's parents. Ellen hid the envelope behind the folds of her skirt, and as soon as Alexander had gone she excused herself and went to her room which, sadly, was no longer on the first floor. Ellen's mother said she wanted to have the downstairs bedroom for herself since Kenneth's snoring often kept her awake. Ellen knew the real reason was that her mother feared she would sneak out of the house to see Alexander, and she was right. Ellen would now have to pass her mother's door to leave the house, and this was why she told Alexander that she couldn't meet him at the falls. Ellen ached for him every night, and she didn't know how much longer she would be able to obey the courtship rules.

Ellen opened the envelope that Alexander had given her, and inside was a drawing of the two of them bundled under her dress in their secret place by the falls. It was signed in Alexander's usual way with the added note, "I long for your touch, I love you, Alen, Alexander." This was one picture Ellen would never let her mother see.

THE FOLLOWING SUNDAY WAS THE FIRST SUNDAY THAT THE BANNS announcing Alexander and Ellen's intention to marry would be read by Father Brennan at the Roman Catholic Cathedral. Most of Kenneth and Louise's friends went to George Street Methodist Church, so it was unlikely that they would find out about the banns at the cathedral.

Ellen was already taking instruction in the Catholic faith from Sister Mary Angela, three mornings a week. She told her mother that she and Cheri were making a dress for Cheri's sister, who was getting married in October, and that the only time they had to sew it was before they went to work. Cheri's sister was, in fact, getting married in October, and Cheri was making a wedding dress, but the dress was for Ellen. She was still counting on her mother's blessing by September thirtieth.

When Ellen arrived at the Presentation Convent on Friday, she was surprised to see Alexander waiting for her in Sister Mary Angela's office. She usually allowed them to be alone together for a few minutes at the end of each lesson, and it was certainly the biggest incentive for never missing a session.

"Alexander asked me to let you be together at the beginning of our lesson today," said Sister Mary Angela. "I'll give you five minutes only." She smiled at them and left the room.

As soon as the door closed they were in each other's arms, their lips and bodies pressed together. When they came up for air, they were both panting as if they had run across the Ten Mile Barrens.

"Alen, I have something to give you," said Alexander. "Close your eyes and don't peek."

Ellen closed her eyes. Alexander took her left hand in his and she felt a ring slip onto her finger. Her eyes flew open. On her third finger was a replica of the plaster ring he had made for her, but this one was in real gold with a diamond that caught the light from the stained glass window, shooting out sparks of red, blue, and rose as she moved her hand.

"Oh, Alexander! It's exquisite. But when did you have it made? Who made it?"

"I took my design to Langmead's on Water Street. George Langmead is a very fine jeweller, and he said he liked the challenge of replicating my design. He worked day and night to make it so quickly. I wanted you to have it before the banns were read in church this Sunday."

"I love it! I am so happy."

"Alen, will you marry me even without your modder's blessing? I am not sure she will ever accept me."

"She will, Alexander. We will be married on September thirtieth, I know we will."

They kissed again and didn't hear Sister as she came into the room. She started singing, and they broke apart. She laughed and shared their joy when she saw the ring. Ellen barely listened to her lessons about the rules for the confessional, she was too busy staring at her ring—the sin of pride.

thirty

The morning of Ellen's nineteenth birthday, she woke up and vomited into her wash basin. She sat on the edge of her bed and faced the fact that she was carrying Alexander's child. She knew before then. Her monthly periods had always been regular, almost to the hour, and when August twenty-second came with no sign of it, she was on alert. She had other symptoms, too: her breasts were very sore, she felt tired in a way she had never experienced, and the taste of tea and toast was bitter in her mouth. She remembered hearing her mother say to Mrs. Parmender that women who were carrying a child often couldn't stomach the things they usually liked to eat and drink. Usually there was nothing Ellen liked better than tea and toast.

Ellen didn't know if she was ready to be a mother, but at least her mother would have to allow Alexander to marry her now. She resolved to tell her right away. It was her day off, and her mother had planned a small birthday dinner party for her. Would she go ahead with it or cancel everything? There was a possibility that she would disown her, but Ellen didn't really give that a serious thought. She knew she was loved and they would get through this.

Ellen waited until she heard Kenneth leave the house for his morning walk, and then she came downstairs. There wouldn't be a better time to tell her mother. She was sitting in the parlour, at the breakfast table, reading the *Ladies' Journal* and sipping on tea. Ellen sat opposite her.

"Mother, I need to talk to you," she said.

Louise smiled at her and leaned over to give her a kiss. "Happy birthday, dear. I can't believe you're nineteen. I was married to your father and you were on the way when I was your age. It doesn't seem that long ago."

"That's what I need to talk to you about. I need to get married, Mother. Soon, I can't wait. I'm carrying Alexander's child." Ellen said it straight out before she lost her nerve.

Louise sucked in her breath and her face registered shock. "Oh, Ellen, no. How is that possible? When? I've been careful to have you chaperoned." She looked at her and then sighed, her shoulders slumping. "You were with Alexander before you told me about him, then," she said. Ellen nodded her head, not daring to meet her mother's eyes. "So moving your bedroom upstairs and watching you carefully has been for nought. Bolting the barn door after the horse has left. I see. Does Alexander know? Does anyone else know?"

"No, I haven't told him or anyone else yet. I thought I might be with child, but this morning I threw up, and now I'm sure that I am."

"Well, this changes everything. I still have many reservations about Alexander, but I can see that he loves you and you love him. I see the way you look at him—the way I looked at your father. When the Hann women fall in love, it's for keeps. I just hope and pray, for your sake, that Alexander is the same. But I do not want you to tell anyone about this, except Alexander. Publicly we will approve your marriage and we will announce your engagement in the paper. There will be talk because it is so soon after his release from prison, but we will put a brave face on it. You are not that far along, so no one has to know that you are expecting. Lots of women have early births." Louise counted the months off on her fingers and then turned to Ellen sharply. "Tell me you weren't with him before he was released from prison."

"No, Mother."

"One small blessing, then. I calculate around the middle of May. We'll announce the wedding date tonight at your party and you can stop hiding that ring you've been wearing." Ellen looked up, startled.

She thought no one had noticed it. Her mother took up her hand and examined the ring. "It is quite unusual. At least Alexander has done something right."

Ellen noticed that she had called him Alexander and not Mr. Pindikowsky. Thank God. She was sure there was a saint that she could thank, too. She'd ask Sister Mary Angela.

"I just thought of something," said Louise. "What about the banns? They have to be announced three times in the Catholic Church. That's going to make your marriage later." She picked up a calendar from the bookcase and started looking at dates.

"September thirtieth, Mother," Ellen said quietly. "The first banns were read last Sunday, and Father Brennan has agreed to marry us then."

"What? Without my permission?" Louise shouted.

"I was hoping you would give us your blessing by the end of the month. I kept telling you we didn't want to wait."

"Well, you didn't, did you?" Louise sighed, loudly. "Now that you are in a delicate condition, I want you married as quickly as possible."

They heard Kenneth out in the hall, and Louise told Ellen to leave them alone while they discussed the situation. She went back to her room to lie down. She was still feeling sick, but she was happy about telling her mother about the baby. She hadn't disowned her, and now Ellen could finally be with Alexander, openly.

Louise had decided to go ahead with the party. Ellen couldn't wait for evening to arrive so she could tell Alexander her . . . their news. She decided to wear her rose-coloured dress, the one that she'd worn at her mother's wedding. Alexander hadn't seen it yet, and the colour would make her look less pale.

When Alexander arrived, Ellen was waiting for him at the front of the house. She took him by the hand and walked toward the river. He was mystified as she led him to a spot that wouldn't be overlooked from the house.

"Happy birthday, my darling Alen," Alexander said. "Your modder is allowing us to be alone? Is this a birthday gift from her? If it is, I love her for that." He took her face in his hands and kissed her thoroughly. For a few seconds, Ellen forgot her news.

"I have a surprise for you," she said, gazing into his eyes, today more green than grey. "Actually, I have two surprises. Mother has agreed to let us marry on the thirtieth of this month and . . ." She didn't get a chance to say anymore as Alexander picked her up and swung her around, making her so dizzy that she was in danger of throwing up. He gave a loud whoop of joy and she knew he could be heard at the house. "Alexander," she said, laughing, "put me down, I have something else to tell you." He set her down, not taking his eyes from hers.

"I don't care what the other surprise is. Just knowing that we will be getting married is enough. But tell me anyway."

"Alexander, I'm carrying your child." Ellen placed her hands over her stomach and then looked into his face, waiting for his response.

He stopped smiling, his brow formed into a frown, and her heart stopped. It was the longest two seconds of her life. And then his face split into a glorious smile that started her heart beating again.

"It is true? You are carrying my child? Oh, Alen, I am the happiest man in the whole world. I love you so much." He crushed her to him and kissed her slowly, turning her to liquid. She wanted him so much, but they had to return to the house. It wouldn't do to be absent from her own party. Now that her mother had capitulated, Ellen didn't want to anger her. She promised herself that she would find a way to be with Alexander that night.

Alexander held her hand, caressing it with his thumb and causing her blood to flow toward him as they walked back to Riverside. When they walked into the drawing room, Louise, Kenneth, Cheri, and Robert Baird all shouted out "Happy birthday!" Jeanette came forward with champagne for everyone. It was the last of her mother's wedding champagne, and Ellen was touched that she was offering it to them. One thing about her mother: when she gave in to something, she did it completely.

Louise cleared her throat. "Kenneth and I have an announcement to make." She turned toward him, and he said, "Ellen and Alexander are officially engaged and will be married on September thirtieth at the Roman Catholic Cathedral." Louise held up her glass. "May their love be forever and may they live long in health, wealth, and happiness."

Cheri, who was privy to all the former objections, gulped her champagne and said, "My God," and then clapped her hand over her mouth and said, "Sorry, excuse me." She rushed over to Ellen and gave her a hug, whispering in her ear, "How in the world did you pull this off?" Ellen whispered back that she'd tell her everything at work the next day. "You'd better," she said, releasing her and holding out her hand to Alexander.

Robert was properly introduced to Alexander, who looked a little bewildered as Robert shook his hand. It was a lot to take in. Within twenty-four hours Alexander had gone from a barely tolerated suitor to being the centre of attention.

Robert surprised everyone, except Kenneth, by saying that he wanted them all to go outside so he could take a picture to commemorate the occasion. Apparently, ever since Kenneth and Louise's wedding, Robert had been fascinated with the whole photographic process. Ellen remembered that he had spent a long time talking to Mr. Vey after the pictures were taken. Kenneth was very interested in photography, too, and he had helped Robert with the purchase of his equipment. Kenneth told them that they had an agreement. Robert would learn how to work the equipment and then teach Kenneth, who thought it would make a wonderful hobby. Robert, however, was very serious about the craft and was considering opening a photography studio as soon as he had mastered the art. In the meantime, he would continue to work at Bowring Brothers as the manager of their shoe department.

They all stood outside for their picture since Robert hadn't yet mastered indoor photography, which was much more complicated because of the lighting required. He had them stand in the garden with their backs to the river. He said he wanted to capture the river as part of the composition, and Alexander and Ellen were secretly delighted, considering their romantic history. The resulting photograph replaced the Champagne Picture in Ellen's heart.

At dinner, Ellen's stomach rebelled and she could hardly eat a thing. She noticed that Cheri kept glancing over at her and registered that fact. Usually Ellen ate everything in sight. She was able to eat a little of her birthday cake, deep chocolate with boiled icing. Her mother made the icing because she was the expert on getting the icing to the perfect consistency.

Cheri was the last to leave and she whispered to Ellen, "Would you happen to have a cake in the oven?" Ellen nodded and she smiled. "You wicked girl! I'll see you bright and early tomorrow. I have some adjustments to make on the dress."

When Alexander left, Ellen told him to meet her in their usual place at twelve o'clock. She was determined to be with him that night, and she would find a way.

As it turned out, it was easy. Kenneth had his arm around Louise when Ellen came back into the house after saying goodbye to Alexander.

"Ellen," said Kenneth, "I told your mother that I've given up snoring. I think it was caused by that lingering cough I had. Anyway, you can have your old room back if you'd like it. We're going to have an early night. It's been quite an exhausting and eventful day. I wish you and Alexander well. Happy birthday, Ellen." He smiled at her and winked when Louise wasn't looking.

"You should get some rest, too, Ellen," her mother said. "Don't stay up reading your new books all night." She kissed her and followed Kenneth upstairs.

Ellen wasn't long bringing her belongings back to the downstairs bedroom.

thirty-one

When Ellen met Cheri at work the next day, she barely let her take her coat off before she was peppering her with questions. She gave her almost all the details.

"It's the most romantic thing ever," she said. "And your ring, Ellen, imagine, it's the only one like it in the whole world. I'm only sorry that you had to get in the family way to get your mother to allow the marriage. I'm sure she wouldn't have otherwise."

"I didn't plan it, though, and I had no idea it was so easy to conceive. It must have happened the first time we were together. I'm meeting Alexander at the cathedral for the eleven o'clock service. Mother wrote a note to Mabel explaining why I would need to get time off from work. Last week I was sick for the first reading of the banns, but this week we'll sit together. I don't know what to expect. Alexander said that last Sunday, when Father Brennan read the banns, there was a lot of whispering and head turning. He made sure he left the church quickly after the service. He's such a good-looking man, I'm sure a good many women would overlook his criminal record to marry him. They probably hate me, especially since I wasn't baptized a Catholic. But I don't really care about all that. As long as I can be with Alexander, I'll be happy."

Cheri looked wistful. "Do you think Robert likes me?" she asked.

"I think he's very handsome and so interesting. He kept me entertained at your party with funny stories about working at Bowring's, and he explained how his camera works and how he intends to set up his photography business."

"I don't think he would bother to entertain you if he didn't feel attracted to you. After all, what's not to love? He'd be lucky to have you. And since he's well over six feet tall, you'd always have to look up to him, way up. What man wouldn't want that?" Ellen joked. "But I thought you were resolved not to get married until you were older so that you wouldn't have many children."

"Oh, yes . . . well . . . did I tell you that I saw him on Regatta Day?"

"No, you did not. Keeping secrets, are we?"

"You're a fine one to talk. Since Alexander's been released, I've hardly seen you. Robert literally bumped into me at one of the raffles. He dropped his ticket, and when he bent over to retrieve it, he knocked into me. He seemed happy to see me, and he even bought me an ice cream at Wood's Confectionery stand. Then we watched some of the races. Robert had a bet on the Beck's Cove boat and they won. He was so excited. He hugged me and then he walked me home. But he still hasn't asked me out or anything. Why do you think that is?"

"I think he's just shy. Maybe you'll just have to be a little more encouraging. Alexander told me that he watched the races from the window at Her Majesty's. He had the best view of the lake, but it was no comfort to him. He won't even walk by the prison now that he's free."

"Well, you can't blame him for that. He probably would have gone mad if he hadn't been let out to do the frescoes. Does he have other jobs booked for after he finishes work at the Presentation Convent?"

"He's going to see if Mr. Fairmont at the Athenaeum will hire him. He could do set design as well as frescoes. Kenneth has already said that he'd give him a reference. The Athenaeum is sold out for most concerts and plays, so I'm sure they can afford his work. I'm not worried about that. Alexander doesn't have a lazy bone in his body. He'll always find work to do. Besides, I'll have my hat business, too. I can handle that and look after our baby, I'm sure."

Cheri laughed. "You really don't know much about babies, do you? Never mind, you'll find out. Now, try on your dress. I brought it over with me this morning. I can see just by looking at you that I'm going to have to adjust the bodice. You're already bigger there." She slipped the cream-coloured satin over Ellen's head and started pinning.

WHEN ELLEN ARRIVED HOME THAT EVENING AFTER WORK, HER MOTHER was full of plans as she had expected. In the note she had written to Mabel she had included notice that Ellen would be quitting her job at The House as of September twenty-fourth. That meant she had just five days left to work there. Everything was happening so quickly that Ellen was overwhelmed.

"When Alexander comes over tonight, Kenneth and I need to talk with him," said her mother. Ellen looked at her in alarm. "It's all right, Ellen, nothing to worry about. We just need to iron out a few things."

As it turned out, Ellen was happy with the talk. Louise offered the Victoria Street house to them to live in until Alexander had his business established. She told him that they could live in the house, rent free, until they were able to buy their own house. All they would have to do was to give Har a room when she returned from New York and look after the maintenance and the monthly bills of the house. Ellen hugged her mother and told her how much she appreciated her generosity. Alexander expressed his gratitude also. Louise made sure to inform them both that the title to the house was in her name and Kenneth's. Ellen knew she said this to protect her. If Alexander left her, she would still have a roof over her head. Ellen was pleased that her mother was protecting her and saddened that she didn't have confidence in Alexander's ability to look after her. It was her mother's way of warning Alexander, and he recognized and accepted it as such. They both knew that he would win her over, in time. They weren't going to rock the boat now since they were in a very vulnerable position.

The days before the wedding were filled with planning, shopping, cleaning, and sewing. Louise opened the house on Victoria Street and she and Ellen, with the help of Jeanette, set about cleaning and airing it from top to bottom. Alexander and Kielly painted the bedrooms, the hallway, and the kitchen in their spare time. Louise got to know Kielly and she quite liked him in spite of herself. Ellen knew that her mother held him responsible for aiding Alexander in his *seduction of her*, even though Ellen had told her she was to blame and there was no seduction. She tried to explain that if Kielly hadn't helped her to see Alexander discreetly, she would have visited him during prison visiting hours, which would have been very public.

Ellen hadn't been able to help very much with the readying of the house since she felt very tired and nauseous. She was sick every morning and was only able to manage the rest of the day as long as she rested and avoided certain foods and smells. She did write a lengthy letter to Har telling her about her romance with Alexander and giving her a censored version of the truth. She didn't tell her about her delicate condition. Har would figure that out when she returned to Newfoundland in early November. In her reply letter, Har expressed her sadness that she wouldn't be home in time for the wedding and she sent her love along with a very generous money order, telling them to buy whatever they liked for a wedding gift.

THE MORNING OF THEIR WEDDING, IT RAINED IN TORRENTS. ALEXANDER said the rain was blessing them with abundance. Ellen would have liked to see a bit of sun, but she was grateful for his interpretation.

The Roman Catholic Cathedral was so huge that the wedding party looked dwarfed in the space. Light poured in through the stained glass, casting a kaleidoscope of colours around them. When Sister Mary Angela sang "Ave Maria" in her clear soprano voice, Cheri started walking down the aisle and Kenneth took Ellen's arm and smiled at her.

"Are you certain this is what you want, Ellen?" Kenneth asked.

"More than certain," she replied, smiling at him.

They started walking down the aisle and everyone turned toward them. It was a small group: apart from Father Brennan and Sister Mary Angela, there were Alexander, Kielly, who was Alexander's best man, Martha, Kielly's wife, Ellen's mother, Cheri, and Robert Baird.

Alexander was smiling and gazing at Ellen with such love as she approached the altar. He looked very handsome; his hair had grown out from the prison cut, and it fell slightly over his forehead, making him appear much more youthful. He wore a morning coat of dark charcoal grey that fit him perfectly. He looked completely at ease in the imposing church, and Ellen realized that this type of architecture suited him. When she first saw him at Government House, she thought he belonged in grand rooms. That thought was reinforced today.

Ellen walked toward him proudly, knowing that she looked her best. Cheri had done a spectacular job with her dress. The front fell in a continuous cascade of softly layered cream satin outlined in lace that looped around into a bustle and short train at the back. She carried a bouquet made up of ivy leaves and cream-coloured gladioli. Her hair was swept up into a soft coil, and she wore a long veil attached to a princess headdress that she had designed.

Cheri was dressed in russet taffeta which suited her to perfection. Her hair was draped around the bonnet Ellen had made for her last Christmas and coiled in a bun at the nape of the neck. Even Kielly, standing next to Alexander, looked good in his black morning coat.

When Ellen reached Alexander's side and saw his love for her reflected in his eyes, everyone else retreated from her consciousness and only the words that Father Brennan had them repeat penetrated their world. When Alexander placed the gold wedding band on Ellen's finger, she saw that it was engraved with their *A* monogram. They were married, and Ellen was filled with contentment.

The bells pealed as they left the church. The rain had stopped and Robert had everyone stand on the cathedral steps while he took a group photograph, as well as two photographs of Alexander and Ellen. Then, they all climbed into the waiting carriages and went to Kenneth's house for their wedding luncheon. Riverside had been the reception place for two weddings and a birthday party in the last few months, and it was becoming forever linked with happy events.

Mrs. Parmender once again made the wedding cake, and together she and Jeanette served the meal. Mrs. Parmender gave Ellen a big hug and said she would miss her over at The House, and she made her promise to visit her. Ellen knew that when she did visit she would make sure to look at her portrait in the ceiling. As far as she knew, Miss Hamilton was the only one who had noticed it so far. Ellen loved the fact that she and Alexander would be a presence at The House for years to come.

They left Riverside at around three o'clock and took a carriage to

Victoria Street, where they would be blissfully alone. Alexander had to work the next day, so every minute was precious to them. They chose to take the bedroom on the third floor because it was large and had a smaller adjoining bedroom that they could make into a nursery. Har would still be in her old room on the second floor when she came back from New York and they would all have their privacy.

Alexander's hands were trembling as he put the key to the house in the lock and opened the door. Then he scooped Ellen into his arms and carried her across the threshold. She had always felt happy entering this house, the only home she had ever known, but now it felt different, it was theirs, a haven away from prying eyes. They could, at last, be uninhibited in their lovemaking.

They didn't make it to the third-floor bedroom for quite some time. Their clothes were discarded in record time and they were soon gasping on the floor by the parlour fireplace. Ellen wondered fleetingly if her mother had ever done anything so outrageous, and then she smiled—of course she had. She was her daughter, after all.

When they finally made it to their bedroom, Alexander laid her gently on the bed and stretched out beside her. He took the last pins from her hair and spread it out over the pillow.

"I have dreamed of this moment for so long, Alen. You are so beautiful and I love you with all my heart."

"I love you, too, Alexander, now and forever." Tears of joy spilled from Ellen's eyes, and he kissed them away and then mapped the rest of her body with his hands and mouth. This time when he entered her, they moved together as one, each part of their bodies molding and cleaving to one another until they cried out each other's names in explosive relief. It was so wonderful not to have to silence their joy! When they gathered their breath, Alexander placed his hand on her stomach, caressing it slowly. "You know, Alen, now that you are in the family way, I don't know if it is proper for you to behave in such a wanton manner." He was grinning at her and laughing, and she hit him with her pillow, which started a chase around the bedroom and ended once again in a tangle of sheets.

When Ellen opened her eyes the next morning, Alexander had already left. She had a vague memory of him kissing her. Right away her stomach churned and she vomited into the bowl at the side of the bed. Alexander must have put it there before he left. Then Ellen noticed a note beside a plate of crackers on the bedside table. Alexander had written, "Eat the crackers to settle your stomach. I love you, Alen, Alexander." Even though the note was hastily written, he had still joined their *A*'s together. She was the luckiest, happiest woman in the world. If only she didn't feel so tired and nauseous. Last night's lovemaking had worn her out. Not that that was going to stop her from repeating the activities that night. She'd just rest up a bit and she'd be fine. She relieved herself and lay down again, snuggling into the blankets and sheets that were full of Alexander's scent. Ellen realized that she didn't have to do anything or go anywhere—a new experience for her.

thirty-two

It was Saturday morning and Alexander was not working. He had worked longer hours in the days leading up to the wedding so that he could get ahead of schedule at the Presentation Convent. The next two days would be a honeymoon for Alexander and Ellen, and they were going to spend them doing exactly as they pleased.

Alexander said he was taking Ellen out walking, starting with breakfast at the Atlantic Hotel located at the east end of Water Street just across the road from Holloway Street. They were having an Indian summer, so they needed to wear only their light clothing, which was a relief. Ellen wore her blue dress and bonnet, Alexander's favourite, and he wore his dark blue suit. She thought they looked perfect together. She took his arm and they headed out the door in full daylight. It was so wonderful to be free from all restrictions. They were a respectable married couple out strolling around the city.

When they arrived at the hotel, they walked through the lobby to the dining room and sat at a table by the window overlooking the waterfront. There were a number of sailing ships lined up in the harbour, and Ellen wondered if bad weather was expected. St. John's unseasonably good weather was unusual and could come to an end without warning—all that was needed was a change in the direction of the wind from southwest to northeast.

Ellen looked at the menu, and nothing appealed to her. The thought of eggs or toast and tea made her queasy. The only thing that she wanted was apple pie. Not the usual breakfast fare, but she knew they had some, as she had seen a whole pie under a glass dome at the front counter.

"Have you decided what you want, Alen? I am ravenous, and I'm having the full English breakfast with double sausage." He rubbed his hands together in anticipation.

"I think I want apple pie."

Alexander looked at her quizzically. "Apple pie? You want apple pie? Is that our baby talking?" he whispered, smiling indulgently at her.

"I'm afraid so. You have what you want, Alexander, but I really just want apple pie. And coffee, no tea."

The waiter came over and Alexander gave him their order. "We will both have apple pie and coffee."

"Are you sure that's what you want?" the waiter asked. "The full English breakfast is on special today."

"Yes, we are sure. The apple pie with coffee."

The waiter walked away, shaking his head. "Alexander," Ellen said, "you didn't have to do that. You should have the full breakfast, if that's what you want."

"No, I just realized that today, October the second, is Apple Pie for Breakfast Day, so we must both have it." Alexander was in a playful mood, and Ellen was delighted to play along.

"Is that a Polish tradition?"

"It is now, for sure. Every October the second from here on we must have apple pie for breakfast. It will be an Alen and Alexander tradition and we will honour it with our son or daughter next year and every year after." He took Ellen's hand across the table and brought it to his lips. She noticed people staring at them from the other tables. She thought, *Let them stare, they're just jealous.*

After their strange breakfast they did some window shopping along Water Street and Duckworth Street, and then Ellen told Alexander she was tired and needed a nap. He said he could do with a rest, too. From the look that passed between them, neither one of them would be doing a lot of resting.

ALEXANDER FINISHED HIS WORK AT THE CONVENT ON SCHEDULE. HE and Kielly had already met with Mr. Fairmont at the Athenaeum, and Alexander was in the process of making sketches for the murals that he proposed for the theatre walls and lobby of the building. If they were approved, he and Kielly would start work there immediately. Alexander felt pressured to get the sketches done and approved as quickly as possible, since he wanted to demonstrate to Ellen's mother that he could support Ellen. Louise was always polite to him, but the ice was still there. Not quite as thick as it had been, but Alexander still felt its chill.

He was sitting at the dining room table with watercolour papers, paints, and brushes strewn all over it. Ellen left him alone to create. She knew that talking to him at this crucial stage would disrupt his creative flow. She had work of her own to do, anyway, since she had acquired more hat customers.

Alexander had made up hand-lettered business cards for her, and they were quite beautiful. Ellen thought that their design alone helped her business. The card showed a profile sketch of Ellen wearing her bonnet-hat with the title "Ellen's Millinery" penned in calligraphic text. Then below, "Original hat design for women and children," followed by their Victoria Street address in small lettering. Alexander had hand-painted each card with his signature vines and flowers. He had made fifty of them for Ellen, and she only had a few left. Her mother and Kenneth had distributed them to their friends and acquaintances, and Alexander had left a few of them at the Athenaeum. From this advertising, Ellen had three orders for hats to finish by the end of the month: a child's bonnet with a double satin bow at the side, another bonnet-hat for an elderly lady, who said she was distantly related to Kenneth, and a princess wedding headdress, similar to the one she had worn at her wedding. Ellen was very happy with the work, and once she had completed the orders, she would start on new designs.

Ellen's mother said she needed to hire a maid soon, one that would help with the heavy work when the baby came. Ellen knew she'd have to hire someone before Har came back, but she'd been able to manage the housekeeping chores so far with just the two of them, and she loved the privacy. Once she hired a maid, she would have to go back to whispering, and she hated the thought of that. She would hire someone who was good at looking after babies, too. She didn't think they'd be able to afford a regular maid as well as a nursemaid.

Alexander stood up and stretched. "As Kielly would say, my back is gone. I find it harder to sit than I do to climb around on scaffolding. I need to get these sketches done, Alen, but I'm stuck. My muse has deserted me." He started pacing up and down the hallway.

Ellen decided it was time for her to give him some encouragement. She laid down her sewing and walked over to him, wrapping her arms around his waist. "I think what you need is a ham sandwich. That'll get your mind going again," she said.

"You are quite right, Alen. I don't know what I would do without you," Alexander said, kissing her. "I will slice the bread since you always cut it crooked." He smiled at her.

"If that's all you have to complain about, then you're a lucky man."

They ate in companionable silence, and as Ellen chewed, her eye fell on a book resting on the table in the hallway. She hadn't looked at it for ages. It was *The Complete Shakespeare*, a book that Har had given Ellen and her mother at Christmas about five years previous. Ellen had an idea. She picked up the book and handed it to Alexander. "Why not paint some scenes from Shakespeare's plays at the Athenaeum? Everyone is familiar with Shakespeare, and it would give the perfect touch of magic to the place. You wouldn't have to worry about getting permission from the writer, either."

"Alen, you are a genius. That is what I will do. I will do the most familiar plays, like *Romeo and Juliet*. You can be my model for Juliet. I will paint the balcony scene."

"It's a good thing I'm not showing my condition yet. Juliet was in enough trouble with her family over Romeo."

"The story does have a familiar pattern to it, doesn't it?"

Alexander and Ellen laughed together and went back to their work.

thirty-three

Ellen woke up two weeks later and felt quite strange. She couldn't quite place the feeling, and then she recognized it—she felt good. The nausea was gone. She sat up gingerly and waited for the vertigo to claim her, but nothing happened. She was free! And she was starving! She dressed as fast as she could and headed for the kitchen. She made herself a breakfast of four slices of bread toasted over the stove, a crock of strawberry jam, and a pot of tea. Ellen savoured every mouthful, and she decided that she and Alexander would celebrate that night. She would prepare his favourite dish of beef stew with dumplings smothered in gravy. Meals lately had not been very complete or appealing, since just the thought of handling meat had turned Ellen's stomach. She was sure that Alexander was subsidizing the meals she cooked with visits to the restaurants located around the periphery of the Athenaeum, where he had been working on his frescoes for the last week.

Mr. Fairmont had been thrilled with the Shakespeare theme, and Kielly and Alexander had work that would last until at least the end of February. Ellen's mother made a special visit to congratulate Alexander. There was now only a skim of ice left on the surface of their relationship.

Ellen couldn't wait to tell Alexander about her new state of health, so she packed a basket with enough food for Alexander, herself, and Kielly and walked the short distance to the Athenaeum. Her surprise visit was a huge success and they had a lively lunch, full of jokes and laughter. It felt like the old days back at Government House when Ellen would serve them their tea. It was hard to believe that it was only a year ago.

As Ellen left the Athenaeum, she took time to watch the construction of the Church of England Cathedral across the street on Church Hill. She was in awe of the skilled work of the masons who worked on the building. The nave of the cathedral had been completed in 1850, but they were now adding the transepts, which already you could see would give it balance and a beauty to rival the Roman Catholic Cathedral. St. John's was becoming more beautiful all the time, and Ellen was proud of its growth. Alexander didn't often talk about his life in Poland, but when he did he spoke of the large cities and the buildings dating back hundreds of years. She had a hard time imagining such history.

That night, after Alexander and Ellen enjoyed their dinner, they lay in bed talking lazily about how their lives would be in the future. "We could build a house near Rennie's River," Ellen mused.

"Or maybe we will live in a big city somewhere," said Alexander.

"You mean leave Newfoundland?" It was a startling idea for Ellen. Newfoundland was the only place she had ever known.

"Would that be so terrible? We could maybe live in New York City, where your friend Har is now."

"I've always wanted to travel, but I can't imagine it."

"We don't have to think about it yet. We have our baby to be born first. I am so happy that you are not feeling sick anymore, Alen. I hated to see you so miserable."

"I know you did, and I love you for that. You know, Alexander," Ellen said, smiling, "it seems that whenever I'm with you, I'm forever looking at the sky or ceilings."

Alexander laughed and said, "I have a remedy for that." He scooped her up, and in a moment she was floating in his arms, naked above him. He lowered her slowly, kissing her lips as her legs straddled his body. Ellen thought they had already experienced all the joy there was in lovemaking, but that night Alexander expanded their repertoire.

thirty-four

Har was arriving home on November the tenth and Ellen still didn't have a maid. She was sitting at the dining room table, pondering what to write about her hats for her newspaper advertisement, when her mother popped in for one of her impromptu visits. She had everything worked out, she told Ellen, and all she had to do was to agree to her proposal. Apparently their former maid, Dora, had returned to St. John's a few days before and had visited Louise to see if she knew about anyone looking for a trained maid. Dora had been at her home in Trepassey ever since Ellen's mother's wedding, tending to her sick father. Sadly, he had died a couple of weeks ago, and Dora decided that she wanted to live in St. John's once more. Louise proposed that Jeanette would come to work with Ellen, and Dora would work at Riverside.

"When the baby comes, Jeanette will be able to help you look after her, too," she said. Ellen's mother always referred to the baby as her, or she, insisting that the baby was a girl. If she was wrong, Ellen knew she'd be able to explain away her prediction.

"Besides, Dora and I are used to each other. After all, she was with me for ten years. I've already run the idea past Jeanette, and she said she'd be more than happy to work for you as long as you're willing. I think she's a bit bored at Riverside, and I know she'd like to be closer to the centre of town."

Ellen didn't know Jeanette very well, but she liked her and she was sure they'd get along. For once she was grateful for her mother's interference. So that was settled and Jeanette moved in, taking the small room next to Har's at the front of the house. Alexander and Ellen had lost their privacy and would have to behave in a circumspect manner.

Ellen mourned their freedom, but she was looking forward to seeing Har and hearing all her New York stories. Har loved to read books, but she could tell a good yarn, too. Ellen often suggested that she write her stories down and get them published. Har seemed pleased with the praise but said she wasn't interested in being in the public eye. "I don't have the face or the personality for it," she quipped.

When Har's ship arrived, Alexander and Ellen went to the dock to pick her up and help her with her bags. Ellen gave her a big hug and introduced her to Alexander. She shook his hand and then whispered loudly to her, "He is the most handsome man I've ever seen. I can see why you fell for him."

Alexander was grinning broadly. "I'll find us a carriage," he said.

"There's no need," said Har. "If you can carry my bags, I would really like to walk. It will help me find my land legs again, and I can reacquaint myself with the city. After living among so many big buildings, it's good to see the hills of St. John's. I like to see the shape of the place where I live. In New York City it's pretty flat, so all you can see are buildings. Except for Central Park—that is quite wonderful. I went there as often as I could."

They walked back to Victoria Street, Har regaling them with stories of New York. Once they arrived, Alexander excused himself to go back to work and Ellen caught Har up on all the family news. Ellen decided to wait another month to tell her about her condition, since in keeping with her story she shouldn't really know about it yet. She hadn't visibly lost her figure, even though she had had to let out the waists of her dresses and lace her corset less tightly. She introduced Har to Jeanette and told her that Dora was back in town working at Riverside.

"It's wonderful to be home again," said Har. "I've missed you so much. I can't wait to see your mother and Kenneth again."

"You won't have to wait long, then. They're coming for dinner tonight. That's if you're not too tired."

"I'll just have a little lie-down and I'll be right as rain again," she said.

Ellen kissed her and went downstairs to set the table. It was too late in the season for dogberry leaves or flowers, but there was a new barrel of apples stored in the cellar, and Ellen brought seven of them up and arranged them on the table. She wove gold and green ribbons around them, completing the centrepiece. Jeanette complimented her on the arrangement, saying that it looked like it belonged on a fancy hotel table.

It was the first time Alexander and Ellen had hosted a proper dinner since they were married, and Ellen felt strange seated at the head of the table with Alexander opposite her. She didn't know how her mother felt about it, but if it bothered her she didn't let it show. Ellen knew she was happy to have Har back home again. She had become like a sister to Louise, who had no family except for Ellen, and now Kenneth and Alexander.

It was a lively evening with lots of laughter and stories. Har kept them all entertained with her experiences in New York City. She made the city sound interesting and not frightening at all. She did admit to having her purse stolen once, but said it was her own fault as it was late at night and she wanted to save money by walking home instead of taking a hansom cab. After that, she thought taking a cab was a bargain. She said the cabs were a lot more comfortable than Earle's cabs here in St. John's. The whole city of New York was a building site, she told them, and you had to be careful walking on the streets for fear of being hit by falling construction materials. She had taken a ride on the newly constructed Third Avenue Elevated Railway, the El, just to be able to see parts of the city in relative safety. It was a very exciting place, but also noisy and dirty. She said she would go back there to visit, but not to live. She liked the quiet and slower pace of life in St. John's.

Alexander, Ellen noticed, was fascinated with Har's stories of New York City. She finally had to implore him to stop asking her questions and let her eat her dinner. He apologized and left her alone until they'd finished dessert. Ellen wondered if his questions had anything to do with their talk the other night.

thirty-five

Winter descended on the city like a growling bear, and by the middle of December, Ellen was sick of waking up to fresh mounds of snow. She wanted to go out and do the shopping, but Alexander was terrified she would slip on the ice and lose the baby. She tried to tell him that it wasn't as easy as that to lose a baby once it had established itself, but he was adamant. To compensate Ellen for missing out on their luncheons at the Athenaeum, he came home for lunch a couple of times during the week, and in the evenings he would take her out for short walks, keeping a firm grip on her arm. He also insisted that she wear her ugly boots that gave her a firm purchase on the icy roads. She was missing her independence but loving Alexander's protectiveness at the same time. He did win considerable approval from Ellen's mother for his solicitude, so that was a bonus.

    Christmas was wonderful because Ellen had Alexander home for a few days. He surprised her with an unusual present. He had made an elaborate hat stand from plaster. The elegant head was painted gold, and across the face and twisting around the neck he had painted his signature flowers, leaves, and vines. It was unique and elegant. Ellen placed her newest hat on it and put it in the window, knowing it would catch the eye of any passersby and would advertise her business.

Ellen had sewn a dozen handkerchiefs for Alexander, each one embroidered with their special *A* monogram. It was lovely that they had both created gifts from their hearts and their hands.

Har and Alexander had become firm friends, and they often played whist in the evenings after supper. Jeanette was called in so they would have the requisite four players, and they were all becoming addicted to the game. Har's Christmas present to Alexander was a very old and battered copy of Edmond Hoyle's 1724 book, *A Short Treatise on the Game of Whist*. Har said she spent a lot of her spare time in New York City hunting around bookstores, and she had found this treasure and couldn't resist buying it. A few pages were missing, so she purchased the book relatively cheaply, considering its age. Alexander was touched by the gift, and in return he gave Har a small painting of the Narrows.

Ellen and Alexander went to midnight Mass at the Roman Catholic Cathedral on Christmas Eve. The candlelight and music throughout the church were breathtaking. Sister Mary Angela sang "Ave Maria," and it brought back happy memories of their wedding day. After the service, Ellen and Alexander wished her a happy Christmas and gave her a small gift. Every Sunday since their wedding they had made a point of visiting with Sister Mary Angela for a while, and they both considered her a friend. People still stared at Alexander and Ellen and whispered about them when they attended Mass, but they hoped that in time they would be accepted by the congregation.

BY FEBRUARY, ELLEN COULD NO LONGER HIDE THE FACT THAT SHE was expecting, and she was more and more confined to the house. On Saturdays, if the weather co-operated, Cheri and Robert Baird would come over to talk and play whist. She and Robert Baird were officially engaged and planning a June wedding. Robert was still working at Bowring Brothers, but he was determined that by June he would have his tintype business ready to go. Go was the operative word, since he had decided to have a travelling business, taking photographs all over the island. The tintypes were the perfect medium for that since they didn't require the long exposure times of daguerreotypes and could be developed quickly. More importantly, they were relatively cheap. For those with a little more money to spend, he would sell silver- and gold-plated lockets to hold the miniature photographs. These he knew would be a popular seller. For the summer months he could travel to all the church garden parties and have a tent set up to develop the photographs on the spot. Many Newfoundlanders had never been to the city of St. John's, and he felt assured that there would be a large market for the pictures. There were already three traditional photography businesses in the city, but no one was as yet providing the kind of services that he envisaged. He felt that he could make enough money in the next few years to buy a house and settle into a permanent photographic studio in one of the larger towns like Cupids or Carbonear. Cheri was really excited about the business, and she would be his assistant as he travelled around the island.

Cheri was still working at Government House, and she kept Ellen informed about the news there. Governor Glover's term of office was finished, and he had been stationed to serve in the Leeward Islands in the Caribbean. Sir Henry Maxse had taken over the post as Governor for Newfoundland, but he was hardly ever in the colony, preferring to spend his time in Germany. It was very dull at The House compared with when Governor and Lady Glover were in residence, and Cheri was looking forward to her new career as photographer's assistant.

LATE IN JANUARY, ALEXANDER HAD TO STOP WORK ON THE SHAKESPEARE murals because he was needed to create a stage set for the performance of Gilbert and Sullivan's *The Sorcerer*, which was scheduled to run until the end of February. At that time of the year, theatre management could be guaranteed a full house because there was little else to do during the winter months. The only reason for a cancelled performance would be if the weather was too inhospitable to allow people to get to the theatre. Alexander arranged for Jeanette and Ellen to attend a few of the rehearsals. They really enjoyed the whole process of staging the play as well as being able to listen to the soprano lead, Clara Fisher. They were so lucky to have a world-class vocalist living in St. John's. Every time she sang, Ellen got goosebumps.

It was the first time that Jeanette had seen any of Alexander's artwork, and she was very impressed. Looking around, Ellen realized that he had completed half of the frescoes: *Julius Caesar*, *Hamlet*, and *Romeo and Juliet*. He had *The Tempest*, *A Winter's Tale*, and *A Midsummer Night's Dream* left to do.

Jeanette noticed that Juliet looked like Ellen and Romeo resembled Alexander. "You're a very lucky lady, you know," she said. Ellen had to agree with her.

thirty-six

On Monday, the eleventh of March, Jeanette called upstairs to Ellen and said she had a visitor. There was no way Ellen would have guessed that Miss Hazel Murphy would be her visitor, but she knew who she was. She owned a ladies' millinery and clothing shop on Duckworth Street.

"Good morning, Miss Murphy," Ellen said. "It's a pleasure to meet you. May I offer you some tea?"

"No, thank you, Mrs. Pindikowsky," she said. "I'm here on a matter of business. I saw your hat in the window, and I'm interested in purchasing a number of them for my store. That is, if you have any in stock."

"I'm very pleased that you like it. I don't have any inventory at the moment since it's a new design and I haven't taken any orders for it as yet."

"So much the better," Miss Murphy said. "I'd prefer to sell the hats exclusively in my shop. I'm sure you want to keep your custom business, but if you would sell this design only through my shop, then I think we could both benefit from the venture. I would pay you the amount that you have designated on your price tag, but I will obviously sell them for at least thirty per cent more in my shop. That is why you'd have to give me exclusivity on that design. I wouldn't want to be undersold, you understand."

"Of course not, but I'll need some time to think about it," Ellen said. "I will give you a firm answer by the end of the week, if that is satisfactory. I would like to discuss it with my husband. In the meantime, I'll remove the hat from the window, and I won't take orders for that particular style."

"Thank you . . . and one more thing. The gold hat stand in the window is very unusual. Do you mind my asking where you bought it?"

"My husband made it for me. He's a very gifted artist, as I'm sure you're aware."

"Yes, he is. Do you think he would make me three of those hat stands for my shop?"

"I don't know. He's very busy, but I will ask him when we discuss the hat proposal."

"Thank you, Mrs. Pindikowsky. I look forward to hearing from you."

Ellen showed her to the door. When it closed behind her, she gave a whoop of victory. She couldn't wait to tell Alexander about her commission that night.

When Ellen told him her news he was very happy for her, but he wanted her to be sure that this was what she wanted. He said she would, in effect, be working for someone else. Ellen assured him that she would still do her custom orders, but she thought that the order for the spring-summer straw hat would be just the thing for when the baby came and she would have less time to see customers. Repeating the design would make the work go faster than custom work, and that would improve her efficiency.

"That would drive me crazy, doing the same thing over and over again," said Alexander, "but if you think it will help you when the baby comes, then it is a good idea. You are such a clever, talented girl. I am very proud of you, Alen." He gave her a lingering kiss and placed his hand on her burgeoning belly. "I can't wait to see our baby."

"I'm excited about that, although I'm not looking forward to the birth. Mother said that even easy births are hard, and I've never looked after a baby before."

"I'm sure you will be a wonderful modder," said Alexander. He led her into the parlour and pulled her down on his lap. She rested her head on his shoulder and cuddled into him, enjoying his warmth. She saw the hat stand on the mantelpiece and remembered Miss Murphy's other request.

"I think it was your hat stand that made Miss Murphy notice my hat," Ellen said.

"I'm sure the stand had nothing to do with it. Your talent shines out."

"No. In fact, she liked the stand so much that she wants to order three of them, if you're willing to make them."

"You are serious?"

"Yes, but I told her you were very busy and you may not want to make them. You don't have to make them if you don't want to."

"I will do anything to help you. You know that. I will be finished work at the Athenaeum at the end of the month, and I will make the stands then. I am hoping that Kielly and I will find more large work to do soon. We have a couple of small jobs to do at the Atlantic Hotel, but that is all." Alexander looked worried, and Ellen tried to reassure him.

"I'm sure there will be lots more work with all the new construction."

"Yes, I'm sure there will be. Anyway, you are not to worry about anything. You must look after yourself and our baby. That is what is most important now."

After supper, Ellen yawned a few times and said she thought she should go to bed early. Alexander said he was tired and needed an early night, too. They said good night to Har and made their way up to their third-floor haven, and Ellen had Alexander all to herself.

thirty-seven

Alexander and Kielly were sitting at a table at the back of the Ship Tavern just west of Telegram Lane. They had finished work at the Athenaeum three weeks before and were meeting to discuss their business strategy for the next year.

"What do you see us doing in the next few years?" asked Alexander.

"More of the same, I guess," said Kielly. "There probably won't be a lot of fresco work to do, but I'm sure we could find stencilling or mural work in some of the grand houses that are being built on Circular Road and Kings Bridge Road."

"And that would satisfy you? You would be happy with that?"

"Why not? It beats being a prison guard, hands down."

Alexander sighed. "I remember you saying when I was in prison that you envied me. But now I am the one envying you. I can't stand doing this painting and stencilling work. Alen even has me making hat stands, for God's sake. I want more. I hated being a prisoner, but I loved doing the work at the Colonial Building. High up on the scaffolding, doing the gilt work, I feel at home. That is what I love to do. I am a fresco painter and I cannot be satisfied with anything else. I want to work on grand buildings like the ones Har talks about in New York. I will never find such work here. Newfoundland is just too small. I want to work in big cities where I will be sure of the kind of work I was born to do."

"Have you talked about this with Ellen?" asked Kielly, his forehead creased with concern.

"No, I haven't. I can't torment her with this now. Our baby is expected in the next few weeks, and I cannot burden her with my troubles."

"Don't underestimate her, Alexander. She's a very strong woman, and I'm sure she would understand your feelings. I'm certain she would move away with you. Not right now, obviously, but maybe in a year from now. I'll continue with the business here. There's enough work to satisfy me. I'll never be the artist that you are, but I'm content with my life here. I was born here and I never want to leave."

"That is another thing. I will never be accepted here. I have tried to make friends, but it is difficult. People like my work and are polite to me, but I am still a criminal in their eyes. I hear the whispers when I walk in the streets. I do not want our child to be whispered about as he grows up. I will not have it. If I go to a place like New York, I can have a fresh start where no one will know of my past."

"I understand how you feel, Alexander. I know you're probably right. This town has a long memory, and your work has made you famous here."

"I am famous and infamous, all at the same time," Alexander said, his tone bitter. "Please don't mention this talk to Alen. I will tell her how I feel, but not until our baby has arrived safely and she has recovered. I am concerned for her. I hope everything will go well. How come you and Martha don't have any children?"

"She is an only child and her mother was an only child. I guess she's just one of those women who have a hard time conceiving. We've certainly tried hard enough," said Kielly, chuckling.

"I'm sure you have," Alexander responded, smiling for the first time since they started talking. "Speaking of all that, I must go home to Alen. She hates being confined to the house, and I'm taking her for a walk as soon as it gets dark. She's so big now that only the dark can disguise her condition."

They parted company at the door, and Alexander decided to put away his worries for now and concentrate on Alen and his baby. He felt his optimism return, and by the time he reached Victoria Street, anyone would think he didn't have a care in the world.

thirty-eight

Ellen was cutting out fabric at the dining room table and her back was aching from all the bending over. A flash of memory showed her Kielly, holding his back at Government House, and she smiled.

"What are you smiling about?" asked Jeanette, who was folding clothes at the other end of the table.

"Oh, just a happy memory. I seem to be daydreaming an awful lot lately, and I'm having a hard time focusing on my work."

"It's probably the baby. Most women get dreamy, especially in the last part of their pregnancy. My sisters were all like that when they were expecting."

"I've never heard you mention them before. How many sisters do you have?"

"I have three, all a good bit older than me. Their children are grown up now, and they all still live in Brigus. I was the only one to move to the city. It's been almost a year since I've seen them," she said, sounding sad.

"Why did you decide to move to St. John's?"

"I was engaged to a man in Brigus, Edward Rice, and he was lost on the ice six years ago. He went sealing, hoping to get a large quota of seals so we would have enough money to get married and buy a house. The truck system never allows for fishermen to get ahead. We'd never have the cash to buy land for a house of our own, only credit or, in a bad year, debt, to the local merchants. Going to the ice was his only way of earning real cash instead of credit to the local merchants. He didn't want to go, and I blame myself for letting him go. Every year, even if the weather is good, men are lost. It's a hard way to make money. People are always saying that swilin' makes men out of boys, but it makes corpses, too. It did with my Edward. He never came back. The ice was raftering and shifting, and then it opened up and he fell through. The ice closed in again before anyone could get to him. They never recovered his body." Jeanette said the words tonelessly, like she was reading from an instruction booklet.

"I'm so sorry, Jeanette. I can't imagine how horrible that was for you. If I lost Alexander, I don't know how I would manage."

"First I cried all the time, and then I went numb. I couldn't bear to live in Brigus anymore. People looked at me with pity and kept asking me how I was. I felt like I was a museum exhibit. I know they meant well, but I couldn't stand it. That's when I decided I'd move to St. John's. I think I've been living in a frozen trance up until now. Seeing you and Alexander together has woken me up. I think I'm ready now to try to find someone again. So, if you know of any likely candidate, feel free to match me up." She smiled.

"I will, for sure," Ellen said. Then she sighed and sat down, feeling weak all of a sudden.

"You should probably take a rest now. You're looking rather tired, if you don't mind me saying so. Carrying around that baby weight all the time is hard work."

"I wish I could take a rest, but I'm hoping to finish these hats for Miss Murphy before the baby comes."

"I could help you with them, if you like. I like sewing, and my mother always said I had a neat stitch."

"That would be a wonderful help, Jeanette. I'll pay you extra for your time when Miss Murphy pays me." Ellen began explaining the design for the hats.

"I'm making bias ribbons from these printed and plain materials, and then I'm going to braid them together to trim the hats. Once they're sewed onto the crown of the hat, I'll wire some of the ribbons to make a stylized bow at the back. The wiring gives the bows an added dimension and the hats a unique flair. If you could sew the ribbon seams, turn them out and press them, it would save me a lot of time and energy."

"I'd love to do it. I'm fascinated with your ideas, and I love the hat."

"Thanks, Jeanette. Designing the hats is the part I like best. Doing all the sewing I find a bit tedious."

"Well, I love sewing, so we should make a good team. I'm so glad I came to work for you."

"I haven't started cracking the whip yet," Ellen said, laughing. They continued talking, and Ellen was glad, at last, to know Jeanette's story. She had always been pleasant and friendly with her, but she felt her reserve, too. Now that reserve seemed to have fallen away, and they relaxed in each other's company.

thirty-nine

The baby came early—not the official early, but two and a half weeks before her real due date. That would make the baby's conception date a little suspect, but Ellen was hoping people had short memories about when she and Alexander were married.

Ellen was sewing at the dining room table, working on the last three hats for Miss Murphy's order. She felt so uncomfortable. She stood up to stretch, and fluid ran down her legs. "Damn," she said, before she could stop herself.

Jeanette came running out of the kitchen and stood in the doorway to the dining room. "What's wrong? I've never heard you swear before."

"I just peed. I couldn't stop myself." Ellen hardly had the words out of her mouth when another gush of water left her body, pooling on the floor.

"Your water's broken. Your baby's coming," said Jeanette, her voice matter-of-fact.

"What, now? But it's not time. I haven't finished the hats."

"Babies come when they want to. Have you had any pains yet?"

"No, but I feel sick."

"I'll help you upstairs and get you into your nightgown. You'll feel more comfortable, and then I'll send word to your mother."

"You don't need to do that. She was coming over this morning, anyway. She should be here within the hour."

"That's good. There's plenty of time. A first baby usually takes a long time."

"I'm so glad you're here, Jeanette. I don't know what to do."

"Nature looks after that. Don't worry, you'll be fine."

Jeanette tucked Ellen into bed, and she slept until a searing pain brought her to full consciousness. She cried out, and within seconds she heard her mother running up the stairs. Her initial feeling of panic abated as soon as her mother came into the room. She told her that she and Jeanette had everything under control. Dr. Smith would be a bit delayed because he was attending another birth out in Topsail, but he would be here by mid-afternoon. There would be plenty of time, she assured Ellen.

Louise insisted on having Dr. Adrian Smith. She said he was an excellent doctor with modern methods, and she especially agreed with him on his doctrine of cleanliness and the use of carbolic acid for sterilizing his instruments. There were other doctors who didn't even wash their hands when going from one patient to another. Louise believed that that was the cause of many infections. Both she and Dr. Smith were proponents of Dr. Joseph Lister's treatise on the matter.

When Dr. Smith arrived, Ellen had been in labour for about five hours. The pain went from bearable to excruciating, and she just wanted the birth to be over. The doctor examined her and said that the baby was in the proper position and that she should deliver within a few hours. Alexander was on his way home, and Ellen longed to see him. She needed his reassuring smile, his love, his presence. When she heard him bounding up the stairs calling out "Alen, Alen," her heart lifted. Her mother, Jeanette, and Dr. Smith left the room and gave them a few minutes of privacy. Alexander sat on the bed and took Ellen in his arms, covering her face with kisses and calling her his *kochanie*. Then a hard contraction shook her body and she cried out, scaring Alexander half to death. He ran out of the room, calling for Dr. Smith. When the doctor realized that she was fine, he tried to reassure Alexander, telling him the birth was going well. But, in the end, they had to ban him from the room. Ellen couldn't help crying out, and

Alexander couldn't help panicking and shouting in angry Polish at the doctor. He paced outside the door for a while, and then Ellen heard his music box playing the Chopin nocturne.

The music box was one of the few possessions that Alexander had brought with him from Poland. Ellen loved it and found it fascinating. The hexagonal-shaped cherry wood base contained the windup musical mechanism. The top part consisted of six hinged doors made from tiles painted with a magnolia blossom motif. The doors formed a gazebo-like structure, and the top of the gazebo had a button that you pushed to activate the music and the doors. Once the music started playing, the doors slowly opened, revealing scenes of the city of Warsaw painted on the back sides of the tiles. As the music slowed, the doors would fold back to their original position. Ellen never tired of playing it, and it never lost its magical appeal. Alexander played it outside their bedroom door, and Chopin's nocturne, Opus nine, Number two, soothed them both with its haunting melody. It was Alexander's way of letting Ellen know he was with her in spirit.

Their baby, a beautiful little girl, was delivered before daylight left the sky. When her baby daughter was placed in her arms, Ellen thought her heart would burst with love. Alexander was dancing around, overwhelmed and delirious with joy. Their daughter had a loud, piercing cry and weighed six pounds, four ounces. Dr. Smith examined her, smiled, and congratulated them on their very healthy baby. He told Ellen she had done wonderfully well and should make a quick recovery.

After the doctor had left, Ellen's mother came into the room to check on the new family. The baby was already suckling at Ellen's breast and Alexander was on the bed with his arm around them both. Ellen's mother gazed lovingly at her, the baby, and then Alexander. The last bit of ice had finally melted. She kissed all three of them and left the room, saying she would be back in a few minutes to settle the baby in her cradle and let them get some rest. After that she would go home to reassure Kenneth, who was beside himself with worry. She would return in the early morning.

Alexander took the next couple of days off from work. Kielly could handle the simple stencilling job that they were doing at the Atlantic Hotel. Alexander used the time to finish the baby's room. He had painted a beautiful mural of a starry sky on the ceiling and a nature montage of animals, birds, trees, and flowers on the walls. In one corner he had painted a waterfall and river. Love was painted into every brush stroke.

Alexander and Ellen had talked about names for their child before her arrival, but now that she was here, only one name seemed right—Johanna. It was the female form of Johann, the name of Alexander's teacher and mentor. Her full name was to be Johanna Mary Ellen Pindikowsky. Ellen's mother approved, and Har was delighted with the name since, strangely enough, Johanna had been her mother's name.

Alexander wanted Johanna baptized as soon as possible, and Sister Mary Angela arranged for the baptism to take place on May the first. It was a private affair with Father Brennan officiating.

Kenneth and Robert fought over who would take Johanna's first photograph, with Kenneth winning out. Jeanette had surprised them all by making a Queen of the May wreath for Johanna in honour of her May Day baptism. She had sewn together white silk flowers in a tiny circlet that they placed on Johanna's head before her picture was taken. She looked like an angel. More pictures were taken, and Ellen's mother had one put in a locket. She said she was saving the second side of her locket for her second grandchild. Ellen told her she needed a breather first, and she laughed. "I'm so happy," her mother said as she put her arm around Ellen and Alexander. Kenneth caught Ellen's eye and winked at her.

MAY PASSED BY IN A BLUR OF CARING FOR THE BABY. BEING A MOTHER was all-consuming. Ellen accomplished very little, and still her days and nights were filled to the brim. Johanna was a good baby, but she still needed to nurse every two to three hours. She would cry and Alexander would pick her up and bring her to Ellen. When it was time for her to be burped, Alexander would put her on his shoulder, rubbing her tiny back, and she would obligingly belch. Once, Ellen drifted off to sleep, and when she awoke Alexander was singing to Johanna a lovely lullaby in Polish. She asked him what the words meant, and he translated them for her. She tried to sing the song in Polish, but her tongue just couldn't master the words. She wrote down the translation, and they would both sing the lullaby to Johanna in Polish and in English. The song never failed to soothe her and send her to sleep.

Alexander was such a relaxed father, and Ellen was amazed that he helped so much with her. From what she understood, his behaviour was quite unusual. Most fathers left childcare completely to their wives. When she mentioned this to Alexander, he said that he was so grateful to have Johanna and Ellen that he could never do enough for them. He reminded her that he had no other family. She and Johanna had fulfilled a dream for him and made him feel connected to life in a way he hadn't experienced since he was a boy. He looked so vulnerable saying this that Ellen leaned over and kissed his lips. The heat that sparked between them made Ellen forget motherhood in favour of womanhood. Alexander placed their daughter in her cradle and, as she slept, they explored each other's bodies as if for the first time.

forty

A week after Johanna was born, Alexander and Kielly received a new commission that challenged Alexander and made him feel more optimistic about working in Newfoundland. Sir John Williams had built an imposing family house on Circular Road, and he wanted a large fresco in his dining room. Kenneth was an acquaintance of Sir John, and he had recommended Alexander and Kielly for the job. Alexander was again in his debt.

Sir John had travelled to Paris and had fallen in love with the city. He wanted the fresco to depict a composite of the places he had seen, and he showed Alexander a number of photographs and etchings that he had collected. Alexander worked hard to get the right balance of buildings and green areas, using the River Seine as the unifying element. Sir John was very impressed with Alexander's drawings and offered him a generous payment for the finished work. Alexander was happy with the commission, and he felt good once again about working in Newfoundland. He thought that maybe everything would work out and that he and his family could have a fulfilling life in the colony.

He and Kielly had done all the preliminary work, and Alexander was about to start on the painting, when Kielly was called away to a family funeral in English Harbour. He would be gone for about five days, so Alexander would have to work on his own. Alexander didn't mind, since the work was at a stage where he could easily work alone. He would just have to prepare all his pigments before he started and do a little more climbing up and down the ladders, but it was nothing he couldn't manage. In fact, he was looking forward to the quiet of working alone. Alexander loved Kielly, but he was a gregarious man and kept up a constant chatter most of the day. Alexander preferred to work in quiet, especially when he was doing intricate work. He wanted this fresco to be perfect, hoping that Sir Williams's friends would see it and want his work in their homes.

Wednesday morning, the day after Kielly left, Alexander heard what sounded like arguing coming from the upstairs bedroom. He couldn't make out what was being said, but from the tone he knew something was wrong. He heard Sir Williams's footsteps on the stairs, and then he was striding purposefully into the dining room. Alexander was completely unprepared for what he said.

"Mr. Pindikowsky, please come down from the ladder. I need to speak with you."

Alexander climbed down and stood waiting expectantly in front of Sir John. He came straight to the point.

"My wife's diamond earrings are missing. She said she left them on the mantelpiece after we came home from the concert Monday night. She went to get them last night and they were not there. Do you know anything about them?" His tone was not exactly accusatory, but it wasn't friendly, either.

The room started to spin, and Alexander had to take a few deep breaths to calm his heart rate. He felt like he had when he was arrested at the Temperance Coffee House in 1880. The same cold knot formed in his stomach, his English words left him, and for a full, long minute he couldn't say anything. Finally, he spoke. "I don't know anything about the earrings, Sir Williams. I didn't see them."

His hesitation in answering had cost him, and now Sir John was looking at him with distrust. "You are absolutely sure you know nothing about the earrings? At this time I am still willing to accept that you may have misplaced them."

"I am sorry, Sir Williams. I truly know nothing about them. Maybe Kielly knows something. He will be back on Monday."

"You leave me with no choice but to terminate your employment, Mr. Pindikowsky, and you must leave immediately. I'll be calling the police to investigate the theft, and they will contact you for questioning. I'll be talking with Kenneth later today about the situation. He vouched for you, you know."

"I know he did. And I didn't do anything wrong. I am sorry that you do not believe me. I will leave right away." Alexander picked up his jacket and left the house. As he walked away, he felt all the eyes of the household on him. He was devastated. The work had been going so well, and now everything had collapsed around him. His reputation was lost once more, and the thought of spending time in jail again was unbearable. At least the last time he had been guilty of the crime of forgery. This time he was innocent, but who would believe him?

Alexander wasn't ready to face Ellen and her family yet. He walked to the Fort Amherst lighthouse and sat on the rocks, hoping the sound of the sea hitting the shore would soothe his nerves.

ELLEN HAD JUST PUT JOHANNA DOWN FOR HER NAP WHEN KENNETH and her mother surprised her with a visit. Her welcoming smile froze on her face when she saw their expressions.

"What's wrong? You both look pale as ghosts," she said.

"Where is Alexander?" asked Kenneth.

"He's at work, of course, over at Sir John Williams's house. You know he's doing that fresco work for him."

"Well, not anymore," her mother said in a tightly controlled voice.

"What do you mean? You're scaring me. What's wrong?"

"Come into the parlour and sit down," said Kenneth. "I'll ask Jeanette to get us some tea." He went out into the kitchen, and Ellen sat with her mother on the settee.

"Alexander was let go from his job," she said. "Apparently, Lady Williams's diamond earrings are missing and Alexander is suspected of taking them."

"That's ridiculous," Ellen said. "Why would he do that? He would never do such a thing."

Her mother looked at her pointedly, and Ellen knew what she was thinking. "Whether he did or he didn't, he's under suspicion because of his criminal record. I was so afraid of this when you married him, and now, here we are. I don't know what's going to happen. Sir John came over to the house to speak with Kenneth as soon as he let Alexander go. Kenneth tried to get Sir John to wait until Kielly came back before he started a police investigation, but he wouldn't be persuaded. He said the earrings were quite valuable and he needed to get them back."

Kenneth walked into the room and cleared his voice. "I see your mother has filled you in on what has happened. I wish Alexander were here. I'm afraid that he may have run off. That will certainly make him look guilty. I have guaranteed Sir John that I would make sure that he stayed in town. Now, I don't know what will happen." He started pacing the floor.

"I can't believe you're acting like this," Ellen said, rising to her feet. "Where is all the family goodwill that has been present since Johanna's birth? It seems as if you both believe that Alexander might have stolen the earrings. I thought that you trusted him. He does not deserve your doubt. We are a family and we must stick together. Remember, Alexander has no other family. We are all he has. I know Alexander. He would never do this. He never told you, but the reason he forged those cheques was because his aunt Paulina, in Poland, his only living relative, was desperate for money. Her husband was part of the underground Polish National Movement and he was arrested. She needed the money to try to get him released. Needless to say, she didn't receive the money, and Alexander found out that his uncle was executed. He told me not to tell you. He didn't want to sound like he was making excuses for breaking the law. But I'm telling you this because you need to know that he is innocent. He would not steal for himself. He works hard and he wants to earn his way in this world. He deserves your full support."

Kenneth and Louise looked at each other and then at her. Her mother was the first to speak. "You're right. We panicked, and we have been as quick to doubt Alexander as everyone else. I wish he had told us about the reason he forged those cheques. Kenneth and I have always wondered about it. But we will stand behind him now."

"Yes, we will. Do you have any idea where he might have gone, Ellen?"

"He usually goes down by the sea when he's worried. I'm sure he'll be home soon. He would never desert me or Johanna."

On cue, the front door opened and Alexander walked in, his face looking haggard. Ellen rushed into his arms and told him that everything would be all right and he had the family's full support. When Kenneth and Louise both echoed her words, his face relaxed and he smiled. "Thank you, thank you. I am lucky to have such a family."

forty-one

The next morning, Alexander stayed home and tried not to think about what would happen if Sir John Williams pressed charges. He wondered if one of Sir John's household staff members had decided to take advantage of the fact that he had a criminal record and would be the prime suspect in a theft. Kenneth had suggested this to Sir John, but he dismissed the possibility, saying that his staff had all been with him for many years and were, therefore, completely trustworthy. Alexander's greatest hope was that Lady Williams would find her earrings and realize that she hadn't left them in the dining room. His next hope was that Kielly had seen them and put them somewhere for safekeeping. This was a slim hope, since Sir John claimed that the place was searched thoroughly.

That afternoon, the police came to the door for Alexander. They took him to the penitentiary for questioning. The look he gave Ellen as he left the house broke her heart. She knew how much it would cost him to have to go back to that place. She even heard the police guard laughingly make a joke about Alexander being "no stranger to the prison." She could have willingly strangled him.

Alexander did not come home that night. He had been charged with the theft of the earrings, and because he had already served time for a felony conviction, bail was denied him.

The next morning, Ellen was waiting at the penitentiary doors when Superintendent Quinton arrived. At first he was not inclined to allow her to see Alexander, but Ellen wasn't going to be dissuaded. When she saw Alexander in his cell, hunched over with his head in his hands, it was all she could do to keep her tears at bay. For his sake she had to put on a brave face, and she was a good actress after all her dissembling in the past year. She held Alexander in her arms while he protested her being there.

"Alen, my *kochanie*, you shouldn't be here. I never wanted you to see me in a jail cell, and now you are here. It is more than I can bear. You must forget about me. Maybe you can get an annulment. Everyone would understand. I have brought nothing but shame to you and your family and our family, our baby."

Ellen knew she had to be courageous now, and she summoned all her will to make her voice strong. "Alexander, I have never heard you talk such rubbish before! I am your wife, and I meant my marriage vow, for better or worse. We're just going through a worse patch now. But that's all it is. You are innocent and you will be proven innocent. That's all there is to it."

"I wish I had your confidence. Many people will think, once a thief always a thief."

"The ones who count won't think that way. You do have friends. Kielly will vouch for you, and Kenneth and Sister Mary Angela, just to name a few. Kenneth is going to get you a good lawyer today. Everything will work out, you'll see."

"I hope so, Alen," replied Alexander, without much conviction. "In the meantime, please don't visit. It upsets me to see you here."

"Don't talk nonsense, Alexander. I'm not a child. We're in this together, and it won't be for long. Kielly is due back tomorrow, and he may know about the earrings, and all this will be over."

"Oh, Alen, what would I do without you? I am so lucky to have you. I love you."

Alexander kissed her and held her close. She was even able to smile at Alexander as she left his cell. It seemed she would never be free of the prison. It had taken all her strength to stay positive while she was with Alexander. Now, walking home, her spirits plummeted and she allowed herself to fear the future.

forty-two

The next day, Kielly was called in for questioning by the police. He went over everything he could remember from the time he and Alexander had started the work at Sir John Williams's house until he left to attend the funeral in English Harbour, but he couldn't shed any light on the theft. As a former police officer he was accorded respect by Officer Bradbury, but there was a thinly veiled undercurrent of something he couldn't quite place. Was it pleasure at his situation? Did his former colleague take pleasure in the failure of his new enterprise? This feeling made him all the more determined to figure out a way to make this right, for his sake as well as Alexander's.

Martha hadn't said very much, but there was censure in her silence. He knew she was thinking that he should have kept his safe job at the penitentiary. Her face set in a hard line reminded him of something that was hanging on the very edges of his consciousness, teasing him. He decided to take a long walk around Quidi Vidi Lake. If he kept his feet busy, he might free his mind to focus on what was niggling at him.

ELLEN WAS JUST ABOUT PARALYZED WITH NERVOUS TENSION. ONLY holding Johanna in her arms seemed to relax her body from the tight strings that compressed her every breath. She missed Alexander and worried about him constantly. She visited him at the penitentiary and gave him new pictures of Johanna that Kenneth had taken. She wanted Alexander to remember always that they were a family. The fact that he had mentioned an annulment, if only in his despair, had frightened her to her core.

Her mother had been coming to the house every day to see Johanna, but she avoided talking to Ellen about Alexander or his situation.

Jeanette walked around the house like she was walking on eggshells. Since Ellen wanted Johanna in her arms for comfort, Jeanette used her time to cook fancy meals no one had an appetite to consume.

Cheri came over and tried to distract Ellen with gossip from The House and Har bought new books for her to read, but she was beyond all that. She was exhausted trying to hold everything together and keep optimistic. Johanna wasn't sleeping well, either. She was reacting to the tense atmosphere.

IT WAS LATE MONDAY AFTERNOON AND ELLEN WAS SITTING IN THE parlour pretending to read the paper. Really, she was scanning it hoping not to see anything about Alexander. His arrest had ended up on the front page, but since then Kenneth had been able to use his influence to keep his name out of the papers. The court date had not been set yet, but as soon as it was, Kenneth's influence would run out. It would be just too juicy a scandal to let go. Ellen couldn't let her mind leap to the trial. It was simply too painful to contemplate. Just a short week ago, she had thought her life perfect.

There was a knock on the door and Ellen literally jumped out of her chair, her nerves were so on edge. It was Kielly.

"I'm glad you're home, Ellen," he said. "I've got something on the edge of my mind that I need to tease out. I've been out walking, and that hasn't helped. There's information about the earrings that I think I know, but my mind won't grab it. I thought if I set up your dining room and parlour to resemble Sir John Williams's place and I walked through everything Alexander and I did last Tuesday, before I went away, I might be able to remember."

"It's worth a try, Kielly," Ellen said. "It's certainly better than sitting around waiting and worrying."

Kielly started moving furniture against the walls, and within fifteen minutes he had a reasonable facsimile of the layout of Sir Williams's dining room, even though it lacked the grand scale of the mansion. Ellen provided some sheets to use as drop cloths to further enhance the authenticity.

Kielly mimed through the preparations for the plaster and the pigments that he and Alexander had done, trying to remember every detail of that day, including their conversations. Ellen could see that Kielly was becoming frustrated and that the effort had not stimulated his memory.

Jeanette came into the room with a tea tray. She laid it down on the table that had been pushed over next to the mantelpiece. "You're tired and overwrought, the both of you. You need a good cup of tea before you collapse." She started to leave the room, and Kielly shouted, "That's it, that's it! I knew there was something."

Jeanette and Ellen stared at him. "Miss Hawkins, Lady Williams's maid. She came into the room and went over to the mantelpiece, and then she left again, muttering under her breath. I didn't hear what she said, but she gave me a stern look just like the one Martha gave me yesterday that triggered all this. She must have taken the earrings off the mantelpiece."

"But why didn't she say anything?" Ellen wanted to believe Kielly's theory, but it didn't explain why Miss Hawkins hadn't come forward.

"She's been with the family for years and she's as old as Methusaleh. Her memory is probably going and she forgot. The family trusts her completely, so maybe they didn't question her."

"Kielly, I hope you are right," Ellen said. "What should we do?"

"Leave it to me. I'm still on good terms with the police, and I'm sure I can get someone to go over and question Miss Hawkins and try to tweak her memory."

"Thank you, Kielly. I feel the first bit of hope since all this started."

"It's my neck, too, so I want this settled once and for all. Our future business depends on clearing both our names." Kielly left, saying he would sort everything out with the police.

AS IS OFTEN THE CASE, THINGS DIDN'T WORK OUT AS THEY HAD HOPED. Kielly had gone to the police with his theories, but there was no immediate follow-through. Miss Hawkins was very sick with a high fever and could not be questioned. At her age, it was thought she might not recover, and Ellen prayed harder than she ever had for a stranger's return to health.

Alexander was becoming more morose every day. The trial date had been set for the following Tuesday and no new evidence had come to light. Mr. Saunders, Alexander's lawyer, was going to go with the defence that Alexander had been set up. He would argue that one of Sir John Williams's servants had taken advantage of the fact that Alexander was a convicted felon and had stolen the earrings, knowing that Alexander would be the most likely suspect. He would state that the thief had used the opportunity of Kielly's absence, when Alexander was working alone, to steal the earrings. It was not a strong defence, and it was unlikely to sway a jury who didn't know Alexander, but it was the best he could do. Mr. Saunders was hoping to convince the jury of Alexander's innocence by emphasizing the fact that Alexander could be trusted. He would remind the jury that he had worked on the ceilings at Government House and the Colonial Building while he was serving his sentence for forgery and that his behaviour was exemplary. He would let the jury know about the fact that Alexander had been hired to work on the Presentation Convent ceilings shortly after his release from jail, and Sister Mary Angela was going to testify on his behalf.

Mr. Saunders debated with himself over whether or not to bring in the fact of Alexander marrying a local girl, and having a baby to support. This information could backfire, since Ellen was so much younger than Alexander and she had married him so soon after his release from prison. Sir Kenneth was going to act as a character witness, but because he was Alexander's father-in-law, his testimony would be seen as biased. It was going to be a tough defence, and Alexander's freedom would depend on winning the jury over to his side. Everything would hang on the jury and whether they would have sympathy for Alexander.

Saunders, who had a great reputation for winning his cases, admitted that he did not like the odds. He would do his best, but without empirical evidence, he was not optimistic about the result. All the workers on Sir John Williams's estate had been questioned and their stories had not revealed anything that could be used to make them suspects. It was very unlikely that the theft had been the result of an outside job, as there was no evidence of a break-in and no one was woken during the night. Also, Sir John had a faithful Labrador dog, and he had assured the authorities that Grog would have barked loudly if any stranger had come into the house. The cards were very neatly stacked against Alexander. They all hoped that Miss Hawkins would recover and solve the mystery of the earrings before the trial.

Nothing was right in the Pindikowsky household. No one had been sleeping, not even little Johanna. Alexander was in despair, and Ellen was unable to stir him from his depression. Each day when she visited him at the penitentiary, he slipped further from her grasp and she could no longer cheer him. She contented herself by holding him in her arms, but his passion was lost to her.

forty-three

It was the day before the trial. Two officers arrived at Ellen's door, and her mind leapt to every dire thought that had visited her in the last two weeks. She feared that Alexander had taken his life, and she feared-hoped that he had escaped. When she opened the door, her legs were barely supporting her and she didn't—she couldn't—say anything. All her physical strength was needed to breathe.

"I'm Officer Tobin and this is Officer O'Brien. We have come to inform you that the earrings have been found and your husband is cleared of all suspicion," said Tobin. "He will be released as soon as the paperwork is done. Miss Hawkins has recovered, and when we questioned her this morning, she right away knew about the earrings. She said she had seen them on the mantel and didn't want them left in the room where, in her words, a convict was working. She had put them in a brass jug on the top shelf of the kitchen cupboard. She meant to take them to Lady Williams when she was going upstairs after breakfast, and then she had suddenly become ill. Sir John has dropped all charges and asked us to come straight down here to tell you. He said to give you this note." Officer Tobin fished in his pocket and handed Ellen an envelope. "We'll be going now. Sorry for your troubles."

They left quickly, and as soon as the door closed, Ellen slumped onto the floor and Jeanette came running. She still couldn't speak, but joy was starting to bubble up inside her. Jeanette had heard the police officers' news and she pulled Ellen up and spun her around, laughing. Ellen decided not to wait another minute. She was going to run to Her Majesty's and Alexander.

When she opened the door, Alexander was there grinning at her. He swept her into his arms and her world tilted back on its proper axis. When they caught their breath, Ellen handed Alexander the letter from Sir John Williams. It contained a full apology and a request to have a meeting with Kielly and Alexander the next morning at nine o'clock.

"Come on, Alen, put on your coat. We're hiring a carriage and going on a ride to celebrate. First we're going over to Kielly's house to tell him our news and thank him for remembering Miss Hawkins. Then we're going over to Riverside to tell your modder and Kenneth. Jeanette, could you get Johanna ready, please? She's coming with us. This is a family celebration."

Ellen's Alexander was back and she was more relieved than she was willing to admit. It was a very happy end to a black time, and when they told her mother and Kenneth their wonderful news, the lines in their faces dissolved, making them appear young again.

The meeting the next day with Sir John went well. Alexander and Kielly agreed to finish the work they had begun. Sir John loosened his purse strings and paid them handsomely for the work time that they had lost on his account and paid them a significant bonus. It would have been satisfying to refuse to finish the job, but they needed the money, and the fact that they had a written apology from Sir John would go a long way to smoothing the way for future business opportunities. Their lives returned to normal, and Ellen was very grateful for days filled with reassuring domestic tedium.

forty-four

Cheri's marriage to Robert was taking place on June the eighth and Ellen felt really disappointed that she wouldn't be able to attend their wedding. They were to be married at Cheri's home in Cape Freels, and it was too soon to be travelling with Johanna. Louise's decision, to have a party at Riverside for them before they left, made Ellen feel marginally better about the situation.

It was a lively party with lots of laughter and music. Kenneth had bought a piano for Louise on her last birthday. She had made an off-hand comment that she wished she had learned to play the piano, and he had surprised her with the piano and lessons from Miss Iris Whiteley to go with it. Louise, so far, had learned to play only two pieces: the Strauss waltz *Tales from the Vienna Woods*, and the popular ballad "I'll Take You Home Again, Kathleen." She knew them by heart, but if she stopped playing in the middle of the piece, she couldn't continue and would have to start at the beginning again. They all liked tormenting her about it, saying she was like a train with a full head of steam—completely unstoppable. When she played the waltz, Alexander took Ellen in his arms, twirling her around the room until she was dizzy. She remembered the Christmas Ball at Government House when she dreamed of dancing with him, and she smiled at the memory.

Cheri and Robert left late in the afternoon, and already Ellen missed Cheri. They wouldn't be home again until November, since they were starting their travelling photography business right after their wedding. Robert had a horse-drawn wagon rigged up with all his equipment. Cheri said they would even sleep in it when they weren't close to a town. She was excited about it, and everyone jokingly called them the Gypsies.

Alexander and Ellen went for a walk to their favourite spot by the falls after she had nursed Johanna. Her mother said she would settle her to sleep. As they walked out the door, Ellen's mother and Kenneth were both cooing over Johanna like she was the only baby in the world. Kenneth had taken so many tintype photographs of her that Har said, "She'll have her face on jam crocks yet." Everyone doted on Johanna so much that Ellen feared she would become very spoiled. When she said as much to her mother, Louise replied, "You can't spoil a baby," and covered Johanna's little face with kisses. She was so happy that she and Alexander were finally friends.

It had been a rare warm, sunny June day, and they delighted in it, knowing that they could still have frost before summer officially began. Only newcomers to the island and the foolishly optimistic planted annual flowers before the middle of the month because of this fact of life in St. John's.

Alexander and Ellen sat by the falls in their little hollow and Alexander took her hand, bringing it to his lips. "Alen . . . how would you feel about living in New York?"

His words startled her. She wasn't prepared for the brief panic that she felt. "What do you mean, Alexander? What's wrong with here? Why do you want to live in New York?" Ellen's voice was high-pitched, betraying her alarm. She knew she had been too happy.

"I need to go there to work. I didn't want to trouble you before the baby came, but Kielly and I are barely making enough money for the two of us. The fresco for Sir John Williams brought in good money, but I don't know how many other jobs like that we will receive. Your order of hats for Miss Murphy brought in more money then I made in the month before Sir John's commission. I know your modder will continue to let us live rent free, but I don't want that. I want to support us properly, as a man should." His voice was pleading.

"I'm sure there'll be more jobs soon. I can ask Kenneth. With all his connections, he'll know of someone who needs mural work done."

"No, Alen. Kenneth has already given me so much help. I do not want to ask him for more. And that's not the only reason I need to go to New York. I need to do important work. I want to work on grand buildings. I want to be known for my work as an artist, not just a wall painter."

"What about Kielly? Have you talked to him about this?"

"Yes, I have. He will continue to work here. He is happy enough with small jobs, and there would be enough work for him by himself."

"What about Johanna? Here, she has family. We would know no one in New York, and Mother will be devastated."

"It is you and Johanna that I am thinking about. I see how people look at me and whisper about me. I thought it would get better and people would forget about my prison term. But now I see that they won't. I don't want you or Johanna to be tarnished by me. You know what happened with Lady Williams's earrings. Right away I was blamed. If I go to New York, I can have a fresh start. No one will know of my past, and we can live happy and free."

Ellen didn't say anything for a while. In her heart she knew that Alexander was right. People would never accept them; they would always be whispered about. Ellen could cope with that, but she would never want their daughter to be exposed to it. "When will we leave?" she asked.

Alexander's face, which had been scrunched up into lines of tension, relaxed. He smiled and kissed her. "You mean I can go? We can live in New York?"

"Yes, but I don't like this talk of *I*'s mixed in with *we*'s. What's that about?"

"We will all be together, of course, but I need to go first and get work and a place for us to live. Then I will send for you and Johanna. She is too young to travel yet. We cannot risk it."

"Then wait until she is old enough. In three or four months it will be fine to travel with her."

"It's not just about Johanna. I can't be worried about you when I am looking for work. You will be safe here with your family and I will be free to find work and get established. I need to go soon and get work before the winter comes. I will send you letters . . . well, short notes and drawings every day. And you can write me long letters. We won't be separated for long."

The thought of being separated from Alexander for a day, let alone months, caused Ellen's heart to ache, and tears spilled, unbidden, onto her face. She was powerless to stop them. Alexander started kissing them away.

"*Kochanie*, don't cry. I can't bear to see you cry. I won't go. It is selfish of me. I will stay and work here, just don't cry. Please don't cry. I never want to make you sad."

Ellen took a deep breath, and while her tears fell she told him that she understood, that she didn't want to stand in his way, that she wanted him to do the work he loved and be the artist he was meant to be. Her heart was breaking, but she would never forgive herself if he stayed and lived to resent her. She wanted his love and she would do anything to keep it, even letting him go.

"Alen, you are so wonderful. I love you. I promise, I will make a life for us that is worthy of your trust. I will find work quickly because I will want you and Johanna with me as soon as possible. It will be very hard to leave you, but our future will be assured. There will be lots of work in the big cities in the United States. We don't have to settle in New York. That can be our starting place."

"When do you think you will leave?" Ellen asked, holding her breath.

"There is a ship leaving on July the third—the SS *Portia*. I will try to be on that one."

"I am missing you already," she said.

"I can see I need to prove to you that I am still here." Alexander gave her the look that liquefied her, and they made love as the music of the falls echoed in their ears.

forty-five

St. John's, July–October 1882

When Ellen and Alexander told Louise about their plan to move to the United States, she was so angry and distraught that she wouldn't even look at or talk to Alexander, and she started referring to him as "he" and "him." Finally, Har intervened, pointing out a few well-thought-out truths.

"Louise," Har said, "you should be proud of Alexander, instead of berating him. He wants to be independent and provide a good living for Ellen and Johanna. He knows you would help support them, but he wants to be independent. You usually admire initiative. I know that you will miss having Ellen and the baby close by, but New York isn't so far away anymore. Ships leave every other week from here, and it only takes five days to get there. If I can go there, you can, too. When the House of Assembly isn't in session, Kenneth and you can go for an extended visit, and Ellen will come home to visit, too."

"I know you're right, Har. But I can't imagine Ellen and darling little Johanna not being near me."

"She's not gone yet, you know, and besides, while Alexander is establishing his business, you'll have Johanna and Ellen all to yourself."

It was this last argument that won Ellen's mother over. She still wasn't happy about the move, but she was at least talking to Alexander again. She even proposed that Ellen move in with her again once Alexander left. Ellen refused that right away. She would be lonely without Alexander, but she wouldn't be treated like a child again. She was a married woman and a mother and she wanted to establish that her life was with Alexander now, and she would follow him wherever he decided to live.

TIME DISINTEGRATED DURING THE NEXT FEW WEEKS UNTIL IT WAS only two days before Alexander's departure. For once Ellen was hoping for bad weather, but the next week was looking clear of fog and storms.

Kielly and Martha had been over to Victoria Street for a farewell dinner, and it was an evening of reminiscing. Ellen didn't know if she'd be seeing much of Kielly and Martha once Alexander left. If Martha and she had become close, it would have been different. Ellen liked Martha, but she and Ellen didn't really have much in common. Martha was about fifteen years older than Ellen, but if they had enjoyed the same things, that wouldn't have mattered. Martha wasn't interested in the arts at all, and when Alexander, Kielly, and Ellen started discussing plays, or music, or design ideas, Ellen could feel Martha becoming restless and bored. The fact that Ellen had a child now also made their relationship difficult. She knew that Martha and Kielly desperately wanted children, and seeing her with Johanna must have been difficult. Alexander was the mortar that held them all together, and Ellen knew that Kielly would miss Alexander terribly. Also, he relied heavily on Alexander's artistic expertise. Before Kielly left that evening, he even asked Ellen if he could come to her for design advice once Alexander left. She assured him that she would be more than willing to help if she could.

During the next two days, Alexander and Ellen spent as much time together as they could, savouring every moment and making passionate love every night. Ellen was like a camel drinking water, trying to store up Alexander's love for the time when she would be alone.

They took Johanna with them in her pram and walked to Bannerman's Park. They visited their tree to check on their initials and noticed that other lovers had placed their initials there, too. They vowed that they would bring Johanna back to visit their tree when she was older. They weren't sure if they would ever tell her their whole story, but they could decide that later.

Alexander reached into his pocket and brought out a small velvet jewellery box. He opened it, revealing a beautiful gold locket. It was engraved with the letter *P* monogram on the front and their special *A* monogram on the back.

"I want you to wear this so that we will always be together," he said.

Ellen opened the locket, and inside was a tiny painting of her and Johanna on one side and Alexander on the other. The paintings were exquisitely rendered—his best work.

"When you close the locket, we are united as a family. When you wear it, it will remind you that we will all be together very soon. Never doubt that, my *kochanie*." Alexander clasped the locket around her neck.

"I will wear it always until we are truly together again. I love you so much. I don't know if I can stand us being apart." Ellen had to blink hard to keep her tears away.

"It will be very hard, but soon we will be together again and we will have a long and happy life. I know this, Alen. I want you and Johanna to have a good life, and I want you both to be proud of me. I promise I will do this. I know I can. I just need this chance in New York."

"I have something for you, too, Alexander." She passed him a braid of hair that she had made from her hair and Johanna's. Her dark, baby-fine hair stood out against Ellen's copper strand. She placed it in the silk pouch that had once held her plaster ring.

"I will keep it with me always," said Alexander. "It will bring me luck."

THE MORNING OF ALEXANDER'S DEPARTURE CAME TOO QUICKLY. Ellen said her goodbyes at the house since she knew she wouldn't be able to witness him stepping onto the ship.

Kenneth arrived with his carriage to take Alexander to Bowring's dock. He gave Alexander a letter of reference that included a note from Prime Minister Whiteway. This would be a wonderful help to him in getting work. Sister Mary Angela had written a letter of introduction as well, which would help him in finding possible work in the Catholic churches in New York. Alexander was extremely grateful and touched by their confidence in him.

When he kissed Ellen and Johanna for the last time, he couldn't keep the tears from his eyes. They were united in their misery. Ellen drank him in with her eyes, and as he waved from the carriage, she held her locket to her lips. He was gone and she was devastated. If she hadn't had to look after little Johanna and have her warm softness to hold, she would have gone mad.

forty-six

The days were bearable because looking after Johanna kept Ellen occupied, but her nights were excruciating. She missed Alexander in countless ways: his touch, his laugh, his smile, his voice, his hair, his eyes, his body folded around hers. She tried to remember how she lived before he was in her life, but her brain refused to draw a picture. She was part of Alexander now, and she was a different being from the girl she used to be.

Johanna missed her father, too, and when she was fretful, Ellen played the music box for her and sang Alexander's lullaby to her in English. She would mix in the few Polish words that she could pronounce, and Johanna seemed to respond to them. The words, in both languages, told her she was loved.

Little One

I love you little precious one, sleeping in your bed,
my darling little baby nodding your downy head,
dreaming dreams of angels sent from heaven above,
watching over baby, spreading wings of love.

I love your tiny fingers curling around my hair,
darling little fingers, never knowing care,

*dreaming dreams of angels sent from heaven above,
watching over baby, spreading wings of love.*

*I love you little precious one, with your funny smile,
treasured little baby, ours for just a while,
dreaming dreams of angels sent from heaven above,
watching over baby, spreading wings of love.*

    Ellen's mother knew how lonely she was and came over every day to see her and play with Johanna. She took her to shows at the Athenaeum, but that only made her long for Alexander even more. His murals contained his very essence, and Ellen kept looking at them instead of the stage and remembering their carefree picnic lunches. She wore her locket every day and opened it so often she feared that she would wear out the clasp. She wrote Alexander a letter before she went to bed each night, telling him about Johanna and the details of their days. Ellen kept them in her shell box, waiting for Alexander's letter and a forwarding address. She knew it wouldn't be possible for her to receive a letter for at least two weeks, but she checked the mail anyway.

    Ellen did receive letters from Cheri, and she was grateful for them. Cheri sent her a photograph of her wedding, and she looked so happy with all of her large family circled around her. She also sent a picture of herself on the white sandy beach in Cape Freels. She was holding up her skirt, revealing her bare legs. The waves were lapping over her feet and her toes were buried in the wet sand. She had attached a note to the picture: "More guts than a one-cent fish—the water is freezing." Ellen remembered talking with her about Cape Freels and the sandy beaches the previous year when they were working at Government House, and she felt sorry that she hadn't made the trip out to the cape that they had planned. Life had definitely taken a turn that neither one of them could have imagined. Maybe Alexander, Johanna, and Ellen could go there someday. After the events of the last year, she believed that anything was possible.

A MONTH HAD PASSED AND ELLEN STILL HAD NOT HAD A LETTER from Alexander. She blamed the fact on the weather, the mail, and the ships' schedules. When Har received a letter from New York, she looked at the postmark and was devastated to find out that it had been mailed only two weeks before. She told herself that Alexander was busy working and finding his way around the city and that she'd get his letter the next day, or the next day, or the next day.

Shortly after Har had received her letter, Ellen started lying about her mail. Even when the weather was bad, she went to the Market House post office to collect her letters. When Har said there was no need, as she had to pass by there on her way to work, Ellen said she wanted the fresh air and it wasn't very far, just a five-minute walk from Victoria Street. She didn't want Jeanette or Har to know that Alexander's letters hadn't arrived.

Ellen went to the Reading Room Library at the Athenaeum and devoured all the news about what was happening in New York City. She would enhance Alexander's imaginary letters to her with references to buildings going up in the city or funny advertisements or transportation problems on the Elevated Railway. She said that he was waiting on a special contract for a church just outside the city and, if he was able to get that work, they would be able to move there and be with him. She was afraid to give the name of a church in case one of Kenneth's or Har's friends knew about it. If they questioned her, Ellen quickly changed the topic. Also, they all knew Alexander's written English was not good, so she used that as an excuse for the lack of details in his letters.

Ellen couldn't admit to them how fearful she was becoming. What if he was sick or injured? What if he couldn't find work and was too ashamed to tell her? She refused to let her mind rest for even a second on the other unthinkable—what if he no longer loved her? It was impossible for her to stop loving him, and she had to believe that his feelings for her were the same. Every time a doubt entered her mind, she thought back to all the days they had spent together, and she knew in her heart that he loved her, and that was what sustained her. The reason she wouldn't tell anyone that she hadn't received a letter from Alexander was that she couldn't bear their pitying looks or the unspoken question of his loyalty, love, and intention.

forty-seven

Miss Murphy saved Ellen's life by redirecting her focus. She came over to Victoria Street for a business meeting the last day of August. She wanted Ellen to design another hat for her to sell exclusively in her store. The spring-summer straw hats had been a great success, and she wanted to have an equally successful fall-winter hat. They discussed the use of fabrics, trims, and the cost of the hat. Ellen told her she would have a sample ready for her approval by September fifth. As she was getting ready to leave, Miss Murphy turned to her and inquired, indirectly, about Alexander.

"I don't suppose you have any more of your husband's hat stands available to sell, do you, Mrs. Pindikowsky?" she asked.

"I'm afraid not," Ellen answered, hoping she wouldn't question her further.

"I wonder if he would make four more of them for me? A few of my customers have requested them for their private use."

"My husband is in New York at present," Ellen replied, mustering as much dignity as she could. "He has a very large commission there and won't be back for a few months."

"I see," said Miss Murphy, looking at her sharply. "Thank you for your time. I'll see you on the fifth."

After she left, Ellen had a sour taste in her mouth. Now, all of the city would know that Alexander was no longer living with her. How many would believe that he was coming back or would send for her? She tried not to dwell on that but to concentrate on her new hats. She hoped that by now Alexander did, in truth, have a large commission.

Ellen told Jeanette about their hat order, and she was very enthusiastic about it. It was great to have someone to talk over her ideas with, and Ellen would need her stitching skills. Jeanette had done a beautiful job with the straw hats, and Ellen now considered her a business partner, even though it wasn't official.

Ellen had been experimenting with a new hat shape that would have a wide brim turned up at the front and sloped down on either side covering the ears and the back of the neck. She was always mindful of the wind when she was designing hats to be worn in Newfoundland, and the contour of this hat would keep it anchored without needing a ribbon tie. The crown would pull down over the head and a couple of hatpins would be all that was needed to keep it secured on the head. It would be a more elegant look than the bonnet. The upturned brim in the front would show off the curled fringe which was the latest hairstyle. Ellen hadn't cut a fringe for herself yet because Alexander liked her hair the way it was. He said that a fringe would cover up her beautiful brow, so she would keep it the way he liked it.

Jeanette and Ellen tried different fabrics on the hat, but they decided that velvet suited the style perfectly. The embellishment would be a bow of a lighter shade of satin so that a dark green velvet covering would be adorned with a pale green bow providing a subtle contrast. Black ostrich feathers would be the accent on all the hats, whatever colour they used. That would give the hats more versatility as they would go well with the black garments which were a staple in everyone's wardrobe.

Miss Murphy was very pleased with the design and the fabric selections and ordered five hats in green, five in blue, and five in maroon. Jeanette and Ellen set to work and established a routine that worked around Johanna's schedule.

Louise came by every day during the week and gave both of them two uninterrupted hours to work on the hats. She loved the design and wanted Ellen to make her one for Christmas. Ellen had to tell her mother that she'd have to buy it from Miss Williams because of their exclusive arrangement. She said she'd be happy to, seeing as the money would be coming back to Ellen.

Even though Jeanette was technically Ellen's maid, Johanna's nanny, and Ellen's business employee, they were also becoming good friends, and the normal societal restrictions between employer and employee were blurred. Ellen was glad of that because she desperately needed a confidante since Cheri was unavailable to her. She really missed her, and though she wrote to her regularly, it wasn't the same as having her within visiting range.

The one thing that Ellen hadn't confided to Cheri was the fact that she still hadn't heard from Alexander. It was the first time she had kept a secret from her. She felt since Cheri had married, she no longer had her to herself. She thought that Cheri might tell Robert about the lack of correspondence from Alexander and he might inadvertently mention it to Kenneth, and hence, Ellen's mother. One thing was certain—she did not want her mother to know that she hadn't received a letter from Alexander. Also, she was hoping she would get a bunch of letters all coming at the same time, and this belief kept her going.

One afternoon as Ellen and Jeanette were stitching the hats, Jeanette brought up the subject of New York City.

"I envy Alexander and Har," she said without preamble.

"Why?" Ellen asked, wondering about the link between Alexander and Har.

"They've both been to New York City. It seems like such an exciting place. I'd love to go there."

"Well, then, you can. When we get paid for the hats you'll have enough money for a ticket, and when Alexander sends for me and Johanna, you can come with us. You could help me with Johanna in New York, as well as here, or you could find work there. If you wanted to, you could work in a millinery shop. You've learned quickly and your stitching is perfect. I have to admit, it's even neater than mine."

Jeanette blushed. "Thank you for saying that, Ellen. Do you really think I could go with you? You're not joking with me, are you?"

"Of course not. You'd be a great help. Mother would be pleased, too, knowing that I'd have a friend from home. You know she doesn't want me to go. But I thought you were afraid of the sea."

"I am, but I want to go to New York so much that I'll just have to get around my fear. Just thinking about making a new life in New York gives me goosebumps. And maybe I'll meet someone there. The only men I've met here are fishermen, and I'm never going to be with a man again who has to go to sea to earn a living. I'm done with that. Once I get to New York, I'm going to see if I can find a man who hates the sea as much as I do, and maybe we'll get married."

"Alexander might already know someone who would suit you. I'll ask him the next time I write."

"When are you moving there? Does Alexander know if he's got that contract with the church yet?"

Ellen could have kicked herself. She had really complicated her life by making up Alexander's contract and his letters. Now, Jeanette was going to keep asking her questions, as well as her mother and Har. She sighed. "I still haven't heard," Ellen said. "He should know by the end of the month, I think."

"We would want to leave before the winter weather sets in. I wouldn't want to be caught in a storm."

"We'll worry about that later. For now, we'd better keep working on these hats or we won't get them finished in time."

"I'm so excited, I can barely stitch."

"Don't tell anyone about our plans yet, Jeanette, especially Mother. I don't want her thinking up ways to stop me from going."

"Don't worry. I'll keep quiet."

Hardly had the words left her mouth when her mother came in with Johanna, who was wailing loudly. "She started to cry just as we turned down the hill. I'm sure she can smell your milk, Ellen. Or is it cream you're feeding her? She's getting as round as a berry," Louise said, tickling Johanna's tummy. "I don't know where you store your milk, Ellen. Your breasts aren't much bigger than they were before you were in the family way. When I was nursing you, I was huge."

It was true that Ellen hadn't changed much in size. She went back to almost her normal weight shortly after Johanna was born. Jeanette said she was lucky because her sisters had never gotten their figures back after they had their babies. The truth was that Ellen was actually losing too much weight. She usually had a healthy appetite, but the stress of not being with Alexander and not hearing from him was taking its toll. She fretted, and this caused her to lose weight. Her mother noticed, of course.

"You've lost more weight, haven't you, Ellen?" She looked at her closely. "I know you're worried about Alexander, but you have to think about Johanna and not let yourself get sick. I'll get some of Achibald's Tonic for you. It's supposed to work wonders."

"I'm fine, Mother. Look, my hair is shiny, so I must be healthy."

"Well, improvement calls out for more."

"Yes, Mother," Ellen said, and winked at Jeanette. It wasn't the first time she had heard her mother's favourite adage.

"I'll make some tea. Har should be home soon, and I want to talk to her."

"I'll make the tea," said Jeanette, jumping up from her chair.

"No, stay and sew. I know you and Ellen have to get those hats done by the middle of October, and time is passing. Besides, I want my tea good and strong, and you tend to make it too weak. As my mother used to say, a poor cup of tea is water bewitched, tea begrudged, and good milk poured away."

"You're the only one I've ever heard say that expression, Mrs. Robinson," said Jeanette. "I thought I knew all the Newfoundland expressions."

"It depends on where we all came from originally, I guess. My mother was from Dorset, England, so maybe the expression is common there. I never asked her about the expression. It was just something she always said, just part of our family history."

Ellen fed Johanna, settled her in her cradle, and joined her mother and Jeanette for tea. It was just right.

forty-eight

The next few weeks were filled with sewing and sleepless nights. Johanna had a cold and Ellen was terrified it would turn into pneumonia. Every time Johanna coughed, Ellen woke, fearing that she had a temperature. Louise stayed at the house for three nights so Ellen could get some rest. She was worried about Ellen's weight loss and the dark circles under her eyes. Ellen, in turn, was worried about Johanna because she would take only a little milk and then fall asleep. She thought of living in the United States without her mother close by, and she knew she would miss her calm presence. But being without Alexander was even more intolerable. Ellen ached for him with every fibre of her being. She clung to the fact that when she did go to New York, Jeanette would be with her.

Johanna quickly recovered, and Ellen was so grateful for this. She was nursing every couple of hours, trying to make up for her lack of appetite while she was sick. Ellen was a bit sore from all the nursing but relieved that Johanna was strong and healthy again. She went back to sleeping regularly, and Ellen and Jeanette were able to return to finishing the hat order.

Ellen still hadn't received a letter from Alexander and her anxiety was becoming harder to hide. Her mother asked pointed questions and Kenneth quizzed her on the places where Alexander had found work. He wanted to know the name of the church where Alexander was hoping to get a commission. He said he might know someone who would be able to facilitate the contract; he just needed an address. Ellen told him that she was expecting a letter in the next couple of days that would give her all that information and hopefully word of his success. At other times, when the questions became too much for her, she would feign a headache or say that she heard Johanna crying. It worked, but she was exhausted keeping up the pretense.

Then, on October the first, Ellen pulled herself together and surprised Jeanette by making an apple pie.

"Are we having company?" she asked.

"No, but tomorrow is October the second."

"So?"

"It's Apple Pie for Breakfast Day."

"What? I've never heard of it. You're playing with me, aren't you?"

Ellen told Jeanette about October the second of the previous year, when she was expecting Johanna and wanted apple pie for breakfast. She told her how Alexander had declared the day Apple Pie for Breakfast Day. She wanted to celebrate the day so she would feel closer to him, and she would even give Johanna a taste of the pie. Jeanette thought it was a great idea and said she envied Ellen the fact that she had such a fun-loving husband. Ellen agreed with her, but the memory of that day made her long for Alexander that much more. The previous year she would never have dreamed that she would be spending the day without him.

AFTER THEY HAD FINISHED EATING THEIR PIE, ELLEN TOLD JEANETTE that she would share the hat profits equally with her. Jeanette was delighted, saying that with the money she had already saved, she'd have more than enough for her ticket to New York and some new clothes. Ellen had never seen her so happy.

They delivered the hats to Miss Murphy's shop on October the fifteenth, and Jeanette and Ellen celebrated by going to Delgado's for ice cream. They had two scoops each—vanilla and chocolate. It was a real treat. They took Johanna with them, and she had her first taste of ice cream. She lapped it up with her little tongue and then laughed out loud. The sound of her laughter was so infectious that Jeanette and Ellen joined in. It felt good, and Ellen realized she hadn't laughed since Alexander had left.

A week later, Ellen took Johanna in her pram and went again to Miss Murphy's shop. She knew her hats would be displayed in the store window by that time. It was cold but sunny and they were both bundled up, Ellen with a warm hat and scarf, Johanna with two warm blankets and a knitted wool coat. Three of the hats were displayed on Alexander's hat stands, one in each colour. Seeing their work together made Ellen happy and sad at the same time. She missed Alexander so much.

Ellen strolled down Water Street to Smallwood's shoe store. She caught sight of herself in the store window, and suddenly she knew with certainty what she had to do. She started up Prescott Street to see Sister Mary Angela at the Presentation Convent.

forty-nine

St. John's, October–November 1882

As soon as Ellen reached home, after walking from the convent, she fed Johanna and settled her in her crib for a nap. She hurried downstairs to find Jeanette and tell her about her plan.

"Pack your bags, we're leaving for New York on the next ship," she said in a brisk tone.

"Are you serious?" Jeanette asked. She smiled at Ellen like she'd just given her a thousand-pound note.

"I'm serious. I was just at the post office and I received a letter from Alexander," she said, the lie falling easily out of her mouth. "He landed the church contract and he wants me and Johanna there as soon as possible. I'm so excited," Ellen said, and at least these words were true.

"Have you told your mother yet?"

"I haven't had time, but we'll tell her when she comes over this afternoon. You're still going with me, aren't you, Jeanette? You're not going to back out?"

"I'm scared of the sea trip, but I'm determined to go and start a new life."

"That's good, because you're my charm against Mother's objections. If she knows you will be with me to help with Johanna, she'll be easier about it. Is the paper around? I need to see when the next Bowring ship is leaving for New York. All their ships stop in Halifax, but it's only for a day and then we're at sea again. If the weather is good we'll be in New York in five days. Imagine! Five days after we leave, I'll be with Alexander."

"I know you've missed him terribly. He must be missing you and Johanna, too. He'll hardly recognize Johanna, she's grown so much since he left. You did send Kenneth's tintypes of her to Alexander, didn't you?"

"I did, but as you know, pictures don't tell the whole story, and she changes every day. Have you seen the paper?"

"The paper's in the kitchen. I'll get it."

Jeanette handed her the *Evening Telegram* and she spread it out on the dining room table, turning the pages to the ship schedules. "The *Juliet* is leaving on November first. That's only five days from now, but that's the one we're going to be on. I'm going down to book our tickets right away, Jeanette. You can pay me later." Ellen put on her coat and headed out the door. Now that she'd made up her mind to go, she was full of nervous energy. "I'll probably be back before Johanna wakes up."

"Good luck," said Jeanette. "I can't believe I'm going to New York!"

Ellen's first destination was the Union Bank on Duckworth Street. She withdrew enough money to pay for her ticket and Jeanette's. Then at Bowring Brothers shipping office, she purchased second-class tickets to New York City. The cheaper tickets would be easier for Jeanette to pay, and Ellen, too, wanted to save as much money as she could since she didn't know what would await her in New York.

All the new Bowring Brothers steamships were named after characters in Shakespeare's plays, and Ellen thought that sailing on the *Juliet* was a good omen, considering the fact that Alexander had painted her as Juliet in his mural at the Athenaeum. Ellen was a nineteenth-century Juliet, going to New York City to find her Romeo. The romance and rightness of it appealed to her.

Ellen started rehearsing what she was going to tell her mother. She knew that she'd have to give her the details of Alexander's commission, so she decided to use the name of the church that Sister Mary Angela mentioned, the Church of the Sacred Heart, the place where she thought Alexander might have found work. In her mind, she repeated the name of the church and made up a detailed description of the fresco work that Alexander was doing. She was glad that she had learned enough about fresco work, when Alexander was at Government House, to sound plausible.

Ellen's mind was spinning with all the things she would have to do in the next few days. She'd have to tell Kielly about her departure and say goodbye. He hadn't had a letter from Alexander, either, and she knew he was hurt about it since he believed that she'd been receiving letters regularly. She had told Kielly that Alexander had asked her to pass on his news to him. She had even made up a few Alexander-styled jokes to make the messages more believable. Since Kielly was well aware of the fact that Alexander found writing English difficult, he seemed satisfied with her explanation. Ellen had missed her calling; she should been an actress at the Athenaeum.

Ellen's deceit would have to extend to Jeanette, at least until they reached New York. She'd have to tell her the truth about her situation then. She felt bad about her lies, but she was desperate. And she still hoped that Sister Mary Angela would find out some news of Alexander before she left. She had contacts in New York City, and she could inquire about Alexander through the archdioses.

When Ellen arrived home, her mother was already there. Ellen nursed Johanna and then told her her news.

"I was dreading this day," said Louise. "Can't you wait for a few more weeks, Ellen? Johanna is barely six months old, and she had that awful cold."

"Mother, look at her, she's the very picture of health."

Louise smiled at Johanna, who held out her chubby arms to her. Ellen's mother lifted her into her arms and kissed her. "She really is healthy and beautiful. I'm going to miss her so much. What am I going to do with the two of you gone?"

"You can always visit us. Kenneth said that he was looking forward to taking you to England for a visit. I'm sure you can convince him to come to New York instead."

"I know, but it won't be the same as seeing you all the time," said Louise, sighing.

"You know I need to be with Alexander, and Johanna needs her father. We need to be a family again."

"I know that, Ellen. I'm just being selfish. I will miss you so much."

"I'll miss you, too, Mother. But I have to go to Alexander. I need to be with him."

"I understand, Ellen, but I don't have to like it."

"And I'll write you often, don't forget."

"Kenneth and I will visit you next spring, as soon as the House of Assembly closes session. Now, on to practical matters. We'll have to go shopping. Johanna is going to need more sweaters and blankets and some warm bonnets. I'm not having her getting cold on that ship. And you'll need a warmer coat for yourself. I'll get Kenneth to pick up your tickets."

"Mother, I already have the tickets. I bought them this morning."

"Before you even told me? I hope you bought first-class tickets. Did Alexander wire you enough money?"

"I have plenty of money, Mother, don't worry." Ellen quickly changed the subject, not wanting her to know that they didn't have first-class tickets.

"Jeanette and I are going to start sorting out everything we'll need to take with us. What about the house and Har?"

"I'll talk to Har. It won't be difficult to find someone willing to do the cooking and cleaning. I'll speak to Mollie Parmender over at The House, and she'll know someone, I'm sure. I won't think about selling the property yet. You and Alexander may still decide to come back here to live."

"Don't count on it, Mother. And don't hold on to the house just for our sakes."

"I won't, but I might keep it for an investment, anyway. I can always rent it out."

Ellen was thankful that her mother had such a practical streak. Once she accepted a situation, she didn't waste time mooning over a decision that she didn't like. Ellen felt she'd cleared another obstacle and was much closer to being with Alexander. She tried to block thoughts about him being sick or injured or worse. No matter what reality awaited her, she had to know for certain, for her sake and Johanna's.

fifty

Jeanette and Ellen spent the next couple of days in a frenzy of sewing, sorting, packing, and repacking. It was difficult to know what to take with them, and Ellen didn't want to have to lug around too many trunks. Jeanette said it wouldn't matter because Alexander would be there to help them. Ellen couldn't tell her that they would probably be on their own until she could find him. She'd have to educate herself and learn about transportation and lodging houses in New York without arousing any suspicion.

Jeanette was so chatty that Ellen had a headache. It was unlike her to be so garrulous, but she was in a fever pitch of nervous excitement. "What if I'm seasick? What if we're both seasick and we can't look after Johanna?" she asked, her brows meeting in a line of worry.

"I'm sure that won't happen, and if it does, we'll ask for help. We won't be the only ones on board, you know, and the porters are well used to seasick people." She wasn't really sure at all, but she had to play the part of the calm, collected person. While Ellen talked she folded a blanket around Alexander's music box, and her shell box, padding them to make sure they were protected.

"They take up a lot of room, don't they? Couldn't your mother send them on later?" Jeanette asked.

"No, they're going with me, even if I have to leave out some clothing. We'll need the music box to settle Johanna, anyway. You know that when she gets in one of her fussy moods it's the only thing that will soothe her. In fact, I think I'll put it in my carpet bag for easy access." Ellen didn't tell Jeanette, but the music box soothed her as well, and she needed to keep her nerves in check. She wasn't at all sure what would happen in New York, and her stomach was in knots.

Two days before they left, Ellen went to the bank, closed out her account, and arranged to have the money wired to the Manhattan Bank in New York City. Har assured her that it was the best one to deal with, and Ellen trusted her advice, especially on money matters. Har had been really helpful. In a little notebook, she had written down all kinds of important information about getting around in New York City based on her experiences. She penned addresses for boarding houses, hotels, lists for places to see and places to avoid, the correct cab fare, and how much to tip people. She also included the names and addresses of a few of the friends she had made in the city, and she told Ellen not to hesitate to call on them if she needed anything. She said she had told her friends about her, and they would welcome a visit. She even included a couple of hand-drawn maps. One of them showed a crude drawing of the Manhattan Bank.

"I know Alexander will show you around, so you probably won't need the information, but it never hurts to have more information than you need when you're going to a strange place," she said.

When Har handed Ellen the notebook, she gave her a look that made Ellen think that she suspected that she wasn't telling the whole truth about her situation. Ellen was grateful for her help and her discretion.

Then, the afternoon before they sailed, a young boy came to the door and gave Ellen a letter. He said no reply was needed and that Sister had paid him. He ran off and Ellen quickly opened the letter. "Come and see me at once" was all that was written on the paper. It was signed, Sister Mary Angela. Ellen called out to Jeanette and told her that she had to go on an errand and would be back in an hour. She threw on her coat and ran up Victoria Street, stopping only once to catch her breath before she continued her climb to the Presentation Convent. Sister Mary Angela was waiting for Ellen when she arrived, and she ushered her into her office and closed the door before she spoke.

"I have an address for Alexander." Ellen's face registered her relief, and Sister quickly added, "He's not there now, but he did do some restoration work at St. Peter's Roman Catholic Church back in September. Here's the address." She handed Ellen a piece of paper, and she grabbed it like a lifeline. "You can start looking there, and I will keep trying to get more information for you while you are travelling. If I find out where Alexander is working at the present time, I will try to send a telegram to him and let him know that you and Johanna are on your way."

"Thank you, thank you, thank you," said Ellen. She hugged Sister Mary Angela as tears streamed down her face.

"Have faith, my child," Sister Mary Angela said as she kissed her cheek. "I have a good feeling about this. I know that you will find Alexander and all will be well. Just trust in God."

"I will, and I'll write to you as soon as I find him."

"You'll be in my prayers. God speed you on your journey."

Ellen left the convent in a state of euphoria and walked down to Victoria Street. She felt that she would be able to find Alexander with this lead. She tried not to let herself believe that Sister Mary Angela would be able to contact Alexander and that he would be waiting for her when she reached New York, but she prayed for this all the same.

fifty-one

Kenneth made two trips with his carriage the day of Ellen's departure to New York. The first trip he took the trunks and Louise with him. Louise waited with the luggage and made sure it was brought to their cabin while Kenneth went back to Victoria Street to pick up Ellen, Johanna, and Jeanette. They had already said their goodbyes to Har when he arrived

It was a beautiful morning and the weather was supposed to stay relatively good for the next week. Ellen thanked God for that! There were countless shipwrecks around the coast of Newfoundland, and they were fully aware of the dangers of the trip to New York in spite of the cheerful brochures published by Bowring Brothers, which led passengers to believe that the worst that could befall them would be a lump in their porridge.

Jeanette was like a coiled spring and her face was a bluish white. After all her chattiness in the last couple of days, she'd now gone totally silent. Ellen gave her hand a squeeze to reassure her, and it was as cold as an iceberg. She prayed that Jeanette wouldn't desert her at the last minute.

When they reached Beck's Cove, the traffic was terrible—carriages, carts, and people were everywhere. This was the usual Water Street bustle of activity whenever a passenger ship as large as the *Juliet* was leaving port. There were just as many people going to see people off as there were passengers. It was like a huge party. Ellen couldn't even imagine what it would be like in New York. Her nerves were stretched to the breaking point, and to make matters worse, Johanna hadn't slept well the night before and she was cranky. She knew something was afoot and she was reacting, instinctively, against it. Ellen just wanted to be aboard the ship and out the Narrows. Leaving the only home she had ever known was torture.

They finally made their way to the dock and were preparing to say their goodbyes when Kenneth leaned over and handed Ellen two tickets. "I've upgraded you both to first-class," he said in a low whisper. "Not a word to your mother. She thinks you're already in first-class. Don't even think about refusing them, it's too late. And besides, I won't be able to rest easy unless I know that you and Johanna will have the best care available on board."

"Thank you, Kenneth. I'll miss you, you're the very best. Look after Mother for me." Ellen gave him a big hug and kissed his cheek.

"I will, and you look after yourself, too. Give my best to Alexander."

Now it was time to say goodbye to her mother, and Ellen didn't know how she could do it. She was thankful that Johanna was in her arms because she would act as a buffer to the pain of leaving her mother for the first time in her life. Ellen leaned over to kiss her mother, and she and Johanna were encircled in her arms.

"If you need me, I'll come as fast as I can. Don't hesitate to ask me to come to you, no matter what. Promise me, Ellen." Tears were falling down both their faces, and Johanna started to cry.

"I promise," Ellen said, barely able to form the words.

"Look after them, Jeanette," Ellen heard her mother say as they walked up the gangplank to the deck of the *Juliet*.

Ellen kept looking at Kenneth and her mother, from the deck of the ship, until she couldn't see them anymore. Her face was streaming with tears and she had a lump in her throat that wouldn't allow her to speak. Jeanette suggested that they make their way to their cabin, and Ellen followed her wordlessly.

Their room was beautiful and more spacious than Ellen had

thought possible. She silently thanked Kenneth for his thoughtfulness in upgrading them to first-class. There were two bunkbeds and a small cot for Johanna. They had a separate washroom with a stack of fluffy white towels. Their window was large and they had a good view of the harbour. Johanna looked all around, her eyes taking in all her surroundings. Then her face screwed up and she started to cry at full volume. Ellen thought that she sensed her world had changed and she didn't like it, not one bit. Ellen took her in her arms and nursed her, even though she shouldn't have been hungry yet. Johanna settled down and was nearly asleep when the ship's horn sounded, signalling that they were heading out the Narrows, and she started crying again. Ellen felt like crying herself, but then she reminded herself that she was another step closer to Alexander, and she felt her spirits rise.

Jeanette was sitting on the bed, looking frozen. She refused to look out the window, saying that she didn't want to look down and see the sea. The ship's horn blasted again, and Ellen knew it would be a while before Johanna would fall asleep. She told Jeanette that she'd take Johanna with her for a tour around the ship.

Jeanette came to life and said, "I'll put away our clothes and straighten out our belongings. I need to keep busy and try to pretend that the sea isn't heaving beneath us." She started unlocking the largest trunk.

Ellen was surprised that it was relatively calm, considering they were heading out into the North Atlantic and it was the beginning of November. Still, she was careful to hold the railing with one hand at all times, since she didn't want to lose her balance, especially with Johanna in her arms.

As she walked around the ship, she saw a few people that she recognized but only knew by name. She didn't really want to draw attention to herself, so she didn't make eye contact with anyone. The dining room was in a central position and she saw the stewards bustling around, setting up the long tables for dinner. There was a smaller room next to it with a sign that said Men's Smoking Room. Farther along there was a library room, and Ellen knew that that was going to be her favourite place.

She saw many of the people that she once served at Government

House and she felt like an imposter, being in first-class. She was a former maid and now a businesswoman, mother, and wife. She didn't feel like she had the right to be here. Also, she was not looking forward to dinner in the dining room. She didn't want anyone to ask questions about her. As soon as she introduced herself, she knew there would be questions. Someone was bound to know the name Pindikowsky. There was only one Pindikowsky family in Newfoundland, and they were it. This was something Ellen hadn't thought about. Alexander's frescoes were famous in Newfoundland, and the fact that he served a prison sentence was also well known. Ellen understood even better now why Alexander needed to move away from St. John's. She realized that she'd been protected by her family and her world had been a very insular one. Maybe she and Jeanette could eat in their room and avoid the obligatory conversation at dinner.

Johanna was starting to fall asleep, and Ellen quickly walked back to their room. She was relieved to see that Jeanette had more colour in her cheeks and was busy putting the last of their belongings in the small closet and built-in drawers. Ellen noticed that the drawers and the closet had latches on them to keep them closed against the rocking of the ship.

Ellen picked up a brochure that had been placed on the small table that was bolted to the floor. There was a chart of the ship showing where everything was and a list of entertainments and services. She read that as first-class passengers they could request that their meals be served in their room, and she felt the tension in her body release its hold on her.

"Jeanette, would you mind if we eat dinner in our room tonight? I'm really tired, and I don't want to have to make conversation at dinner."

"Oh, thank God. I was dreading it. I don't belong in first-class, and I don't want to embarrass you by doing or saying the wrong thing."

"That makes two of us, then. I don't feel I belong here, either. And I don't want people asking me questions about Alexander. I'm sure someone will mention his prison sentence."

"That wouldn't be very first-class behaviour, then, would it?"

"Working at Government House, I heard a lot of low-class comments from high-class people, so nothing would surprise me."

"What was it like working there?"

Ellen gave Jeanette an edited version of her time working at The House while she changed Johanna's clothes and settled her into her cot. She was asleep in seconds, the motion of the ship rocking her.

There was a bell pull that brought the steward to them, and she and Jeanette ordered their dinner. It was an excellent meal: tomato soup first, then fresh cod with a béchamel sauce and croquette potatoes. Dessert was a sponge cake with cream and blueberry sauce. They ate every bit, and then they decided to go to bed. Ellen took the lower bunk and Jeanette took the top one, and they were both asleep in minutes. The stress of the last few days had exhausted them, and their bodies didn't care if they were on land or at sea—they just wanted to rest.

fifty-two

Johanna woke at six o'clock the next morning, and for the first few seconds Ellen was totally disoriented. Then she felt the roll of the ship and remembered. She heard Jeanette splashing around in the washroom, and by the time she came out, already fully dressed, Ellen had started nursing a very hungry Johanna.

"How do you feel, Jeanette? You're not seasick, are you?"

"Don't say the word. So far so good. I slept like the dead. What about you?"

"Yes, and I can hardly believe it, after our dinner last night, but I'm starving. Why don't you see if there's anyone in the dining room? It's early, so maybe we can have our breakfast before too many people are about. We don't want to be stuck in our room all day."

"I'll be back as quick as I can."

"I'll dress Johanna and have her all ready by then."

Ellen bundled Johanna in the new coat that her mother insisted on buying for her. She decided to wear her coat, too, since the corridors of the ship were quite chilly. When Jeanette came back, she reported that there were only a couple of men reading the papers at one end of the dining room, so it was a good time to eat. She had arranged for a high chair for Johanna so she could have a little freedom. At six months of age, Johanna was already demanding more independence.

As they walked to the dining room, Ellen noticed that Jeanette kept her eyes away from the brilliant blue sea surrounding them. She walked over to the railing to get a better look, but Jeanette wouldn't come; she said she would meet her inside. The weather was still good—sunny and not too windy. Ellen knew it could change in a moment, but she was hoping their luck would continue.

"I'm sorry I didn't join you at the railing," said Jeanette, as she tied Johanna securely into her high chair. "I can't bear to look at the sea. From in here I can imagine that I'm eating at the Atlantic Hotel instead of on the Atlantic Ocean."

"I'm glad you're making jokes, Jeanette," Ellen said, smiling at her. "You must be feeling better."

"We're already closer to New York and I'm happy about that. I just hope the weather stays good."

The food and service were certainly wonderful. They both enjoyed a full English breakfast of kippers, toast, strawberry jam, and tea. It was delicious. Johanna made cooing sounds as she looked around her, full of curiosity. The room was beginning to fill up, and a couple of women came over to admire Johanna, asking her name and saying how pretty she was. Ellen only gave her first name, and she signalled to Jeanette that it was time to leave before too many more questions were asked.

When Johanna took her nap in the afternoon, Ellen decided to go to the library, leaving the baby in Jeanette's care. When she entered the room there were only two people there: a man sitting at the end of the room, and a grey-haired lady going through the bookshelves. Ellen hoped the library shelves would hold Anna Sewell's novel, *Black Beauty*. It had great reviews, and she couldn't wait to read it. She scanned along the shelves to the *S* section and stooped down to the last shelf. "Oh, good, it's here," she said, not realizing that she'd spoken out loud.

"Ellen?" said a voice that Ellen recognized. "Ellen Dormody? Or I should say, Ellen Pindikowsky?"

The voice belonged to Miss Rose Hamilton, one of Lady Glover's art friends, the woman who had seen Ellen's face in the ceiling at Government House. She smiled at Ellen and she couldn't be rude to her, even though she felt the curious attention of the man in the corner. "Hello, Miss Hamilton," Ellen said. "How have you been?"

"Quite well, my dear. Thank you for asking. You look well, too, although you're even smaller than when you were at The House. I miss those days. I still paint with the art group, but it's not the same without Elizabeth, Lady Glover. It was a great loss to us when she and her husband were transferred to the West Indies. Oh well, time hurries on. Are you going to Halifax or New York, if you don't mind my asking?"

"New York. I'm going to meet my husband."

"Is he working there now?"

"Yes," said Ellen, trying to keep her answers short.

"I'm not surprised you two married. It was your face that he painted in the ceiling, wasn't it?"

Ellen lowered her voice and said, "You're the only one who ever noticed it, and I'd be grateful if you didn't mention it to anyone."

Miss Hamilton looked surprised. "Of course not, if that's what you want, but I don't know why you wouldn't want it known. I think it's wonderful." Then she glanced at her watch and said, "Look at the time, I must go. I hope to see you later, Ellen."

She left quickly, and Ellen was relieved until the gentleman in the corner spoke to her.

"Excuse me, I couldn't help but overhear. Are you Alexander Pindikowsky's wife?"

He didn't give her a chance to answer but introduced himself as Mr. Anthony Perks, a reporter with the *Halifax Times*. He said he knew all about Alexander's prison sentence and his frescoes and he wanted to interview her for a story in his paper. He seemed to think that she wanted her life spread out for all to read.

Imitating her mother's best authoritative voice, she said, "I am not interested in giving you an interview now or ever. Good day, Mr. Perks." She held her head high and left the room as rapidly as she could. She hoped that he would get off the ship in Halifax. She went back to her room and decided that she wouldn't leave it again until they arrived in Halifax. Her nerves were totally frayed, and she didn't want to risk another encounter with Mr. Perks.

Jeanette and Ellen had dinner in their room that evening, and to pass the time, Jeanette asked Ellen if she'd read *Black Beauty* aloud, so they could both enjoy it. Ellen began the story. "*The first place that I can well remember was a large pleasant meadow with a pond of clear water in it."* They were both enthralled from that first sentence. Even Johanna seemed to like it, or she just liked to hear the sound of her mother's voice. She went to sleep without making a fuss, and at one in the morning Jeanette and Ellen reluctantly went to bed. They couldn't wait to continue the story and vowed that they'd finish it before they reached New York.

The next morning, they were awakened by the ship's horn. They had arrived in Halifax harbour. They dressed hurriedly and made their way to the ship's railing along with everyone else. It was cold and cloudy and the wind was starting to blow. They watched people disembark and board. The harbour was larger than St. John's but not nearly as sheltered. The land surrounding the city was hilly like St. John's, but the buildings looked different and the air felt and smelled foreign to Ellen.

Ellen was deeply relieved to see Mr. Perks leave the ship with his luggage. That was one hurdle over with, she thought. Then she started to worry about what she'd do when they arrived in New York. If the weather held, they would be there in two and a half to three days' time, and she decided that she wouldn't tell Jeanette about her situation until the night before they docked. If things worked out badly, Jeanette could always go back to St. John's when the *Juliet* made her return trip.

They were told that they could go ashore for a few hours, but Jeanette and Ellen decided that they'd rather stay on board. They didn't like the idea of walking in an unknown place unaccompanied by a man, especially with Johanna. What if someone decided to pickpocket them? Ellen tried not to think about the fact that they'd be even more of a target in New York City. She was relying on Har's careful instructions to get them safely to the Aspen Hotel. Har had told her that the hotel was in a good neighbourhood and not too expensive. They could stay there for a day or so until she found a boarding house that would accommodate the three of them. That is, if Jeanette didn't decide to return to St. John's. Every time Ellen thought about that possibility, she felt nauseous and her heart doubled its beat. She tried to block such negative thoughts from her mind and reminded herself that she was a mature woman of twenty years. She could manage on her own. After all, her mother managed by herself after her father died. Then she started thinking that Alexander might be sick or dead, and she didn't know how she would survive that, so she tried to stop herself even glancing at that possibility. She redirected her focus on finding him, and the happy ending of them being together for the rest of their lives.

fifty-three

The *Juliet* sailed out of Halifax harbour just before darkness descended. The wind was high and it started to rain; their smooth sailing was over. Jeanette and Ellen retreated to their cabin and the novel. If they didn't have the story of Black Beauty to distract them, they both would have been very anxious. The ship started to roll and pitch, and they stayed up half the night watching over Johanna, making sure she didn't fall out of her cot, and reading. Ellen felt a bit queasy, but Jeanette turned out to be a good sailor and was fine. Ellen was glad that they were on the upper deck because they felt the roll of the ship a little less.

    The wind calmed just before sunrise, and Ellen woke up. She took a walk around the deck to clear her head and get a little exercise while Jeanette and Johanna were still asleep. The ship still rolled a bit, so she was careful to keep a firm grip on the railing. There was no one about yet except the staff, mopping up areas where the sea had washed over the deck during the night. The sky was a watery, greenish-gray colour, and Ellen remembered the adage "Red sky in the morning, sailors take warning." There was no sign of red, so she hoped that they would have good weather for the rest of the trip.

    In the library, Ellen found a *New York Times* newspaper dated October twenty-fourth. She guessed that it was left over from the *Ju-*

liet's last trip. She scanned the paper to familiarize herself with the city through the headlines and the advertisements. Ellen always thought that you could tell a lot about a city by the kinds of things it advertised. What people bought and sold gave you a map of the people and what was important to them. She was surprised to see a very large advertisement for Achibald's Tonic—the same tonic that her mother wanted her to take when she thought she was getting too thin. Mr. Ross Archibald made that tonic in a small factory in St. John's. He was successful enough to advertise in a New York City newspaper, and this fact made Ellen feel better about leaving home and more connected to the city.

Ellen was always interested in the fashion section, especially millinery, and there were some sketches of the latest hats from a shop on Fifth Avenue called Marie's Millinery. She wasn't impressed by the designs, and she egotistically thought that Ellen's Millinery offered better merchandise at decidedly better prices. A hat with fewer trimmings and cheaper materials than her latest fall-winter hat was selling for seventy per cent more than what Miss Murphy charged. If she revived her hat business in New York City, she'd charge more, too, she thought. Why not?

There was a story about the P. T. Barnum's Circus and their latest acquisition, Jumbo the African Bush Elephant, who was drawing great crowds at Madison Square Gardens. She read about how he'd travelled to New York the previous March and cost ten thousand dollars in United States currency. Ellen was having a hard time imagining a live elephant, weighing thirteen thousand pounds, in the hold of a ship coming across the Atlantic from London, England, especially with rough seas like last night. The article told of all the thousands of English schoolchildren who petitioned Queen Victoria to keep Jumbo at the London Zoo, all to no avail. Ellen couldn't believe that she hadn't read about this in their local paper. Of course, she had been expecting Johanna, then, and she hadn't been paying much attention to world news at the time. She realized that now that she'd be living in a big city, she'd have access to shows like P. T. Barnum's Greatest Show on Earth, and she made a mental note to take Johanna to see Jumbo at the circus.

When Ellen left the library to join Jeanette and Johanna for breakfast, she took the newspaper with her, knowing that Jeanette would want to read about Marie's Millinery Shop. Ellen wanted to keep her interested in New York City life and what it offered so that she'd stay with her, at least until she found Alexander.

Jeanette was really excited about the fact that they'd be in New York City by late the next morning, and Ellen was a nervous wreck. She kept reading *Black Beauty* to help distract herself and to put off making her confession to Jeanette. Too soon she was reading the last sentence of the book. "*My troubles are all over and I am at home; and often before I am completely awake, I fancy I am still in the orchard at Bertwick, standing with my old friends under the apple trees.*" Ellen wished her troubles were all over.

"What a great story," Jeanette said. "I'll never be able to look at a horse in the same way again."

"Yes, the story really makes you think about them in a whole new way. I've always liked horses, but I've never spent a lot of time with them. I think I'll be giving them a lot more apples in the future."

"Me too. I can't believe we'll be living in New York City by this time tomorrow."

"There's something I need to tell you, Jeanette." Ellen paused to make sure she had her full attention. "I haven't been completely honest with you."

Jeanette looked at her with fear and surprise in equal measure. "What do you mean?"

"I couldn't tell you before. I was afraid you wouldn't come with me if you knew."

"What couldn't you tell me? I don't understand."

"I haven't had a letter from Alexander in a month," Ellen said, telling her a partial truth. She didn't have the nerve to tell her that she hadn't heard from him since he left St. John's, four months ago.

"But what about the church contract?"

"I made it up. I didn't want Mother to worry, so I had to tell everyone that Alexander had steady work and had sent for me and Johanna."

"Does he know you're coming to New York? Did you write him to say you were coming? Is he going to meet us tomorrow?"

"I'm afraid the answer is no to everything you've asked, unless Sister Mary Angela can work a miracle. I don't know where Alexander is working now, so I couldn't contact him. Sister Mary Angela promised that she'd try to locate him while we were travelling. If she finds him, she'll send a telegram to let him know that we're coming."

"So the chances of him meeting us are between slim and none," said Jeanette.

"I'm afraid so. But I'll find him, I know I will. And don't worry, I have enough money saved to keep us for a month, anyway, and I'll definitely find Alexander by then.

"I'll understand if you want to go back home, and I'll buy your ticket if you want to go back." Jeanette was sitting, slumped-shouldered on her bed, and she had gone quiet. Ellen waited for what seemed like hours for her to say something.

"Where will we stay?"

"Does that mean you'll stay with me?"

"Well, I'm not getting back on board a ship any time soon after we get on dry land, I can tell you that. That rocking and rolling last night had me scared. If it wasn't for you reading *Black Beauty*, I would have gone crazy with fright. That horse saved my life."

Ellen was so relieved that Jeanette was staying with her that she gave her a huge hug. "Thanks, Jeanette. You're a real friend. And Har has given me all kinds of instructions on what to do and what not to do in New York City. We'll spend a couple of days at the Aspen Hotel, and we'll look for a boarding house where we can stay while I locate Alexander. I know I'll find him, and then everything will be fine."

"Why did he stop writing? There weren't any storms, so the mail was getting through."

"I don't know. That's why I had to come to New York. I couldn't wait any longer. I'm afraid Alexander might be sick or injured. When he works on ceilings, he's often climbing on scaffolding twenty to thirty feet above ground. He's supposed to wear a tether, but I know he doesn't, and I'm afraid that he might have fallen and hurt himself. I can't bear the thought of him being in hospital with no one to be with him." Ellen started to cry, and then she couldn't stop. She had kept herself in tight control for the last few months, and her confession had released a flood of emotions. Her sobbing woke Johanna, who started crying, too. Jeanette picked her up and brought her to Ellen. She held her in her arms and tried to control her tears. Jeanette wound up the music box in the hopes that Chopin's nocturne would soothe them both.

fifty-four

The ship roared like a lion the next morning. The level of noise and activity was such that Ellen would have been amazed if any of the passengers had slept through it. Her eyes were stinging from all her tears the night before, and while she did get some sleep, her dreams were so full of confused imaginings that she didn't feel rested. She was nervous, and even though she knew that Alexander wouldn't be there to meet them, she still clung to the hope. Despite her confident talk about finding her way around New York City, she was really frightened. She was going to have to call on her acting skills again to get her through this next stage of her journey.

The dining room was full when they went in for breakfast, but they didn't have to worry about anyone talking with them that morning, as everyone was too busy anticipating their new agendas. The sea voyage had been a suspension of reality, and now the passengers had to pick up their lives, for good or bad. You could see by the expressions on people's faces which ones were looking forward to leaving the ship and which ones dreaded their departure. Ellen was caught between both categories, longing to see Alexander and terrified that she wouldn't find him. Up until now she'd been fairly successful at blocking her fears, but now that they were nearing New York harbour, they were surfacing like whales needing oxygen. Jeanette was talking non-stop, and Ellen realized that this was her reaction to nervousness.

"I can't wait to see New York harbour and the Brooklyn Bridge," she said. "I was reading about the bridge in that newspaper you brought to our room. It's supposed to be finished in May of next year, and all of the foundation work is completed. We should be able to see it from the ship. I'm so excited."

"We should get back to our room and make sure everything is packed and ready for the steward to take. Then we can go on deck and we won't miss the first sight of New York City. You're going to have to be next to the ship's railing, though, in order to get a good view. You're not afraid anymore, are you?"

"No, now that I know we'll be in port soon, I'll be fine. And I'm going to look out at the view instead of down at the water. I can't wait to feel land under my feet again."

Johanna was feeling all the excitement, and her eyes darted around in all directions, trying to understand what was going on. Ellen had no idea what it took to dock a ship the size of the *Juliet*, but all the deckhands and service staff were buzzing around at top speed. They were polite, as always, to passenger queries, but you could tell they had things to do and no time for idle conversation.

It didn't take Jeanette and Ellen very long to pack up their belongings. Ellen made sure that she had her United States currency within easy reach. It was a sunny day but really cold, so they bundled up in their coats, hats, scarves, and gloves and went on deck to see the curtain rise on their new scenery, their new lives.

They found a spot near the bow of the ship on the starboard side. The land was a smudge of gray-black on the horizon and then became more distinct, its contours visible. As they approached the mouth of the harbor, they passed a large island that had to be Ellis Island from Har's description. Then they saw the buildings—masses and masses of them. Ellen realized that it was the buildings and not the land itself that created the shape of the place.

"Look," shouted Jeanette, grabbing Ellen's arm. "It's the Brooklyn Bridge! I can't believe what I'm seeing. It's huge!"

Ellen had no words for what she was seeing, only a feeling of awe. The wire cables holding the bridge reminded her of harp strings. She imagined angels plucking them. She felt privileged to witness such a marvel.

Miss Hamilton tapped Ellen on the shoulder, startling her. "Ellen, I'm glad that I've found you before we dock. Have you been hiding? I thought I'd see you before now."

If she only knew how close to the truth she was. "Isn't the bridge wonderful," replied Ellen, redirecting the conversation.

"It is a miracle of engineering. But then, all of New York City is full of building miracles. And speaking of miracles, is this darling child your daughter?"

"Yes," Ellen said, enjoying her proud-mother moment.

"She's so beautiful. She has your eyes but her father's hair. And speaking of her father, does he teach art lessons here in New York? My niece needs a good art teacher, and it would be wonderful if he could teach her."

"I don't think Alexander is going to be doing any teaching in the next while. He prefers to do fresco work. That is his specialty."

"Please take my sister's card, just in case," she said, handing her a gold-lettered, embossed card. "I would love it if you two would visit me while I'm in the city. I'll be staying with my sister until April."

"Thank you, Miss Hamilton. That's very kind of you, but it will depend on Alexander's work."

"Of course, I understand. Are you planning on settling here, or will you be returning to Newfoundland?"

"I think this will be our new home, although the size of the place is overwhelming."

"You'll get used to it. My sister felt the same way when she first came here, but now she just takes it all in her stride. Well, I must say goodbye to my other travel companions. Good luck to you, Ellen. Remember me to your mother."

"I will. Goodbye." She waved and walked to the other side of the ship. Ellen pocketed the card, feeling grateful for Miss Hamilton's words. It was reassuring to know that, if she was in dire straits, she would have someone to go to for help. She prayed that she would never need that help.

The ship approached the dock and they were close enough to see the multitude of buildings that provided the landscape for this place. Ellen understood what Har meant when she said she couldn't see the shape of the land. Everywhere she looked she saw tall buildings, long, low buildings, and short, squat buildings. Construction in all its stages created the backdrop for the city, and the Hudson River cut through the buildings on either side of the harbour like a silvery blue ribbon. Ellen couldn't compare it to anything she'd seen before; it was unique and it resonated with power.

After the sight of the buildings and the bridge, the next assault on Ellen's senses was the noise. It was deafening. It was a combination of shouting, hammering, and clanging interspersed with the cry of gulls and ships' horns as they passed by the *Juliet*. There were ships of every sort coming from all directions, streaming toward the river and the docks. Ellen wondered how their ship would make its way to their wharf and she was grateful that she wasn't in charge. She thought back to the harbourfront confusion that she thought was so remarkable when they had left St. John's. That scene was like an outport fair compared with this one.

New York harbour smelled different from home, too. The familiar smell of smoke, horse manure, rotting fish, and sea brine was overwhelmed by the smell of hot steel, acrid and sharp, that she imagined must come from all the metal rivets needed to construct the bridge and the buildings. She was dizzy trying to assimilate it all. She looked over at Jeanette, who just seemed excited. She hadn't stopped smiling since she saw land. Ellen held Johanna tightly in her arms and nuzzled her neck, taking in her comforting baby softness and warmth.

The ship neared the dock and they were close enough to see individual workers as they swarmed around the wharf securing ropes and calling out instructions to the deckhands on board the *Juliet*. Then Ellen heard a loud scraping sound, the ship lurched to the side, and she grabbed the railing to keep herself from falling. They were docked.

fifty-five

The seething mass of people on the waterfront was something Ellen could never have imagined. Har had said that that had been the biggest adjustment for her—the fact that you never had a street to yourself and there were people everywhere, that you had to line up for everything, a table in a restaurant, a salesperson in a store, a teller in a bank, a librarian in a library. Even if Alexander was miraculously there to meet her, she would never be able to find him in the crowd. Ellen was completely overwhelmed.

Strangely enough, Jeanette seemed in her element, commenting on women's hats and clothes and chattering away. Ellen only heard a fraction of what she was saying until her high-pitched squeal penetrated her consciousness. "Oh my God, oh my God. It's you, Ellen, it's you." Jeanette jumped up and down and pointed to the dock.

"What are you saying? What do you mean?" Ellen was dumbfounded by Jeanette's behaviour.

"Look, look, over there." She pointed again. "It must be Alexander."

That focused Ellen's attention, and she followed Jeanette's outstretched arm as her heart started to pound. Then, Ellen saw it. Far back from the apron of the dock, a large painting was waving above the heads of the people on the wharf. The painting was a replica of Alexander's portrait of her and Johanna, the one that she carried in her locket! Now it was Ellen's turn to squeal and jump around.

"Alexander, Alexander," she shouted, quickly handing Johanna to Jeanette so she could wave her arms. She knew he couldn't see her from that distance, and she was totally frustrated. She wanted to fly over the railing of the ship and into his arms. She was the happiest woman on earth. She could hardly believe that her prayers had been answered.

"Come on, Jeanette, we have to get to the front of the line to disembark. I have to get to Alexander as fast as I can." Ellen forgot how intimidated she was by crowds as she elbowed her way to the front of the line. The deckhands had moved the gangplank into position and had ropes tied across the opening, keeping everyone back until they were ready to let them leave the ship. The ship's officer quickly glanced at their first-class tickets and allowed them to move forward. Ellen had never been so grateful for Kenneth's thoughtfulness in changing their tickets. Passengers in second- and third-class would have to wait until the first-class passengers had all disembarked. Also, they wouldn't have to go through an inspection. They just had to show their tickets and be waved through.

Ellen was crazed with impatience to be with Alexander, and Jeanette had to calm her before she made a complete spectacle of herself and shouted rudely for the ship's personnel to hurry up.

It took a good half-hour before they were able to descend the gangplank to New York soil. From this level Ellen couldn't see Alexander or the painting, and she was scared that he would leave, thinking she wasn't on board.

They finally made it through all the checkpoints, and they went inside a large building where they had to claim their luggage. This took another half-hour, and Ellen was frantic by the time they were allowed to pass through to the exit area. Their trunks were on a cart pulled by a young man who followed them outside. Both Jeanette and Ellen scanned the crowds waiting for their loved ones, but they didn't see Alexander. Ellen started calling out his name, not caring now if she made a spectacle of herself.

Then she heard Alexander's deep, accented, glorious voice. "Alen, Alen," he called out, and she saw him running toward her.

Jeanette took Johanna from Ellen's arms and said, "Go, go."

Ellen ran straight to Alexander. His arms wrapped around her in a tight embrace and her heart leapt toward his. They kissed and laughed with abandon, not caring who was looking. Then they heard Johanna say something that sounded like "dadada," and they turned toward their daughter. She was in Jeanette's arms but reached out to Alexander with a big smile on her face. Was it possible that she recognized him?

Alexander gave a whoop of joy and scooped Johanna into his arms. His accent washed over Ellen like a soft, warm rain. "My leetle *kochanie*, I can't believe you've grown so much. You are even more beautiful then I remember, just like your modder." He smiled at Ellen and his arms circled the two of them. Ellen was delirious with happiness. They had both forgotten Jeanette's existence, and the realization hit them at the same time. Alexander was the first to recover his manners.

"Jeanette, it is wonderful to see you. I am so glad that Alen didn't have to travel alone. But I thought you hated the sea."

"It's good to see you, too, Alexander. I do hate the sea, and I won't be sailing on it again any time soon. If I have my way, I'm here to stay."

"Excuse me, sir," said the young man standing with their luggage. "Will you need me to take the trunks to your carriage?"

"Thank you, yes. Follow me." Alexander led them to the busiest street Ellen had ever seen. There were horses, carts, carriages, wagons, and cabs of every description. Everywhere, people walked so quickly that at first she thought there must be a fire. She said as much to Alexander and he laughed, assuring her that this was the normal pace of life in the city. He seemed so at home and looked as if he'd lived here all his life. Ellen had to remind herself that he had grown up in the large European city of Warsaw. It was Heart's Content and St. John's that were foreign to him.

There was a line of carriages on the street, and Alexander hailed one of them. He and the cart man loaded the trunks onto the back of the carriage while Jeanette talked to the horses and stroked their heads. Then Alexander helped them all get settled inside the carriage, which was equipped with lovely soft leather seats.

"Two hundred one, Fourteenth Street," Alexander told the carriage driver.

Ellen sat as close to Alexander as she possibly could without sitting on his lap, and the feel of his body through her clothing was making her weak with desire. She should've been asking him all sorts of questions, but her mind couldn't seem to function in the haze of her physical need for him. Jeanette was trying not to notice them and was looking discreetly out the window, not saying a word.

"Alen, *kochanie*, I can't believe you are here with me. I will never leave you ever again. I have been so lonely." He took her hand in his, pressing his lips to her palm. "Please excuse us, Jeanette. I have missed my wife so much."

Hearing him say *Alen* and *my wife* flooded Ellen with joy. She had so many questions to ask him, but she wanted to wait until they were alone. Now that he was with her, and she knew he loved her as before and nothing had changed between them, she could wait to hear why she hadn't received any letters. There was no rush, since Ellen was never going to be parted from him again.

"Where are you taking us, Alexander?" Ellen asked, although she really didn't care as long as she was with him. She asked more for Jeanette's sake than hers.

"We are going to Mrs. Oliver's boarding house. I thought you would recognize the address. It is the same one I have had since I came here."

Ellen looked at him and frowned. "But I never knew. I didn't receive your letters."

"Of course, I am being stupid. I forget for a moment that you did not know. I will explain everything later. For now I have taken a large room for us and Jeanette will have my old room. We will straighten everything out in the next few days. I don't know what your plans are, Jeanette, but I would be happy if you could help Alen with Johanna until we get settled. I have paid for everything for the next month, and that should give you plenty of time to decide what you want to do."

"Thank you, Alexander. I will be happy to help for the next little while. Everything has worked out far better than we had hoped." She glanced over at Ellen and smiled

By the time they arrived at Mrs. Oliver's, Johanna was asleep on Alexander's shoulder. He introduced everyone in a whisper, and Mrs. Oliver showed them to their rooms. Jeanette was two doors down the hall from them, and she offered to look after Johanna while she slept. "I'm sure you'd like to have some time alone together," she said, winking at them. They could barely keep the grins off their faces, and when they closed their bedroom door they fell into each other's arms.

"Alen, I must tell you what happened about the letters," Alexander said between kisses.

"Later. Right now, I just want you. Talk can wait."

"I remember now why I love you so much," Alexander said, giving her that look that melted her. They took their clothes off and fell hungrily on each other like the first time they had made love by the river. They muffled each other's cries, mindful of the fact that there were other people in the house and it was still broad daylight. Alexander and Ellen lay in each other's arms, their eyes filled with the sight of each other, their arms and legs entwined. They made love again, more slowly this time, but with increased passion. They had a lot of lost time to make up for, and with any luck, they'd never be compensated for the time they had spent apart.

Too soon they heard Johanna's cries, and they hurriedly dressed. Ellen went to Jeanette's room just as she was coming out with Johanna. Ellen guessed that her flushed face gave her away and Jeanette said, "You look healthy and happy, I must say. I'm so glad everything has worked out. All that worrying was for nothing."

"Thank you, Jeanette, for everything. I don't know what I would have done without you, truly."

"I'm really looking forward to finding my way around this city. I think I'm going to like it here. And I'll help you with Johanna at least for a few weeks. I know you and Alexander must have lots of catching up to do. I'm just going to unpack while you feed Johanna, and then I can take her for you again, if you like. Mrs. Oliver said that she'll be serving us dinner in the dining room in one hour."

"I'll see you later, then," Ellen said, giving her a hug and carrying Johanna back to her room.

Ellen unbuttoned her dress and gave Johanna her breast. She drank thirstily while she gazed at her father. She couldn't seem to get enough of him, either.

"I forget that those luscious breasts are for more than decoration. You are such a beautiful modder, Alen. You have cared for our daughter so well. I am in awe of you. And when I think that you did not receive the letters I sent, I am broken-hearted. What must you have thought of me?"

"I never doubted your love, Alexander. I knew there had to be an explanation. I was afraid that you were sick or hurt, so that is why I was coming to find you. How did you know that I would be on the *Juliet*? Did Sister Mary Angela get a telegram to you?"

"I can't believe your modder let you come. How did you manage that?"

"I'm afraid I lied to her. I told her I had been receiving letters from you all along and that you sent for me because you had a big church commission."

"You are a mystic, then, because I did have a large commission. But it was a private home, a mansion, in what they call upstate New York. I was working for Mr. Bruce Steer. He wanted frescoes in his grand hall and in his dining room. The ceilings were even higher than at the Colonial Building." Alexander's eyes were shining, and Ellen knew he was happy with his work.

"Before I left home, Sister Mary Angela gave me the address for St. Peter's Roman Catholic Church here in New York. She thought you may have found work there."

"I did some restoration work there in September. That is how I received the work from Mr. Steer. He is a member of St. Peter's Church, and he liked what I did there and wanted me to work on his house. I didn't know how long I would be working there, so Mrs. Oliver said she would collect my mail for me when I was gone. That is why I didn't worry about not receiving any letters from you. I was sure that I would collect them when I arrived back in the city. I sent you a couple of letters explaining all this when I was working on Mr. Steer's mansion. His butler mailed them for me. When I came back to the city, I couldn't wait to read all your letters, and then Mrs. Oliver handed me these." He took a stack of letters from the top drawer of the dresser by the window and showed them to her.

"I didn't understand what had happened. The letters were all the ones I had sent you—all returned unopened. I was crazy with grief. Mrs. Oliver saw how upset I was, and she figured out what had happened. Alen, my darling, you know my writing is not so good. Look at the address. I am so sorry."

Ellen shifted Johanna in her arms and read the address on the letters.

Mrs. Alexander Pindikowsky
9 Victoria Street
Saint John

On the letter was the stamp of the post office in Saint John, New Brunswick, Canada.

"If I did not have my New York address on the back of the letters, I would never have known what had happened. I can never forgive myself for the worry you must have felt. I went to the Western Union office and sent a telegram to Kenneth saying I was coming back to St. John's to get you and Johanna. I made sure this telegram arrived to the right place. Then Kenneth sent me a reply saying that you were on your way on the *Juliet*. He said he didn't know why I didn't know that. I was so happy. I tried to telegram the ship, but their wireless was not working. I painted the picture so you would see it and know that I was there, waiting for you. What a terrible mess I have made of everything."

"We are together now, and forever, Alexander. That is all that matters. And we can read each other's letters at our leisure." Ellen passed him Johanna and lifted her shell box from her trunk. "I wrote to you every day you were away. I was just waiting for an address to send them. I pretended I was talking to you." Ellen handed him her letters, and his eyes streamed with tears.

"Alen, you are so wonderful, you know that?" He kissed her and held her close while Johanna said *dadada* again. They laughed together, full of joy.

AFTER JOHANNA HAD FALLEN ASLEEP, ELLEN AND ALEXANDER SAT UP in bed and opened their letters, his first one to her, her first one to him, until they finished the last one, weaving their lives back together with each photograph, drawing, painting, and word.

acknowledgements

There are many people I want to thank for their help in writing this novel. I owe a large debt to my best friend, Cheri Bell Inkpen, who collaborated with me in making up stories and imaginary places when we were children. As adults we remained best friends, and she always supported and encouraged my creative projects. She is no longer in this world, but her joyful spirit is with me and her voice is in this book.

My first draft reader was my sister Joanna Gosse, also a writer (www.joannagosse.com), whose encouraging remarks and careful criticisms greatly improved the final version of my novel. Thanks to my friend Mikki Spracklin, who helped with editing suggestions and even took my rough draft on vacation with her!

I am grateful to Bernice Morgan, Annamarie Beckle, and Trudy J. Morgan-Cole, who read my early novel and gave me wonderful suggestions, most of which I implemented. Special thanks to Larry Dohey, Manager of Collections and Projects, The Rooms Provincial Archives Division, who offered his historical perspective and advice.

Thanks to my family and friends who read my book and encouraged me to get it published: Barbara Winsor, Gertrude Dalton, Bob and Beulah Inkpen, Doreen and Wayne Wells, Stella Francis, Tom Brewer, Julie Duff, Judy Smith, Elizabeth Anne Murphy, and Margarita Peckford. Also thanks to my friends and family who have yet to read my novel but have listened to my angst about the writing process.

Thanks to my book club of seventeen years, The Book Bags—Patricia, Anne, Michelle, Donna, Susan, Angela, and Charlotte—for making me more aware of the writing process through reading books that I might not have chosen to read on my own.

I am very grateful to Garry, Jerry, and Margo Cranford of Flanker Press for publishing my first novel, and to their editor, Robin McGrath, for her insightful comments. Thank you to Graham Blair for the colourful book cover design.

To my husband, Paul, my son, Jack, and my daughter, Adrienne, thank you for encouraging me in all my creative endeavours and putting up with me when the creative gremlins made me cranky.

Last, my thanks to Alexander Pindikowsky for making the history of our province more colourful and leaving the city of St. John's the legacy of his beautiful frescoes.

author's note

This is a work of fiction inspired by historical facts. While I have used the real names of characters such as Governor and Lady Glover, Prime Minister Whiteway, Alexander Pindikowsky and Ellen Dormody, their conversations, actions, and storylines are completely fictitious. Also, the chronology of events in Newfoundland during the years between 1879 and 1882 has, at times, been altered to suit the narrative.

THE HISTORICAL FACTS

Alexander Pindikowsky was a Polish fresco painter who came to Newfoundland in 1879. He was hired by the Anglo-American Telegraph Company in Heart's Content to give art instruction to interested employees of the company and their wives.

Pindikowsky was arrested at the Temperance Coffee House in St. John's on March 10, 1880, for forging two cheques in the name of his boss, Ezra Weedon, one for the amount of £232 and another for the amount of £65. He was convicted of forgery and sentenced on June 15, 1880, to fifteen months at Her Majesty's Penitentiary in St. John's.

Pindikowsky painted frescoes on the ceilings of Government House and the Colonial Building while serving his prison sentence. He painted the face of a young woman on the ceiling of the ballroom at Government House. His prison sentence was commuted because of the fresco work that he did, and he was allowed to remain in the Colony of Newfoundland once he had served his sentence. After his release from jail, Pindikowsky was hired to do decorative painting at the Presentation Convent and at the Athenaeum in St. John's. The Athenaeum was destroyed in the fire of 1892.

Alexander Pindikowsky and Ellen Dormody had a daughter, Johanna Mary Ellen Pindikowsky, who was baptized at the Roman Catholic Cathedral in St. John's, now known as the Basilica of St. John the Baptist, on May 1, 1882. By the end of 1883, Alexander Pindikowsky and his family had moved to the United States.

SELECTED SOURCES

The following sources may be of interest, as they were used to gain background information for *Art Love Forgery*.

Books

Glover, Elizabeth Rosetta Scott. *Life of Sir John Hawley Glover, R.N., G.C.M.G.* London: Smith, Elder, 1897.

O'Neill, Paul. *The Oldest City: The Story of St. John's, Newfoundland*. St. John's: Boulder Publications, 2008.

Smallwood, Joseph R. *The Book of Newfoundland Volume 1*, pp. 170-177. St. John's: Newfoundland Book Publishers (1967) Ltd., 1973.

Internet Sites

A Brief History of the Colonial Building by Patti Bannister: www.heritage.nf.ca/articles/politics/history-colonial-building.php. April 2016.

CBC Weekend Arts Magazine: Alexander Pindikowsky and Restorative Justice Interview with Diane O'Mara: www.cbc.ca/wam/episodes/2012/06/30/wam-june-30-july-1-diane-omara/. June 2014.

Forgery and Romance and Boston Connections: http://archivalmoments.ca/2015/06/forgery-and-romance-and-prison-rehabilitation/. April 2016.

A Virtual Tour of Government House: Ballroom, Drawing Room, Dining Room, Hall and Vestibule: www.heritage.nf.ca/articles/politics/ballroom.php. April 2016.

PHOTO BY VATCHER PHOTOGRAPHIC

Carolyn Morgan was born in St. John's and has lived in the city most of her life. While she was teaching English at a local high school, her story "The Collector" was published in *Canadian Living* magazine (October 2001). Carolyn is a visual artist as well as a writer and teacher. In 2014, she had a solo art show titled Art Is for Apple at the Five Island Art Gallery in Tors Cove, Newfoundland and Labrador. This was a multimedia exhibit exploring the mythology and history of the apple. Her interest in art and history inspired her to write *Art Love Forgery*, her first published novel.